T0129418

Praise for *Midnight Spells Murder*
"Zo continues to be a witty heroine whose life experience and genuine appreciation of Spirit Canyon make her a winning investigator, one whose blogs for the local newspaper deserve to be shared. Readers will be looking forward to the next in this fun series that highlights a charming town, aggressively slothful cat, and a woman finding her Happy Place."
—*Kings River Life Magazine*

"*Midnight Spells Murder* is full of treats, nasty tricks, and a determined amateur sleuth."
—**Fresh Fiction**

Praise for *Open for Murder*
"When you add up a fun setting, characters who would make excellent friends, and an engaging mystery, you get Angela's *Open for Murder!*"
—**Lynn Cahoon, *New York Times* bestselling author of the Kitchen Witch series**

"*Open for Murder* is an absolute delight! You'll adore your visit to the charming Spirit Canyon, where nothing is quite as it seems. The very talented Mary Angela has created a gorgeous setting, a lively cast of characters, and a tremendously satisfying mystery that will keep readers happily guessing."
—**Cynthia Kuhn, author of the Agatha award–winning Lila Maclean Academic Mysteries**

"A great start to the Happy Camper series. *Open for Murder* features a strong protagonist, likable secondary characters, and a compelling mystery with the gorgeous backdrop of the Black Hills."
—**Catherine Bruns, *USA Today* bestselling author and Daphne du Maurier award winner**

"*Open for Murder* is a fun read with a fresh setting, interesting plot twists, great characters, humor, and budding romance."
–*Mystery and Suspense Magazine*

Mining for Murder

Mary Angela

LYRICAL UNDERGROUND
Kensington Publishing Corp.
www.kensingtonbooks.com

LYRICAL UNDERGROUND BOOKS are published by

Kensington Publishing Corp.
119 West 40th Street
New York, NY 10018

All Kensington titles, imprints, and distributed lines are available at special quantity discounts for bulk purchases for sales promotion, premiums, fund-raising, educational, or institutional use.

Special book excerpts or customized printings can also be created to fit specific needs. For details, write or phone the office of the Kensington Sales Manager: Kensington Publishing Corp., 119 West 40th Street, New York, NY 10018. Attn. Sales Department. Phone: 1-800-221-2647.

Lyrical Underground and Lyrical Underground logo Reg. US Pat. & TM Off.

First Electronic Edition: April 2022
ISBN: 978-1-5161-1071-1 (ebook)

First Print Edition: April 2022
ISBN: 978-1-5161-1074-2

Printed in the United States of America

To readers, you are truly golden.

Chapter One

Zo Jones stood outside an estate sale on Mountain View Road, torn between a box of old keys and a box of old doorknobs. Really, she shouldn't buy both. First, she didn't know how well they would sell at her gift store, Happy Camper, and two, she didn't know what she would do with them at her house. She picked up an ornate gold key, liking the weight and color of the metal. Still, they *were* small. If she didn't use them, she could probably find somewhere to stash them…

"I struck gold!" exclaimed Hattie, who was one table over.

Zo joined her. Hattie Fines, Spirit Canyon's head librarian, was, not surprisingly, looking at a small collection of books. What *was* unexpected was the books' location—outside, exposed to the elements. Vera Dalrymple had been one of the most respected historians in the area. The sale boasted a fine assortment of books inside, including one volume that had grabbed the attention of several collectors. Their friend and fellow Zodiac Club member Maynard Cline was inside considering it right now. These paperbacks were either missed or unimportant. Based on the meticulous organization of the estate sale, Zo would guess the latter. "What did you find?"

Hattie turned over a paperback. Pulling down red reading glasses from her short gray hair, she scanned the texts. "Mysteries, romances, thrillers." She looked up. "I'm taking them all."

"Are you sure you need another box of books?" The lift in Zo's voice matched the lift of her eyebrows.

Hattie shelved the spectacles on her head. "Are you sure you need *two* more boxes of doohickeys?" She nodded toward the box Zo had been browsing.

"They're not 'doohickeys'. They're—" Zo glanced at the contents. "Fine, they're doohickeys, but at a bargain price, how can I resist? You know I've been wanting to redo my dresser, and these glass knobs will go perfectly."

"And the keys?"

"The keys…" Zo cleared her throat. "They're so small. They won't take up much room. Those books, on the other hand, they're going to need a home, and if I remember correctly, you used up your last shelf on the Louis L'Amour purchase."

"These are going to the library." Hattie's voice held a note of finality. "Crazy Days is coming, and patrons will snatch these up."

"That's that, then," Zo said with a chuckle. "It sounds as if we've both made up our minds."

Hattie gave her a nod and a smile, and they moved on, looking for their friend Julia Parker, Jules for short. The day was sunny, windy, and hot—a typical July day, but also the best kind of day because Zo was spending it with her friends at the estate sale. She couldn't think of a better way to pass an afternoon.

She pushed her black Ray-Bans to the top of her head to keep her hair back. Though short, her blond, textured hair was flying in her face, making it hard to scan the crowd. Even with her hair problem fixed, however, Zo didn't see Jules, who was hard to miss. At almost six feet tall, with a curvy figure and pink highlights, she stood out in a crowd.

"Let's check inside," said Hattie, reading Zo's mind. "The auction's going to start any moment."

"Agreed." Even Zo's tie-dyed tank top was beginning to feel too warm. It would be nice to get into the air-conditioning.

Zo regarded the arched doorway, warm colors, and hardwood floors as she entered the historical house. Though she took pride in her small collection of antiques, her décor was an amalgam of old and new, shabby chic with a bent toward the West. Vera Dalrymple, however, was a true collector, and Mountain View Manor was one of the most remarkable houses in the area. A Spanish Colonial, it had been built in 1931 for the president of Black Mountain College, who also happened to be a Dalrymple. The house had been passed down through generations, and Vera inherited it many years later.

Zo scanned the entryway. Every piece of furniture looked authentic. From the guéridon table to the nineteenth-century bronze candelabras, the pieces would thrill art enthusiasts, not to mention book enthusiasts, who packed the next room.

Hattie noticed and tugged her elbow. "Here's the library."

Zo followed Hattie to the first room on the right, where six bookcases were enclosed behind glass, and the scent of paper and ink tinged the air. Many of the tomes were old, thick, or delicate. Others were leather bound and pristine. One in particular was encased in a special display box. Zo inched closer, but not close enough to see well. Several collectors were in the way. So *this* was the book causing all the commotion. As a former newspaper journalist, she was glad words could still get people excited. Maybe a little too excited.

A couple of men were bickering about the book, and she recognized Maynard Cline's voice right away. A little bit nasal, a little bit pinched, it matched his personality. She peeked around a man in a blazer and confirmed it was him. *Yep.* Maynard wore creased gray slacks, a starched white button-down, and a perfectly trimmed mustache. There was no mistaking his fastidious dress.

"I plan to bid on this item, and I need room to examine it," Maynard proclaimed. "I will not be hovered over."

The comment didn't surprise Zo, who knew Maynard was fussy to a fault. He was also a huge germaphobe who didn't like getting too close to people.

A small man with round glasses interjected. He was dressed in a black, three-piece suit and a striped bow tie, despite the hot day. His name tag read Cedric Tracey, and it was clear he was with the auction company. "Please give Mr. Cline space. He has the right to an unimpeded view of the item."

"You don't understand," pleaded another man, who was not as well dressed as the other collectors in the room. In his oversized jacket and baggy trousers, he even looked sort of shabby. "This book should not even be on auction. Vera Dalrymple promised Black Mountain College the entire collection. I'm the history chair at the college, and as you know, she retired from the same department."

"The college?" fumed a woman in a straw hat. She stood on the balls of her feet to make herself more visible. "Vera was the historical society's greatest benefactor. If anything, she would want it to come to us."

The comment was met with a sneer from the history chair. "Lies!"

"That will be enough." Cedric Tracey's voice was curt. "We are not here to debate the items on sale. If you wish to bid, you will remain civil or be escorted out. The bidding will begin shortly."

The room fell silent as bidders gathered last bits of information. Oblivious to spectators or even his friends, Maynard carefully studied the book. His mustache twitched with concentration. Zo decided not to interrupt him.

"*My Journey West.*" Hattie read the title out loud. "It sounds familiar."

Zo smiled. "You say that about every book."

"Because it's true," Hattie said. The town librarian for over twenty years, she had a sweeping knowledge of fiction, nonfiction, and poetry.

"We'd better find Jules," Zo suggested. "You heard that guy. They're starting soon."

They walked around the living room, where many of Vera Dalrymple's antiques, including a sizable blue, red, and yellow Louis XV–style tapestry, were displayed. Zo zeroed in on an ancient map of Spain, framed in gilded gold. She loved maps of other places. Maybe it was her own wanderlust, which was always strongest in the summer, or maybe it was the travelers who came here on vacation, who always had stories to share about other places.

Nestled in the heart of the Black Hills of South Dakota, Spirit Canyon was the tourist destination for people who wanted to visit Mount Rushmore, Crazy Horse, and Devil's Tower, just across the state border. Hikers, campers, and wildlife lovers flocked to the area to get lost in nature. There was no better place to forget one's troubles than Spirit Canyon. Besides the colorful canyon itself, the town was an eclectic mix of souvenir shops, specialty stores, restaurants, and ice cream parlors. On any given day, tourists strolled through the downtown area, eating taffy, popcorn, and homemade fudge. Though summer was Happy Camper's busiest season, Zo wouldn't have it any other way. She loved meeting people from different parts of the world. It was the next best thing to taking a vacation herself, which usually didn't happen until later in the year.

Along with a married couple, Zo and Hattie entered the dining room, painted a faint terra-cotta color. The large Persian rug had the same orange hue but also a navy-blue design that made for a striking contrast. The table was heavy and oak, made for formal dinners, and Zo wondered whether Vera Dalrymple had entertained often. She could imagine the history professor inviting the department for dinner and discussing *The Iliad* or perhaps a bit of local trivia. Zo liked imagining how a person lived, piecing together a story one room or item at a time. It was one of the reasons she went to so many estate sales. That, and of course, the doohickeys, as Hattie would say.

The woman next to her must have been considering entertaining opportunities, also, for Zo overheard her tell her husband they could have his entire family over for the holidays if they purchased the house. Zo smiled and kept walking. The house was too big for her budget. Besides, she didn't have a family to entertain, though her next-door neighbor Cunningham's Thanksgiving dinners were getting larger and larger. Last year, he had twenty people stuffed into his tiny house. This year, she'd promised to plan Christmas, and truth be told, she could hardly wait.

Zo didn't know her true birthdate, but she always celebrated it on Christmas Day since she'd been found at the police station in December. The celebration would double as a birthday party.

A familiar voice interrupted Zo's premature planning, and she waited a moment, listening for the voice again.

"That's Jules," confirmed Hattie. "Come on."

Jules was near the center island in the kitchen, talking to a man who could only be Cedric Tracey's brother. He also had on a three-piece suit and was even shorter than his brother. Or his smaller stature was an illusion caused by Jules's height, which was emphasized by her messy top bun.

"I apologize, ma'am," the man said. "It is the way it's done."

Zo tilted her head. At thirty-four and thirty-five, respectively, she and Jules were too young to be called *ma'am*, weren't they? She hoped so.

Jules was just as surprised by the comment. Her brown eyes went from milky to dark chocolate in a matter of seconds.

"The way what's done?" asked Zo. "Hi, Jules."

"The estate," said the man. "We won't open for bids on the house until tomorrow."

Zo was confused. Why would Jules be asking after the house?

Jules must have seen the consternation in her face because she pulled Zo and Hattie aside. The man turned to the married couple, who'd followed them into the kitchen.

"I'm putting in a bid on the house," Jules informed them. "You heard the man. I'm not getting any younger, and I have the money. This is the one."

Zo blinked. "He called you *ma'am*. He didn't call you old."

"Same thing." Jules set her chin.

"It's your choice," Hattie said. "I love it, but it's big. The carriage house alone has to be a thousand square feet."

"It's the perfect size." Jules's eyes didn't waver. Once she made up her mind, it was done. Heaven or earth couldn't change it. "Have you guys seen the wine cellar?"

"Not yet." Zo couldn't wait to investigate, though.

"It's climate controlled, so I can store additional merchandise there. It'll save me almost…three hundred dollars a month." She glanced above Zo's head, as if pulling numbers from the air. "Not to mention the reduction in my electric bill and insurance."

One thing Jules knew was business. If she said a historical manor would save her money, Zo believed it. Jules owned the incredibly profitable Spirits & Spirits, a liquor store that doubled as a voodoo shop. When not selling wines or specialty brews, Jules did tarot card and palm readings. Tourists went bonkers for the place and so did locals.

Since they were kids, Jules had come up with moneymaking ideas that played off the town's name and history. The canyon was said to be a haven, of sorts, for spirits. If tourists felt a little eerie hiking the hills, they blamed it on the famed star-crossed lovers, who were separated by a rock avalanche. To this day, the lovers' spirits wandered the paths, looking for each other in the netherworld. No wonder tourists didn't miss a visit to Jules's store. She had everything from specialty brews to ghost beads to help them make their adventures successful.

"What about your house?" Even to her own ears, Zo sounded more practical than usual. She just didn't want to see her friend get caught up in the excitement of the sale, which she'd done several times herself. An oversized bird painting that hung in her bedroom reminded her of her own zealousness every morning. Since purchasing it, she made herself set a budget *before* going to an auction.

"I'll sell it in a week," said Jules without a blink. "Everyone wants a house on Main Street. It's the perfect size and location."

"True," agreed Hattie.

The couple interrupted their conversation, coming together in a showy embrace.

"Can we, dear? I'm so excited!" The woman's French-manicured nails clutched his shoulders tightly.

"We'll talk to the bank today," proclaimed the man into her hair.

Jules crossed her arms, leveling a glare at the couple.

"It looks like you have competition," Hattie pointed out.

"Fine by me," said Jules. "I've never fought a battle I didn't win."

Zo smiled. Jules always got what she wanted, and if Mountain View Manor was her target, woe be to the man, woman, or both who stood in her way.

A bell announced the start of the auction, and they hurried outside, where small items, like Zo's doohickeys, would go for a few dollars. She, in fact, bought her box for five dollars, while Hattie bought hers for seven. Jules wasn't interested in collectables, so it was a long wait for larger-ticket items to go, including the rare *My Journey West*. They were all interested in seeing if Maynard would acquire the text.

Cedric Tracey opened the bidding on the book to much fanfare, describing it as a once-in-a-lifetime opportunity to own a memoir of one of Spirit Canyon's original settlers. According to him, it was written by the businessman and mercantile owner Charlie Clay, who had ties to the first gold prospectors in the area. Although hand-bound, the book was in solid condition, with few torn or missing pages, and would be a wonderful addition to any book enthusiast's collection.

Paddles went up immediately, and Zo, Jules, and Hattie had a hard time standing still as they watched their fellow Zodiac member continue to raise his, even as the bid reached five thousand dollars. At seven thousand, Zo held her breath. At ten, she practically hyperventilated. When he received the bid at sixteen thousand, she thought she would pass out from excitement. Maynard, however, acted as if it was a pittance to pay for the item. He collected the item with all the aloofness of a cat, shrugging off their congratulations with a mild "Thank you."

Lugging her box to her car, Zo wondered if he was right. Maybe sixteen thousand dollars was a small price to pay for a piece of history.

For if it was truly the first book about Spirit Canyon, who knew what secrets it held? And how much they would be worth to the right reader.

Chapter Two

The next day, Zo returned to Mountain View Manor on her red Kawasaki motorcycle. She'd promised to meet Jules before the start of the house auction, which gave her fifteen minutes. Luckily, Spirit Canyon was a small town, and she zipped into a parking spot with ten minutes to spare. Shaking out her hair, she tucked the helmet under her arm and followed the signs through the backyard gate.

Jules was seated in the front row of white folding chairs, and Zo gave her a wave. About forty people were gathered on the lawn, and Zo wondered if they were bidding or browsing. Mountain View Manor was one of Spirit Canyon's oldest properties. Some of the attendees—okay, most of them—were nosy and wanted to know how much it went for. The minimum bid was two hundred thousand dollars, and it would certainly reach a higher amount.

Scooting in next to Jules, Zo hoped her friend won the bid. The more she gazed at the Spanish abode, the more she thought Jules was the perfect owner for the house. She had the money and talent to take care of the historic property, not to mention the wine cellar. If Zo could share a glass of wine in the vintage vault, life would be good.

"There are quite a few people here." Zo settled into her folding chair. "Are you ready?"

Jules smoothed her bright yellow maxi dress. "Absolutely. I consulted my tarot cards this morning, and the Ace of Pentacles appeared. I am buying this house today. Count on it."

Zo tucked her helmet under her seat. She had no idea what the Ace of Pentacles was, but if Jules saw it as a sign, she would follow it, come hell or high water. Though Zo had little faith in Jules's psychic abilities, she had a lot of faith in her business savvy. If she said she was going to do something, she did it, and often made money in the process. Zo doubted Mountain View Manor would be any exception.

The young couple from yesterday was across the aisle, and Zo pitied them a little when she saw the hopeful look in the woman's eye. Behind them was Russell Cunningham, her neighbor and good friend. She recognized his bushy head of white hair. "Cunningham!" she called. Spotting her, he returned the wave. Zo turned to Jules. "I wonder what he's doing here?"

"Vera Dalrymple was a professor at Black Mountain College," said Jules. "Doesn't he work there?"

"He teaches English—I mean, literature." Cunningham had corrected her enough times for her to remember. His grading complaints were cemented in her skull. She would never forget the spelling of Edgar Allan—*with an a!*—Poe again.

A man walked up the aisle, and the crowd quieted. It was the Tracey brother who had called Jules *ma'am*. He said his name was Sean. After explaining the rules of the auction, Sean opened the bid at two hundred thousand dollars.

His brother Cedric was already up front, seated next to a young woman, about twenty-five, whom Zo heard was Dalrymple's niece. Like the Tracey brothers, she wore upscale attire, which included a designer shirt and miniskirt. Her sunglasses alone cost five hundred dollars. Zo knew because she'd browsed a pair online. She remembered thinking, *Who would pay five hundred dollars for something that could fly off your face?* Now she had her answer. But the woman probably didn't ride a motorcycle, and Vail, Colorado, where she lived, was not Spirit Canyon, South Dakota.

The price of the house went up quickly, and soon Jules and the couple were the only ones bidding. Zo glanced at her friend; she'd never seen Jules so steady in her resolve. Okay, she had, but just once during a séance. Shoulders back, eyes straight ahead, Jules was determined to keep going. The young couple realized it and relinquished the bid, much to the wife's dismay.

Zo and Jules celebrated with a hug, and Cunningham joined in the congratulations.

"Well done, Julia. It's good to know Vera's property will be well taken care of." Cunningham put his hands in his blazer pockets. He'd paired a blue jacket with jeans and dress shoes. It was a change from his normal summer attire, which included Hawaiian shirts and loafers. "She was a respected scholar and wouldn't want the house going to pot."

Jules thanked him before being ushered away by Cedric Tracey to complete some paperwork.

"Did you know Vera well?" asked Zo.

"Fairly well," Cunningham answered. "We collaborated on a few events at the college, and she was an avid historian and book collector." He squinted over her shoulder, the wrinkles around his eyes growing more pronounced. "That must be why Jeffrey Davis is here."

She turned to follow his gaze, recognizing one of the men from the library. "Jeffrey Davis. He was here yesterday. Who is he?"

"A history professor at Black Mountain."

"That's right." Zo studied him from afar. "He mentioned the college."

Jeffrey was talking to Dalrymple's niece. He, like Cunningham, wore a blazer, but on his thin frame, it hung like a sack. He was pointing a finger at her, and she was leaning back to avoid the reprimand.

"Introduce me," said Zo, and they started toward the pair. She hated seeing a young woman berated by an older man and wanted to know what the argument was about.

"So, this is where old professors spend their summers." Cunningham clapped Jeffrey on the back. "How's it going, Jeffrey?"

"Hello, Cunningham." His face didn't change, and his voice was still marked with irritation.

"This is my friend and neighbor, Zoelle Jones. Zo, this is Jeffrey Davis." Cunningham gestured to the woman. "And you, I assume, are Vera's niece?"

She smiled, and Zo noticed the bridge of pink freckles across her nose. They matched her light red hair. "Yes, I'm Cora Kingsley. Vera was my great-aunt."

"Hello," Zo greeted.

Jeffrey crossed his arms. "Tell this girl I'm the chair of the history department."

"He's the chair of the history department," repeated Cunningham matter-of-factly.

Cora's skin flushed. "It's not that I don't believe you, Professor Davis. It's that I don't have the book. It was sold yesterday, as you know. You're welcome to talk to the collector who bought it. I don't know what else to tell you."

Jeffrey settled into his stance, ignoring Cora and speaking to Cunningham. "Vera promised me a rare historical account, and instead, it was sold to a collector, a monied tradesman who probably has no idea what he purchased."

Zo wasn't so sure about that. Maynard was not only monied, he was intelligent. An avid reader, he was knowledgeable on many subjects. He always had something interesting to add to the Zodiacs' discussion.

"I know the man who bought it, Maynard Cline," Zo interjected. "He's a reasonable guy. I'm sure he'd be happy to discuss the matter."

Jeffrey turned a condescending smile on her. "I don't want to discuss it. I want the book. One of my students is counting on it for his dissertation."

"I don't think you have a choice in the matter." Cunningham was as cool as the cucumbers he grew in his garden. He wasn't the type to anger easily, unless he was discussing sentence fragments. Then he became a veritable bulldog.

Personally, Zo liked the occasional sentence fragment. It could punch up a paragraph or give a reader pause. Cunningham saw it pretty much the opposite. He preferred long sentences, carefully punctuated, and thoughtful transitions. Anything else was *uncivilized*.

Zo turned to Cora. "I'm sorry about your aunt. I didn't know her well, but I talked to her a few times at events sponsored by the historical society. She seemed like a nice person."

"Thank you." Cora smiled, appearing relieved to be off the subject of the book. "She was. It's been several years since I saw her. I wish I would have visited more often, especially now."

"Don't blame yourself," Cunningham instructed. "Vera wouldn't. She had a very full life. She expected the same of others."

"What she expected was competency." Jeffrey's lips were a thin, pasty line. "She'd be aghast to know her precious book was sold to the highest bidder, like a prize cow."

Cora's pink cheeks darkened. Either the warm July day was getting the best of her, or her irritation was finally showing through. "I did what Tracey Auctions told me to do. Vera certainly left me no instructions regarding the book. Now, if you'll excuse me, I have more important things on my mind, like my aunt's special necklace. It's missing, and I need to find it before the next owner moves in. The necklace has great sentimental value."

Zo watched her walk in Cedric's direction, either to discuss the missing item or to get away from the old professor. Jeffrey was a headache Cora didn't need right now.

"Take it easy, Jeffrey," advised Cunningham. "She's just a kid who's lost her aunt. Now's not the time for animosity."

"And if the history is lost forever? You know how these things go. People don't really care about books anymore. The man will sell it for twice the amount he paid, Cora will skip town, and the rest of the books Vera donated will sit in the college's basement over the summer. By the time fall comes, the books will be forgotten altogether. I can't allow that to happen."

"Like Cunningham said, you don't have much choice." Zo switched her helmet to her other arm. She was fed up with his attitude, not to mention his poor treatment of Cora.

He lowered his wrinkly lids into a glare. "I might have more choices than you think."

Chapter Three

The excitement caused by the weekend estate sale had faded by Monday, but Zo was already looking forward to another upcoming event: Gold Rush Days. Hattie was celebrating with a display about the South Dakota Gold Rush, and Allison Scott, a geoscientist, would open the event with a talk. Zo couldn't wait to get a sneak peek at the display in person tonight at the Zodiac Club meeting. The group usually met at the observatory at Black Mountain College, but they were meeting at the library tonight to discuss a manuscript Professor Linwood was submitting for publication. It was an introductory guide to local stargazing, and Zo thought it was perfect for beginners. If the university press published it, she would be the first one to offer a book signing at Happy Camper.

She stuffed her marked-up copy of the manuscript in her backpack, along with her notebook, where she had written comments and questions for Professor Linwood. Then she slipped on her fringed sweater. Despite the warm weather, it was often cool in the library. Hattie said women of a certain age expected a comfortable atmosphere. Zo suspected Hattie was one of those women. It was never a degree over 69.

Tossing her backpack over her shoulder, Zo locked the deck door. Cunningham called out to her from his deck, and she gave him a wave. He was back to Bermudas and fruity cocktails.

He held up a margarita glass. "Jules got in a batch of tequila from Jalisco. Join me for one, and I'll tell you about the *jimadores*, who have harvested the agave plant for centuries. I've done some research on the subject, and it's quite fascinating."

"By 'research,' do you mean drinking?" Zo said with a grin.

"Field experience, Zo. Field experience."

She guessed it was as good a reason as any to buy an expensive bottle of booze. "As fun as that sounds, I'm on my way to the library. The Zodiac Club is discussing Linwood's new astronomy book. You should come."

"No, thank you." Cunningham adjusted the umbrella in his drink. "I read enough professors' work during the school year. I read the classics in the summer." The way he said *classics* indicated they were the superior art form.

"Suit yourself." Zo started down the steps and stopped. Squinting, she spotted an orange fluff ball on Cunningham's other deck chair. "Is that George?"

George was the Maine Coon cat she'd adopted from the humane society last year. Sitting in the metal cage, his paws tucked beneath him, he'd looked so domestic at the time. The model house cat. When she slipped her fingers through the crate, he swerved to meet them, and the action tugged at her heartstrings. The name on the little blue card, George, cinched her decision. All the other cats had thoughtful names—Snowball, Simba, Socks—but George was as plain as could be. At the center, they'd run out of time for cute names and scrawled a basic name on the card. At least that's what she imagined happened. She kept the name because she liked him the way he was, and names were important to her.

Her own name had been taken from a necklace that was with her when she was found at the police station. Her adoptive parents kept the unusual name, and last fall, Zo had found out that her name had another part when she found a matching necklace at the opera house: elle. Elle had been her mother's name, which explained the interesting spelling of her full name, Zoelle. It was as if a missing piece had been restored, and Zo had spent the better part of the winter researching her birth mom's identity.

Elle Hart was an actress in a traveling theater troupe. Tracking her a few years after her stay in Spirit Canyon was easy. The company performed at small venues all over the Midwest as part of a program to bring arts to the heartland. Tracking her after that, however, was hard. The theater company went out of business, and Zo couldn't find her name in any other productions. One possibility was Elle Hart was a stage name, and she'd changed it when she changed companies. Without any new information, Zo was left with nothing but a name that meant "strong" and "brave."

Cunningham reached over and scratched George's chin. "He's a very good pupil. He only closed his eyes once during my brief, but necessary, explanation of Aztec history. The tradition of the agave plant wouldn't have made sense without the short detour."

The cat has no shame! She counted herself lucky if he kept her company ten minutes before bounding off to chase a rabbit or hunt for mice—and that was *if* she didn't speak to him. She rolled her eyes. "Enjoy your evening, gentlemen."

"And you, as well," bid Cunningham. George didn't bother looking up. Despite the warm day, the evening had cooled significantly, as it often did in the Hills, so she chose to walk to the library. Buffalo Bill's, the bar and grill kitty-corner from her house, was busy, and an occasional burst of laughter hit her ears as she crossed Main Street. The outdoor beer garden was full of tourists, waiting for the band to begin. Farther up the street, another popular destination was packed with people, and for good reason. Lotsa Pasta was a favorite local restaurant with authentic Italian cuisine. The fresh scents of bread and garlic were always prevalent on this area of the block.

The tiny brick library was on the corner of Main and Juniper, and Zo recognized a few club members' cars parked in the lot, duly noting her ex-boyfriend's motorcycle. Hunter was an expert on just about everything, especially his own feelings. Also there was Jules's Volkswagen Beetle. Zo was excited to talk about her purchase of Mountain View Manor—or should she call it Parker Manor now? A lot of paperwork went with the sale, and she wondered if the house was in her possession yet.

As Zo entered the library, she was struck by the faux-gold nugget that replaced the kids' corner. It provided an enormous backdrop for a display about South Dakota's Gold Rush, which included a sluice, scoops, and pans. Children could pan for gold while adults browsed the impressive collection of historical books and maps that had been blown up for the event. It was the kind of exhibit one might expect in a museum. Never in her wildest dreams did Zo imagine Hattie would turn the library into a gold mine, but she had, and Zo was more impressed than usual by her creativity.

"Wow," Zo exclaimed to Hattie. "You've outdone yourself."

"I have, haven't I?" Hattie crossed her arms as she gazed at the display. Tonight she was wearing a shirt that said, UNDERESTIMATE ME. THAT WILL BE FUN. "I think it's one of my favorites."

"It's better than the idea on censorship." Agnes Butterfield, the library's newest—and grumpiest—employee, sniffed. A paragon of propriety, she wore a gray cardigan and a black polyester skirt. She had an assortment of them in drab colors. "For a while, she was searching all the banned books in America, determined to bring them to Spirit Canyon, if you can imagine."

The dismay in Agnes's voice was palpable, and Zo tried not to laugh. Maybe the polyester was starting to itch. "Actually, I can. I bet they would bring people into the library."

Hattie nodded. "Nothing better than a dirty book to get patrons talking."

Agnes *tsk*ed her disgust and walked away. The farther she walked, the bigger Hattie's smile grew.

"I see you two are getting along much better," Zo joked.

"The woman drives me nuts." Hattie repositioned a book on the table. "It's like working with my mother."

Since both women were in their sixties, Zo thought the remark amusing but didn't comment on it. Instead, she zeroed in on the books Hattie was arranging. "The book that Maynard bought at the estate sale, *My Journey West*. Do you think it has information on all the old townspeople?" Zo was thinking of her own family now.

"I'm sure it includes some." Hattie propped up a dazzling picture book. "From what I gathered, it mentions many of the original founders of Spirit Canyon."

"Maybe the Harts?" Zo guessed.

Hattie shrugged. "Maybe the Martins, too."

The Martins were the family who built Spirit Canyon Opera House, where the other half of Zo's necklace was found. Since 1906, the theater had changed owners several times.

Hattie tapped her chin. "I wonder if Maynard would be willing to lend me the book, just for the opening event."

"Ah . . . " Zo knew how careful Hattie was with her books, but sixteen thousand dollars careful? Zo wasn't sure Maynard would go for that.

"I wouldn't let it out of my sight."

"I know that, but does Maynard?" Zo questioned.

Hattie thrust back her shoulders. "It doesn't hurt to ask."

"No, it doesn't." If anyone deserved to borrow the book, it was the town librarian. Zo hoped Maynard would extend her the courtesy, if only for a few hours.

Jules hollered from the back of the library. "We're starting, ladies!"

Zo and Hattie joined the group in the conference room, where eight club members sat around a perfunctory plastic table. Zo took out her copy of Linwood's manuscript and selected a chair between Jules and Hunter.

Hunter nodded at her marked-up pages. "You've always liked voicing your opinions. I just hope Linwood agrees with them."

Zo dismissed the comment, like she did all comments from Hunter. Linwood had requested feedback. Hunter didn't like criticism because he thought he was perfect. "I'm sure he'll appreciate the time I took to make comments, since he *specifically asked for them*." Zo glanced at his pristine copy. "What about yours?"

He pointed to his forehead. "When I was in grad school, I practiced storing large amounts of information in my memory. It was a four-step process I still practice today: attend, code, store, retrieve."

Zo guessed she needed to invest in the process because she'd forgotten what he said already. After dating him for months, she'd honed her short-term memory skill. It was set to *immediately erase*. But with his beachy blond hair and leather jacket, he was easy on the eyes. And, despite his long harangues, he was always up for an adventure, which was what drew her to him in the first place. That and his motorcycle. At least they could still be in the same room—and the same club—without completely getting on each other's nerves. Focusing on his lips and not his words helped immensely.

"I see you're all good students and brought copies of your assignment," announced Professor Linwood, who sat at the head of the table, ready to work. His long shirtsleeves were rolled up to his elbows and smeared with faint marker stains from the classroom whiteboard.

Although they all had their roles in the club, Zo thought of Professor Linwood as the leader, since he was the chair of the astronomy department and knew how to run the sophisticated telescope in the observatory at Black Mountain College. But Jules was the one who had actually come up with and named the club. She also offered free tarot card readings to the group in October.

"Actually, I didn't print mine," Landon Hess admitted sheepishly. Landon was Linwood's student and their newest member, but Zo already liked him. He'd been with them since January, and she could tell he was a hard worker. More than once, he'd come to meetings in his work clothes. Like Linwood's marker stains, mineral dust from Copperhead Mine often smudged his T-shirt or jeans. She guessed he didn't have the time, or perhaps the money, to print an entire manuscript for tonight's meeting.

Professor Linwood gave him a forgiving smile. "That's okay, Landon."

"I brought my girlfriend, Olivia Nesbitt, though. I hope you don't mind."

"Not at all," said Hattie. "The more, the merrier."

"Hi, everybody!" Olivia gave the group an enthusiastic wave. "Landon has told me so much about the club. I'm glad to finally meet all of you."

Zo waved back with a hello. *So, that's who she is.* Zo didn't know her personally, but she knew her last name. Like the Merrigans, the Nesbitts were one of the oldest—and probably wealthiest—families in town. If her handbag was any indication, the gossip was true. An oversized Louis Vuitton purse sat on the table beside her. Zo appreciated her zeal, even if it was due to her boyfriend.

Maynard Cline was less enthusiastic about the new visitor—and her handbag. He scooted his chair over several inches. It wasn't that he didn't like her; it was that he didn't like being near her. Maynard was particular to the point of being obsessive. He might even suffer from obsessive compulsive disorder, which could account for his fear of germs. He pulled out his hand sanitizer, a powerful brand that smelled like turpentine, and rubbed a generous amount onto his skin, his eyes never leaving Olivia's purse, which was too close for comfort.

One by one, group members gave Linwood their feedback. Zo commented on the introduction, Jules on the inclusion of witches, and Hattie on the typographical errors. Afterward, Linwood brought out a container of cookies. The scent of chocolate filled the air as he popped open the lid.

"Thanks so much, everyone. Help yourself to a cookie." Linwood showed off the chocolate-chip goodies. "My wife made these. I think you'll enjoy them."

"They look delicious," murmured Hattie. "I have lemonade for tomorrow's event in the break room. I should have enough for tonight's celebration, too. It's not every day a Zodiac member finishes a book." She pushed in her chair. "I'll be right back."

When Hattie returned with the lemonade, she asked Maynard about borrowing *My Journey West*. Much to Zo's surprise, he agreed to lend it to her for one hour. He knew how important the event was and what the mention would mean for library interest.

"But you alone can handle the book," ordered Maynard. "No one else is to touch it."

Hattie crossed her heart. "I promise."

"Contractors are scheduled to work on my gazebo tomorrow." He glanced at the yellow liquid in his cup. Perhaps it wasn't up to his exacting standards. "You'll need to meet me at the house. Do you have my address?"

"Can I come with?" asked Zo. Truth be told, she had been wanting to see his house for a long time. He was always talking about it, and architecture was a topic Zo herself wished she knew more about. Touring his place, a structure he'd been crafting for years, would be a start.

"Of course." Maynard took out his phone and texted Hattie the address. "I'll see you both tomorrow."

"Thank you, Maynard," Hattie said. "It means a lot." She proceeded to hand out cups of lemonade. When everyone had a glass, she held up her own. "To Professor Linwood and his new book. I hope it's a bestseller."

The group members touched glasses, except for Maynard, who quickly took a drink to avoid the gesture.

After finishing their refreshments, Zo and Jules helped Hattie take out the trash and put the chairs back into place. Agnes wasn't happy about a few cookie crumbs on the conference room floor and started the old, noisy vacuum, which quickly put an end to their conversations. Zo and Jules waved good-bye and walked to the parking lot, already deserted.

"Hop in," said Jules. "I'll give you a ride."

Zo thanked her and jumped in. "When will you move into the new house?"

"As soon as I can." Jules buckled her seat belt.

Zo looked at her friend. "I thought you wanted to sell your house first."

"I did," said Jules. "But now that I have first month's rent and a deposit on the carriage house, I'm not as concerned."

Jules was good at business, but even for her, this was an incredible turn of events. The ink couldn't have been dry on the paperwork yet. How could she have found a tenant for the guesthouse? "Do you want to explain what you're talking about, or should I guess?"

"Guess," said Jules. "Let's see if our extrasensory course paid off."

Zo didn't know if she would call it a course. It was a four-hour class meant to heighten awareness of the senses. "It was a workshop, Jules, and I can't read your face in the dark."

"Try reading my voice." With the request, Jules lowered her voice several octaves. "Sound is one of the five senses."

The only thing that made sense was Jules's uncanny gift for business. But Jules was waiting, so she ventured a guess. "Okay...it has to be someone you know. Someone in need of a house." Zo twirled around the idea in her head. "It isn't Hattie. She loves her new twin home. It isn't Melissa, though I bet she wouldn't mind a she-shed. Cunningham hasn't fought with Midge in a while, so it can't be him." She landed on a person who was fed up with his living arrangement and stopped. "Oh no. Is it Max?"

Jules put the gear shift in PARK, shaking her head. They were in front of Zo's house. "So, so close, yet a hundred percent wrong."

Zo wrinkled her nose in question. Who else could it be?

"Duncan." When Zo didn't react, Jules gave her shoulders a little shake. "Duncan Hall is my new tenant."

Chapter Four

Zo shouldn't have been surprised. She knew Duncan and Max's living situation was growing tenser by the day, and Duncan and Jules were friends. She and Max had even joked about the possibility of them getting together, but that's all it was: a joke. She didn't think Jules would seriously consider it.

Jules was all business; Duncan was…not. The most important appointment on his agenda was a jam session, or a date. Zo herself was an avid dater, not by choice but by chance, yet even she couldn't keep up with his girlfriends, who cycled through his life like loads of laundry. How well would that go over? Jules wasn't a prude. Far from it. A rule or axiom didn't exist that she hadn't bent, dented, or broken. But when it came to her home and business, she had certain expectations. Zo hoped Duncan was aware of them before he moved in.

"If your gaping mouth is any clue, you think I've lost my mind." Jules's brown eyes sparkled in the light of the streetlamp. Her car was parked under a beam of yellow streaming from Main Street.

"No, I don't think that." Zo rummaged for something to say. "I know you're a fan of money. It makes sense to bring in some more of it with the larger house payment."

"Thank you for making me sound like a witch." She dipped her chin, her eyebrows taking on a crafty look. "I'm a good witch, though. My intentions are purely noble."

Zo crossed her arms, waiting for the rest of the story.

"Fine," said Jules. "It's good income, but I feel bad for Duncan, too. Max practically kicked him out of the house last week for jamming to Foghat." She shook her head. "Who doesn't like Foghat?"

"Anyone who has to be to work by eight a.m., that's who."

"I've never heard you criticize a classic rock band in your life," said Jules. "Admit it." She stared directly into Zo's eyes as if to hypnotize her. "You're falling for Max."

Zo waved away the attempt. "I've been falling for Max for six months. That's no secret. It's the longest I've ever dated someone, so maybe I shouldn't complain, but he's starting to test my patience."

"Do you think it could be you?"

"Me?" Zo was confused. "What makes you say that?"

"It's just a little thing called your trust issue." She pursed her lips. "It appears like a wet blanket whenever you get close to a guy."

"Come on," argued Zo. "You've met some of the losers I've dated."

"True, but Max is not a loser."

"No."

"So, what's the problem?" continued Jules.

Until ten seconds ago, Zo would have answered that Max was the problem. Did Jules have a point? Was she keeping Max at arm's length because she didn't trust him? She pushed away the thought, determined not to replay her past, one foster home at a time. She'd been so close so many times to finding a forever home, and right when she thought it was possible, the chance was yanked out from under her. After a while, she learned not to trust people when they told her things she wanted to hear. Instead, she focused on what *she* could do to change her life. It made her independent, but it also made her lonely at times.

Zo reached for the door handle. "It's getting late, and I think I hear George meowing."

"You're avoiding the question," Jules countered. "If George were here, we'd see him. He's as big as a fox."

Zo zipped out of the car. "I gotta go. See you later."

"You know George is nocturnal!" she called out.

Zo hustled up the steps. Jules was right about George: He was nowhere in sight. If he found his way into Cunningham's house, however, she would kill them both. She refused to play second fiddle to her talkative neighbor when it came to her cat.

She didn't see George, in fact, until the next morning. She was curled up on her deck furniture, drinking her first cup of coffee, when he decided it was time to come home for breakfast. He sauntered to the back door, tossing a look over his shoulder to make sure she was watching him, which, of course, she was.

"I just sat down," Zo grumbled. "You have the worst timing."

He glanced at the door handle.

"Fine." Zo set down her coffee mug on the outdoor table and went inside to feed him. When she finished, she left the screen door open as she knew he would want to return to the great outdoors. Looking around, she understood why. The cornflower sky and hunter-green ponderosas painted a pretty picture this morning. The tall trees cut along the smooth blue backdrop like the teeth of a saw. Beyond city limits, the rocky canyon walls were a glow of pink, bathed in a rich pastel color of warm summer sun. If the calm weather was any indication, tourists would be out in full force.

Her prediction turned out to be right. When she went downstairs to open Happy Camper an hour later, three guests were already waiting.

She paused for a moment, still hardly believing this was her giftshop. Loaded with natural sunlight from the oversized windows, Happy Camper was filled with anything a tourist or townsperson might want. Bison prints, books, and positive messages were her most popular items, but used memorabilia like photos and postcards came in a close second. She smiled at the display of antique keys she'd made out of an old wire window frame. *A place could be found for them after all.* They hung above her Happy Camper merchandise, which included personalized mugs, stationery, and water bottles that said things like "HALF-FULL," "FLOWER SNIFFER," AND "GOOD VIBES ONLY."

After opening the door for her patrons, she flicked on the 1940s radio. "Our House" by Crosby, Stills, Nash & Young hummed from the speaker. It, indeed, was not only a very, very fine house but a home, something she had dreamed of as a child. Maybe the adage was true: What you thought, you would become. In her case, it was true. She dreamed of a place like this her entire life. Now it was hers, and it meant everything.

The traffic kept up for the first hour, and Zo was relieved when her employee, Harley Stiles, walked through the door. With a preference for grunge, Harley was always a sight to see, and today was no different. The purple streaks in her black pixie cut matched her purple tank top, which boasted a skull and roses. With jeans and a flannel tied around her waist, she looked like a typical college student, but she was much more than that. She was an employee and a friend on whom Zo had come to depend.

"Sorry I'm late." Harley lifted her cross bag over her head. "The recheck at the dentist took longer than I thought."

"No worries," said Zo. Harley wasn't even late. She just wasn't early, like she usually was. She paid her own way for college and, in the summer, worked all the hours she could spare. "Everything okay?"

"Everything's fine." Harley glanced around the packed store. "What's first?"

"Wrap these, would you?" Zo pointed to the new gift-wrapping paper. It was white with colorful campers and went perfectly with the teal ribbon.

"I don't know where you find this stuff," Harley said, tearing a large piece from the roll.

"Shopping is my superpower."

Harley smiled. "I think your customers would agree."

With Harley in charge of wrapping gifts, Zo finished ringing up several purchases. Her phone buzzed as she handed a bag to the last shopper. She looked at the screen. Hattie was on her way. *Perfect timing!*

Zo informed Harley of her plans and promised to be back later that afternoon.

"Don't forget you're closing tonight." Harley added a bright blue bow to the package. "I have that date."

"I won't," promised Zo. "See you later."

Hattie arrived a few minutes later, dressed in a white pantsuit and gold sequined top that was perfect for today's library event.

"Love the outfit," Zo said, buckling her seat belt. She wished she would have worn something gold. She had on jeans and a ruffled yellow top. Gold was yellow, wasn't it?

"Thanks. You look nice, too." Hattie pressed the link to Maynard's address, and the navigation started. Maynard lived in Canyon Heights, an exclusive community of home owners who shared a pool, clubhouse, and even a guesthouse. It was incredibly posh and so out of Zo's budget. She couldn't imagine when she would get another opportunity to tour the house. *Maybe if I talk Maynard into hosting the next Zodiac meeting...*

When they arrived, Zo was awestruck even though she was expecting something spectacular. From her conversations with Maynard, she knew the house was big, but this was massive—a custom ranch with views she could only dream about. The back was all windows, built to take advantage of the mountain drop-off and the view of the Black Hills National Forest.

Hattie whistled. "I had no idea."

Zo remembered Maynard saying he worked as a surveyor for the government. He must have inherited his wealth, unless the government paid more than they used to. "Me neither." She opened the car door. "I can't wait to get inside."

They inched along a gray wood walkway up to the front door. Twisting and turning, it provided a smooth path over the rugged terrain beneath. Nothing had been done to impede the raw natural beauty of the area. It was as if the house had been placed on the top of the mountain without hurting one tree. In the distance, a gazebo in the half-state of being built was as big as Zo's house, but no contractors were in sight. She and Hattie must have beat them there. *Nice*. They could enjoy the tour uninterrupted.

Hattie rang the doorbell, then knocked. Nothing happened.

Zo peeked in the window, trying not to smudge the pristine glass. Inside was meticulous. No other word described it. The dark hardwood floor gleamed, the glass from a clock reflecting a prism of color. Although spotless, the house was a little severe. At least for Zo's taste. Sure, the architecture might be flawless, but she couldn't spot a chair or nook where one could get comfortable. Why have so much room if you couldn't use it?

She pressed closer, looking for any movement from Maynard. On the entry table was a note. It was conspicuous only because it was evidence that someone actually lived there. She squinted to get a better look. The slip of paper was yellow, so the black ink was easy to read. Did that say what she thought it said? *Merrigan*? As in Chief of Police Brady Merrigan? Zo felt her pulse jump a beat. Could Maynard be in trouble?

She knocked harder. Still no response. "He's obviously not inside. Let's look around back." Zo glanced at Hattie's gold-sequined heels. "Be careful where you step."

Around the corner of the house was nothing but the mountain drop-off. The enormous deck was several feet above their heads. Only a mountain climber was getting in that way. "Shoot. That doesn't help." Zo scanned the area, looking for another way in.

Hattie pointed to a shoe, a flipped men's loafer. "What's that?"

But they both knew what it was. It was Maynard's crocodile slip-on. Zo would recognize the high sheen anywhere.

They inched toward the footwear. Their eyes met. This was his shoe, but where was Maynard? Zo took two baby steps forward and hazarded a glance over the cliff. Down below, in a dirty pile of rubble, was the body of Maynard Cline.

Chapter Five

Zo's first thought was a nonsensical one. They had to get Maynard out of the dirt; he would detest the messiness of the situation. Then she reminded herself that Maynard was dead and, from the looks of it, had been for several hours. The dirt hardly mattered.

The knowledge hit her hard and fast, and she gulped a breath of fresh air, backing away from the edge of the rocky ledge. Her hands trembled, and she shoved them into her pockets. How could he be gone? She'd talked to him just last night. They'd had cookies and lemonade, for goodness' sake. It seemed impossible that he was now lying at the bottom of the mountain. She looked to Hattie, who'd joined her near the cliff. Had she seen him, too?

Hattie blinked. "I can't believe he's dead."

Zo shook her head, trying to make sense of the scene. There had to be an explanation. She rolled through possibilities. "Was he stargazing? Did he see something and get too close to the edge? Was it a wild animal? Was he defending his property?" She scanned the area but didn't find a telescope, binoculars, or gun.

"I don't think so." Hattie glanced back at the house. "Maybe he jumped. Maybe he was in over his head."

"Even if that's true, which I don't think it is, can you see Maynard plunging himself into a pile of dirt?" Zo tried to grasp the reality of the situation. Her mind was having a hard time getting past the soil, rock, and rubble. It shouldn't be anywhere near Maynard, and now he was lying in it.

And the odd shoe. What was it doing there?

Hattie was quick to agree. "I can't. I've known Maynard to wipe off a library table before sitting down. One crumb of food could set him off. This?" She motioned to the edge. "I can't fathom how he could do it."

It started soaking in that Maynard was really dead. It didn't matter how it happened. It had happened. They needed to call someone—but not the ambulance. It was too late for that. From her first glance, Zo had known he was gone. She pulled out her phone. Max was not only her boyfriend, but also a law enforcement officer for the National Forest Service. He would know what to do. "I'll call Max."

He answered on the second ring, and she realized how happy he sounded to hear her voice. She hated telling him the bad news. After she did, his voice changed. So did hers. Although she and Maynard hadn't been close friends, saying the words aloud brought tears to her eyes, and her voice cracked as she explained the situation.

"Are you okay?" he asked.

"Yes, Hattie's with me." Zo reached for Hattie's hand and squeezed. "I'm fine, really. It just doesn't make any sense. His shoe is sitting here, on the edge of the cliff."

"I'm on my way right now. Don't touch anything until I get there, okay? Zo? Did you hear me?"

She had heard him but was thinking about the note on Maynard's entry table. The one that said *Merrigan*. "Why would I touch anything?"

"I don't know," said Max. "Ten years of investigative journalism? Not to mention your two recent involvements with murder?"

"I won't touch anything. I promise."

He clicked off the phone.

That didn't mean she couldn't look around. She walked over to Maynard's loafer and crouched down for a closer look. Hattie joined her. A sizable scuff was on the heel. Very unlike Maynard. Zo pointed to the line of dirt behind the shoe. "See that? It's as if he stumbled backward."

Pulling down reading glasses from the top of her head, Hattie followed the line with her eyes. "Or someone pushed him." The idea hung in the air.

That would explain why the shoe was off. If he had jumped, the shoe wouldn't be on the edge of the cliff; it would be down below with the body. "But wouldn't the person have noticed the shoe?"

"Not if it was dark," Hattie hypothesized. "The forest is pitch black until sunrise."

And even after sunrise. The dark ponderosa pines gave the Black Hills their name.

Zo stood. "I saw a note inside that said *Merrigan*. Do you think Maynard knew he was in trouble? Is that why he wrote down the name of the police chief?"

"If so, why not just call the police? That doesn't make sense." Hattie shook her head. "Maybe it has something to do with the book."

The book. Zo wondered if it was somewhere inside. "Let's see if it's there."

"I thought you told Max you weren't going to touch anything," Hattie reminded her.

Zo was already walking toward the front of the house with Hattie close on her heels. "I'm not. I'm just going to double-check what I saw." She pointed to the table. "See? There's the note. But no book." While Hattie squinted to get a better look at the note, Zo walked to what might have been a bedroom window. The shade was closed. The shades in the formal living room, however, were open.

A slim bookshelf housed dozens of books, perfectly arranged by size, but not the one she was looking for. Then again, she'd only briefly laid eyes on the book. Maybe Hattie would recognize it more easily. She called Hattie over for a look.

"Nope, I don't see it." Hattie's head moved slowly from left to right. "With all those leather binders, I'd recognize the tattered spine."

Gravel crunched behind them, and Zo turned around. Max's old mint-green and white Ford pickup was pulling into the drive. Scout, Max's German shepherd, saw Zo and barked. Though Scout hated George, she loved Zo, and when Max let her out of the truck, she bounded up the path to greet her.

Zo almost lost her balance when Scout jumped up on her. She scratched the dog's pointy ears. Scout was a gorgeous mix of brown and black, and her brown eyes were intelligent and kind.

"Down, Scout." Max was walking up the path.

Scout wagged her tail, her paws on Zo's chest.

"I see the obedience classes are paying off," Zo joked.

"They are," said Max. "It's you. She knows she can get by with bad behavior. You need to tell her to get down."

Seeing Max's pinched face, Zo gave the order, but not before giving Scout a squeeze. Her warm fur felt good after the morning she'd had. It felt as if she could breathe again.

After giving Zo a hug and making sure she was okay, Max continued. "Brady Merrigan's on his way. I briefed him on the situation. Why don't you show me where you found the body?"

"This way." Hattie led them to the rear of the house, where Maynard lay at the bottom of the cliff below.

Max shook his head. "A terrible way to die."

"Especially for Maynard. He was a germaphobe. He would never plunge himself into a pile of dirt on purpose." Zo pointed to the shoe. "See that loafer? Hattie and I believe it's a clue to what happened here. We think Maynard was shoved off the cliff, maybe sometime in the night, which would explain why it's still here. It might have been missed in the dark."

"I'm so glad you have it all figured out. How did you do it?" Max put his fingers to his temples. "Wait, don't tell me. Jules did a séance over the phone, and Maynard's ghost told you."

Zo was about to reply with a snarky comment when Hattie cut her off. "See that line of dirt behind the shoe? If he was pushed, his foot might have caught on a rock, flipping his loafer."

Max bent down to study the mark. Scout looked over his shoulder. "When Merrigan gets here with the investigators, I'll make sure they get a picture."

"Speaking of Merrigan, there's a note inside with his name on it," said Zo. "Very curious, if you ask me. Why would Maynard have written the police chief's name on a piece of paper? And before you accuse me of snooping, I didn't. I saw it through an open window shade."

"Maybe Merrigan knows the victim and will be able to explain." Max stood. Scout was a statue beside him, albeit a statue with a long tongue. "What are you guys doing out here anyway?"

"Last night at our Zodiac Club meeting, Maynard promised to lend me a book he'd purchased," explained Hattie. "For this afternoon's library event. I was hoping it might have information on some of the first gold prospectors in the area."

"Ah," said Max. "So the Zodiacs are involved. I feel like the stars don't always align for the group."

"Are you saying we're cursed, Max?" Zo asked.

"Nope." Max patted Scout's large head. "That's the last thing I'm saying. I don't need any rituals performed on me, thank you very much."

In the distance, a siren grew louder. Tires on the gravel path followed, and Police Chief Brady Merrigan stepped into the sunlight like a solar eclipse. The Merrigans were a famed Irish family in town, known for their charter history. Even if Zo didn't know them personally, as a local, she knew their story. Great-Grandpa Merrigan came to the area years ago, staked a claim, and the clan had lived here ever since. Zo's interactions with them included one failed business venture with Patrick Merrigan and several police encounters with his brother, Brady, who looked disappointed, but not surprised, to see her.

"If it isn't my favorite pair of super sleuths," said Brady, who wore a black cowboy hat that made him look even taller than his above-average height. He put a hand to his brow, pretending to shield his eyes. "And you brought along our trusted town librarian. Isn't this cozy? Hello, Ms. Fines." Hattie crossed her arms. "Hello, Chief."

Scout barked, Zo scowled, but Max didn't react to the comments. "Zo and Hattie came out here to borrow a book. Instead, they found Maynard Cline's body at the bottom of the mountain."

"We think he was pushed," added Zo.

"When I want your opinion, young lady, I'll ask for it." Brady walked to the drop-off and looked over. His two-way radio buzzed with chatter, filling the void in conversation. He returned to the shoe, bending over to study it. A few minutes passed. As he stood, his knees cracked loudly. "This time, though, I agree with you. It looks as if he was pushed."

Zo felt her jaw drop. That was a first.

"Tell me what happened," prompted Brady.

Hattie explained about the book, the Zodiac meeting, and the library event. "I really wanted to show *My Journey West* this afternoon. Lots of people are interested in it."

Brady rubbed his chin, which was free of the black whiskers that plagued him later in the day. "That's the event Zo mentioned in her Curious Camper column this week."

"That's right," Hattie confirmed.

Zo was incredulous. "You read my column?"

"How else can I find out what's happening in town?" Brady returned his attention to Hattie. "We'll search the premises for the book. Was it worth a lot of money?"

Hattie swept a smattering of dust off her white jacket sleeve. "Sixteen thousand dollars, and my gut is that it could be worth more than that. It belonged to Vera Dalrymple, after all, and she was a famed historian."

Brady whistled. "That's a lot of money." He glanced at Max. "It might be our motive."

Zo snapped her fingers. "That reminds me. There was a guy, a history professor from Black Mountain, asking after the book at the estate sale. He said it was supposed to be donated to the department. The auctioneer said if he couldn't calm down, he'd have to leave."

"It's worth looking into," said Max. "Do you remember his name?"

Zo thought back to the argument. "Jeffrey Davis."

A siren sounded somewhere in the distance, and Brady took a step toward the driveway. "That'll be the crime scene investigators. I'll take your statements inside."

"Good," said Zo, following him. "Because I want to show you something."

Brady sighed. "And what might that be?"

"Your last name on a piece of paper."

Chapter Six

Brady was puzzled by the name *Merrigan* scrawled on a yellow note card. He said he knew Maynard worked for the city; he also knew Maynard was his family's neighbor. That was the extent of his personal knowledge of the deceased. To make matters more confusing, a first name wasn't attached to the last. It could have been any one of the Merrigans, and theirs was an extensive family.

Upon closer inspection, Zo, too, was perplexed by the note. The name was underscored three times, forcefully. What could it mean? Maynard's penmanship, like his mustache, was conspicuously neat. He never made unnecessary marks or doodled.

"Maynard was particular to a fault," Zo said. "He must have had a reason to underline your family's name three times."

"Don't look at me." Brady raised his hands. "I have no idea what it's about. I can only assume if that book is about Spirit Canyon, it mentions my family." His chest swelled with pride. "Ours was one of the first families in the area."

"Yes, I know that." Zo shook her head. "Everybody knows that. But why write down the name?"

Hattie tugged at the ankle of her gold heels. "Maybe he was taking notes as he read it. Lots of readers do. Maybe he wanted to share information with your family." She shifted her weight. "These shoes are killing me."

One of the Merrigans lived nearby. Could they be involved? "Which one of your family members lives down the hill?" Zo asked.

Brady tilted his head, revealing emerald-green eyes under the brim of his black cowboy hat. "My *parents*. Why?"

"It seems a little convenient to me. Your name shows up at the victim's house." Zo nodded out the window. "Your family lives close by." She shrugged. "An interesting coincidence for sure."

Brady blinked. "Are you accusing my family of *hurting* Maynard Cline?" Hattie covered her eyes with a hand.

"I'm just saying it's a coincidence. That's all."

Brady pointed to a chair in the living room. "That's about enough from you, Zo Jones. You've had a vendetta against my family ever since my brother Patrick wouldn't renew the lease on your first store. But this time you've gone too far." He threw a look back at Hattie. "Wait here while I take her statement. Trust me when I say it will be quick."

"Don't get bent out of shape." Zo trailed behind him. "You've accused me of murder plenty of times, and I'm still talking to you. You don't have a claim on righteousness, you know."

"Sit."

Zo did as she was told. "And I don't have a vendetta against your family. Patrick came to my Halloween party last fall. We shared a drink. Ask him."

Brady took out a notepad from his shirt pocket. "From the beginning."

"Fine, but before I give you my statement, I want to say something— off the record."

He tapped his pen.

She took the action to mean she could continue. "We both have compelling reasons for finding that book, besides murder." Now that she was closer to the bookshelf, she scanned it as she spoke. Black leather, brown leather, tan leather. No old books whatsoever. "You have your family, and I have mine."

He stopped tapping his pen. "What do you mean? I thought you were an orphan."

Zo really didn't want to tell him. She rarely talked about the subject with her best friends, and Brady Merrigan was not even close to her best friend. Still, they had made some headway last fall, when he revealed he was the one who had found her at the police station. Maybe she could trust him. "My birth mom or her family might be mentioned in it."

He opened his mouth, then shut it. "Really?"

"It's a long shot, but yeah, really."

A moment passed without him saying anything. He untwisted the pen cap. "If I find the book, I promise I'll let you and Hattie know right away."

"And you won't mention it to the press?"

"No. Why would I? We have no idea if it's connected to his death." Brady cleared his throat. "Now, your statement."

Zo gave her account of the morning's events, then waited outside while Hattie gave hers. Max and Scout met her near Hattie's car. It was nice to have a private moment.

Max put his arm around her shoulders, taking time to console her even though he had a lot of work to do. He was a good ranger and a good man, albeit a stickler for the rules. They'd had strong discussions (that's what *he* called them; she called them something else entirely) about her walking tours at Happy Camper many times. After he joined one last fall, however, the discussions had all but dissipated, and their relationship had grown stronger. She only heard a grumble from him now and then about a park sticker or a license. *That* she could deal with. A murder right now? Not so much.

"You survived the inquest," he murmured.

She sank into his warm arms, inhaling his scent, a little woodsy, a little pine. "I held my own."

"I never had any doubt." When she didn't respond, he added, "Are you doing okay?"

She nodded. "Maynard and I weren't close, but it's still hard. He was a friend."

"I'm sorry," Max said. "Is there anything I can do?" Scout licked her hand.

"No, it's nice just being together."

They sat for a moment in silence, watching the crime scene investigators and medics descend on the scene, the cars lining up like ants at a picnic. As they drew nearer, Max dropped his arm, and Zo understood he had work to do. He knew the terrain better than anyone and would probably be helping retrieve Maynard's body.

He turned to face her. "So, how about some more time together? Now that Duncan is moving out, would you like to have dinner at my house?"

The question surprised her, but she tried not to act like it. "You can cook?"

A smile spread across his face. "Are you kidding? I was in charge of dinner Monday through Thursday."

That's right. He was raised by a single mom. Being the eldest, he had to help out around the house. "Okay, sure."

"If it isn't good, we'll go out."

"I'm not worried." She tried a smile. "It'll be great."

"Then why are you acting like it's a trip to the dentist?" Max chuckled. "Seriously, not all men are bad cooks."

Zo wasn't worried about his cooking; she was oddly stressed about the invite itself. With Duncan living at Max's house, she and Max hadn't spent much time there. Their meetups were casual, and the only house they'd been in was hers, and not often. Although it wasn't a big step, it felt like one, and it made her a tiny bit anxious. Avoiding his gaze, she bent down to scratch Scout's ears. "I'm sorry. I'm just distracted. This whole thing is overwhelming."

"I understand. It probably wasn't the best time to extend an invite."

"It's fine, really. I'm looking forward to it." Zo switched topics. "I'm sort of surprised Duncan is moving into Jules's guesthouse. Aren't you?"

"Yes, but in a good way," said Max. "He'll have his own space, which is more than he had at my place. A two-bedroom bungalow does not make an ideal studio for guitar lessons."

Zo nodded. "At least the carriage house is some distance from the manor."

"With some of those kids, Jules will wish it was farther."

"Working together, and now living together?" Done petting Scout, Zo stood straighter. "I don't know. It might be a recipe for disaster."

"Why?" Max checked the status of the police and medics, parking and getting out of their cars. "I think they're really starting to like each other."

"Even if that's true, it's a lot of time together." He tapped his chin, pretending to consider the statement. "Do you know that some couples who like to spend time together eventually commit to spending time together for the rest of their lives? It's called marriage. A lot of people do it."

Zo crossed her arms. "Jules will never get married."

"Why not?"

Zo couldn't believe he thought marriage was plausible, yet she couldn't say exactly why it seemed so implausible to her. Was it the couple or the idea? Without a specific answer, she threw out a guess. "Tax implications?"

The front door shut, and Hattie shot past them, her legs moving fast. "Let's go."

"What's wrong?" Zo hurried to the passenger's side door.

"It's past noon, and Agnes hasn't eaten." Hattie unlocked the doors. "She takes a joint pill at twelve o'clock. On. The. Dot."

"Right. A joint pill." She glanced at Max, whose attention was now turned toward the crime scene investigators. "See you later?"

He nodded. "I'll call you when I'm done."

"I want to know all the details." Zo jumped into the car.

"Stay, Scout," he said.

Zo turned to see Scout staring after her.

Chapter Seven

Zo and Hattie returned in plenty of time for the library event—but not Agnes's afternoon medication. Thanks to their tardiness, and Maynard's untimely murder, she was now one hour behind schedule, Agnes bitterly informed them. She stomped off to take her lunch break before the two o'clock event, leaving Zo to help Hattie with last-minute details like lemonade, cups, and napkins.

"A man has died, and all she can think about is her supplement?" Hattie shook her head. "I don't get that woman."

Zo didn't, either. The only explanation was her type A personality. She seemed to thrive on rituals and details. Schedules were how she functioned, and breaking them upset her more than most people.

Hattie stalked toward the break room, and Zo followed, helping her carry several gallons of lemonade to the dispenser at the table. After giving them a shake, Hattie poured the liquid into the clear containers. Meanwhile, Zo unpacked the yellow cups, plates, and napkins, which went perfectly with the gold display. As the first attendees began to arrive, she ran to Honey Buns to pick up the gold-coin butter cookies. She wasn't surprised to see all the chairs filled by the time she returned with the treats.

In front of the sparkly backdrop, Allison Scott stood ready to speak at the podium. She gave Zo a brief smile as Zo slipped into the remaining seat; then she refocused on her notes. Zo knew Allison from last summer, when she was staying at Spirit Canyon Lodge, a resort Zo's friend Beth owned. Allison was a geoscientist at Black Mountain College and the perfect person to talk about rocks, minerals, and specifically, gold.

She began with a basic history of the South Dakota Gold Rush. The rush started in 1874 with the discovery of gold in French Creek. Despite belonging to Native Americans, the land was explored by General George Armstrong Custer, for which present-day Custer, South Dakota, was named. After the discovery, prospectors flocked to the area, but the excavations didn't stop with Custer. More gold was found near Deadwood and Lead than the original location. Miners were anything if not tenacious, Allison explained.

"Gold wasn't just a mineral," she continued, her plain face growing pink with excitement. "It was a magic bullet that could solve all their problems." Her eyes flickered across the rapt audience. "Money, wealth—greed. It became an unspoken disease among prospectors. Friends turning on friends. Families turning on families. They would do anything to get their hands on the almighty mineral. They'd left everything behind and come out West. They *had* to find gold," she emphasized. "Their lives depended on it.

"Imagine it, if you can. Selling your home, packing up your things, and moving to this rugged country." Allison gestured out the window. "Only to come up empty-handed. Imagine the envy. You had nothing left: no home, no community, no connections. Just the dream of becoming rich. Now what would you do? What did they do? Some of them turned to lying, cheating, and stealing." She flipped over to the last page of her notes.

But Zo had stopped listening. She was thinking about Maynard Cline and his purchase of *My Journey West*. Did the murderer suffer from a lapse of judgment, like the old miners of the Wild West? Or was there something in the book worth killing for? He couldn't have been murdered simply because it was a collector's item. Could he? Maybe the book wasn't involved at all, yet the timing indicated otherwise. Zo guessed Maynard would be alive today if he hadn't attended Vera Dalrymple's estate auction.

Maynard Cline was one of the safest people she knew. He was an obsessive hand washer. He avoided touching surfaces and people. He hadn't even taken one of Professor Linwood's cookies! The last person who should have been at the bottom of the mountain drop-off that morning was Maynard. And yet, there he was. It didn't make sense.

The sound of applause interrupted Zo's thoughts, and she realized Allision's presentation was finished. She joined in clapping her hands.

Hattie walked to the podium. "And thank *you*, professor, for that inspiring lecture. Any questions for Professor Scott?" Hattie waited a moment. "That concludes our program, so help yourselves to cookies. I think Honey Buns did a terrific job, don't you?" The cookies were piled high in pots of gold, and the crowd murmured in appreciation. "But please, no books near the refreshment table. Save your browsing for later."

Hattie took Zo aside as the crowd formed a single line. "How was it?"

"Fabulous," assured Zo. "I loved it."

Hattie nodded to Allison. "I liked her talk."

"It was so interesting," Zo agreed.

"A little help, please," Agnes called from the refreshments table.

"On my way." Hattie leaned toward Zo. "You know what she said when I told her about Maynard? 'He shouldn't have bought the book in the first place. It belonged in a library.' As if he'd committed a crime."

Zo put a hand on Hattie's elbow to stop her from leaving. "You don't think *she* could have done something to Maynard, do you?"

Hattie studied Agnes from afar. "Agnes a murderer?" Her twinkling gray eyes returned to Zo. "I could see it."

With a second complaint from Agnes, Hattie hurried off to help, leaving Zo to seriously consider the possibility. She didn't know Agnes well, but what she did know wasn't favorable. The woman had strong opinions on just about everything. Could she kill someone? Yes, Zo decided she could. With enough motivation, almost anyone was capable of the dastardly deed. But *would* she? That was a whole other question.

Zo ducked out of the event area to peruse the new display of books. Hattie had picked up a bunch at Dalrymple's estate sale. Maybe another jewel was waiting to be discovered.

She was happily surprised to spot Olivia, Landon's girlfriend, even though Landon was not with her. He was probably working, as he did most days, at Copperhead Mine. Or he could have been at class. "Hi, Olivia."

Wearing wedge sandals and a belted khaki dress, Olivia looked up from the display. She flashed a dimple. "Zo, right?"

Zo nodded. "I'm so glad you made it. Thanks for coming and showing your support."

"Me, too. I had a great time at the Zodiac meeting." Olivia's blue eyes scanned the room. "I'm embarrassed to admit that, before last night, I'd never been here."

"Never?" From what Zo knew, the Nesbitts had always lived in Spirit Canyon. How could Olivia *not* have ever been in the library?

"Nope." Her smile was outlined in pink lip liner. "This will be my first time borrowing a book." She flashed a new library card. "I'm going to become a regular now, like Landon."

Landon was always at the library. It was how he'd found out about the Zodiac Club in the first place. He was checking out a book on constellations when Hattie told him about the group. He attended the meeting the next day.

"I enjoyed your column this week, Zo." Allison Scott joined the conversation. Although she was about Zo's age, she looked older in her high-necked sleeveless blouse. Or at least more serious. Her blond hair, wavy and casual, was a nice contrast to the professorial look. "I'm looking forward to Gold Rush Days."

"Thanks," said Zo. "Your talk was great. It reminded me of a question I wanted to ask you."

"Ask away." Allison browsed the books on display.

"Have you ever heard of the book *My Journey West*?"

Allison stopped browsing, looking instead at Zo. "Of course I have. Why do you ask?"

"What did you say the name of book was?" Olivia interrupted.

"*My Journey West*," Allison repeated. "According to stories, it includes the account of one of the first prospectors in Spirit Canyon, Ezra Kind. I've heard the book mentioned in academic circles, but I didn't think it really existed until I saw it mentioned in the estate sale notice in the newspaper."

"Wait—Ezra Kind—the stone guy?" Zo asked.

"Who's that?" added Olivia.

Zo turned to Olivia to explain. "You've seen the sandstone slab by Lookout Mountain? The replica of the one that was discovered in 1887? The original stone, which is now in a Deadwood museum, I believe, was purportedly chiseled by Ezra Kind in his last days of his life."

"I've seen the stone, but I'm still not following," Olivia admitted. "I heard it wasn't even real. That it was done by the men who found it, the Thoen brothers."

"You're right to be suspicious." Allison tucked a blond curl behind her ear. "The stone has always been suspect because the Thoens were stonemasons. Some say they could have carved the rock themselves. Many scholars doubt its authenticity, despite being dated 1834—a full forty years before Custer's expedition."

The date was an interesting aspect of the stone, as were the names of the seven prospectors who, if true, had struck gold in Spirit Canyon forty years before the official gold rush. According to the stone, the group was killed by indigenous people, who presumably left the gold hidden deep in the Hills. But if Ezra Kind had written an entire book before he died, it would include not only forty years of undiscovered history, but also the location of the gold. "Wait," said Zo. "I saw the book. If it had Ezra Kind's name on it, I would have noticed. Or if not me, Hattie would have. I'm sure of it."

Allison shook her head. "It wasn't *written* by Kind. It was written by his friend, Charlie Clay, who came to the area years later, after hearing about Kind striking it rich. He was one of the first settlers of Spirit Canyon. He came, supposedly, looking for his friend's gold."

That's right. Cedric Tracey had said the book was written by the businessman. CLAY MERCANTILE was etched on the side of an old brick building downtown. It had to be the same man, or at least the same family who came to the area years ago.

"So, this book," Olivia continued, "might contain the location of the famed gold?"

"Maybe even a map to it," confirmed Allison.

"If that's the case, why didn't Charlie Clay dig it up himself?" Zo asked.

"I haven't read the book," said Allison. "Obviously. And I'm a scientist, not a historian. But I can only assume Clay *thought* he knew the general location but couldn't find it. One green hill, I'm afraid, looks very much like another to the untrained eye."

"Do you know when he wrote the book?" asked Zo.

Allison tossed her cup in a nearby trash can. "Unfortunately not. You could ask a colleague of mine in the history department, Jeffrey Davis. He knows everything about local history."

Jeffrey Davis. That was the man who had been arguing with the Tracey brothers the day of the auction. Zo would be visiting with him all right, immediately after this.

Finished with their refreshments, attendees made their way to the display. Zo, Olivia, and Allison stepped aside to allow patrons to browse.

It was Olivia's cue to leave. "I have to get going, but it was nice talking to you both."

"You, too," said Zo. "Thanks again for coming. Hope to see you at the next meeting."

"For sure." As she left, Olivia held the front door for KRSO personnel, who must have been there to cover the library event. Although, really, they should have been at the library thirty minutes before to catch Allison's talk.

Justin Castle, a young reporter with shiny black hair and dark eyes, was headed their way now. He could still interview Allison about the discussion, and Zo thought that was his plan—until she spotted his lifted brow, aimed at her.

"Well, well, well. If it isn't one of the Zodiacs. I just heard the news over the radio. Maynard Cline is dead." He motioned to the man carrying the equipment to roll the camera. "Maybe it's just me, but it seems like every time something bad happens in town, it involves someone from your group." He shoved the microphone to Zo's mouth. "Can I get a comment on that, for the record?"

What he could get was out of her face. But Zo kept her cool. Hattie wanted the library event covered. She'd gone to a lot of work and needed locals and tourists to visit the display. Besides, Zo knew Justin was holding a grudge. She'd helped the police solve two crimes recently, and it was a blow to his ego. He was determined to settle the score, but insulting her, or the members of her club, wasn't the way to do it.

"I don't have a comment, but I'm sure Professor Scott would love to discuss her library talk with you. Unfortunately, you're late to the party." Zo grinned. "Again."

"What are you saying? I missed a scoop?"

Zo put the event program in her purse. "You said it, not me."

Justin withdrew his microphone, taking a step closer to her. "I promise you I won't miss anything this time. If you so much as breathe the name *Maynard Cline*, I will be there."

Zo couldn't help it. She whispered the name.

A glare was his only response.

Chapter Eight

Zo knew she shouldn't spur Justin's vendetta, especially since she had a personal connection to the murder. But Justin was so smug, and haughtiness caused a reaction in her every time. This instance was no exception. She understood Justin had a difficult job. Spirit Canyon was the most peaceful mountain town on earth: the towering ponderosa pines, the cascading waterfall, the rocky canyon. Reporting the news here wasn't the action-packed job he'd signed up for. He had to go looking for news where there was none. Unfortunately, that news often involved her.

Riding her motorcycle to Black Mountain College, she put the thought out of her mind. The afternoon at Happy Camper had been a busy one, and she'd taken the bike to relax. Her Fourth of July display was a big hit with shoppers who stopped in to see her new merchandise. She'd placed books by Fredrick Douglass, Maya Angelou, and Ralph Waldo Emerson beside a pale blue hammock with a white tea set. Red-and-white-striped flip-flops completed the look and were incredibly popular, especially with their reasonable price. Before she left, she asked Harley to order ten more pairs.

But now she focused on the curvy road that led to the college. Since it was summer, the road wasn't busy. A carload of students whizzed by, a buzz of laughter spilling out an open window. Some stayed for classes; others stayed for employment. Working for the adventure industry was a fun way to spend the summer and make money. Hiking, white-water rafting, fishing, and spelunking were just a few options, not to mention seasonal positions at popular tourist attractions, restaurants, and shops.

Parking her bike, Zo took in the campus with a sigh. The students who went here really had it made. Secluded by trees, the large buildings were situated in a way that blended in with the topography. It was an oasis of learning, albeit an oasis surrounded by pine—not palm—trees.

Zo approached the campus map, tucking her helmet under her arm. Humanities, Science, History. Her finger stopped on the last department, where Jeffrey Davis was the chair. He'd made that clear at the estate auction. She just hoped he was in his office. With the department's recent haul of books from Dalrymple's estate, she was counting on him being there.

Without the breeze from the drive, Zo realized how warm the afternoon had grown as she walked toward the building made of Sioux Quartzite, which was a pretty pink hue under the umbrella of sunlight. Spirit Canyon's weather was mild, even in the summer. Its elevation kept the humidity low and the evenings cool, but with the cloudless blue sky, she was feeling the heat. She twisted half her hair into a bun to get it off her face, shoving a Happy Camper pen through it to keep it temporarily in place.

Inside, the building was only a bit cooler, probably from the natural rock, not air-conditioning. Zo scanned the sign by the entrance. The history department was on the second floor, and she recognized Jeffrey Davis's office at once. It had a large sign that read CHAIR.

Though the door was ajar, Zo knocked.

"Come in," Jeffrey called.

Despite the warm day, he was dressed in a blazer and slacks, the same attire he'd worn the day of the auction. His long face looked as worn out as some of his old books. There had to be a hundred or more thick tomes in his office. "Hello, Professor Davis. I hope you remember me. Russell Cunningham introduced us the day of Vera Dalrymple's estate auction. I'm Zo Jones."

"Yes, I remember. Come in." He moved a stack of books off the wooden chair next to his desk.

"Thank you." Zo adjusted the pen in her hair as she sat down. "I was at a library event this afternoon. The one about the history of gold mining in the area?" As soon as she said the words, she wondered why he hadn't been there. It should have been an event that interested him. She shook off the question and kept going. "Anyway, I was talking with Allison Scott—she was the guest speaker—and she said you might be able to answer questions about the book *My Journey West.*"

"*My Journey West.*" He planted a shaky fist on the desk. "That should have come to me." He gestured to his bookshelves. "Look around. I own most of the historical books about the area. Many of these wouldn't even be here if it weren't for me." He crooked a finger at her. "But that man had to swoop in with the one thing I don't have—money. If you think I'm going to educate you on the book so you can run the information back to your friend, you're wrong."

She would disabuse him of that notion right now. "My friend is dead."

His eyes grew so wide they lost some of their wrinkles. "Dead, you say?"

She nodded. "We found him at the bottom of the mountain this morning."

"And the book?"

She released a breath. "As far as I know, it's missing. The police hadn't found it by the time I left."

He shook his head, muttering, "No, no, no."

She'd seen Hattie get upset over books, but his reaction was intense. It was as if the information had dealt him a physical blow. For a moment, she thought he'd cry. "Allison thought you might be able to tell me about the book," she prodded. "I'm trying to figure out why someone might have taken it."

"*Why?*" Jeffrey's voice was strained. "There are a hundred reasons. This is why I needed to procure the book, not just for my student. It's impossible for a layman—or woman—to recognize a rare antiquity. It's a one-of-a-kind history."

"Maybe you can explain it to me."

He took off his reading glasses and tossed them on his papers, rubbing the bridge of his nose.

She needed him to focus on the material, and from her years as a journalist at the *Black Hills Star*, she knew specific questions helped. "Allison said the book might include the location of Ezra Kind and his posse's haul of gold. Does it?"

"Very probably," admitted Jeffrey. "Charlie Clay was an associate of Kind's back in Independence, Missouri. Kind wrote him three letters, and one supposedly included the location where they were mining the gold." Jeffrey's sharp shoulders relaxed as he settled into the story. "He wrote to Clay, telling him to come to the Hills, which Clay did, but not until many years later, after it was well known that gold was located in the area." He paused, perhaps considering Clay's actions. "If he found Kind's gold, we don't have record of it. We do have record of his mercantile, where he printed and bound the memoir. He probably meant to print more copies and sell them but never had the chance. His connection to Ezra Kind, however, has been since forgotten."

Zo's eyes lingered on his bookshelf: Frontier History, the Homestake Mine, South Dakota's Gold Rush. As he'd stated, this was definitely his area of expertise. Still, it didn't explain his in-depth knowledge of a book he didn't own or hadn't read. Maybe Vera Dalrymple had told him. "It's a fascinating story, but if you haven't read the book, how do you know so much about it?"

He took in a quick breath, perhaps put off by the question. "It's not a story. That's what I've been trying to tell you. It's history. I've dedicated my entire life to keeping records of the Black Hills, and Spirit Canyon, specifically. I know the difference between fact and fiction."

Zo felt Jeffrey's connection to the topic by journalistic instinct. When people told stories with such passion, something was usually at stake, personally. What was the good professor not telling her? "How do you know the facts, if not by reading the book?"

Jeffrey pointed to a black-and-white daguerreotype on the wall. It was a photo of an old man in a fancy hat with a handlebar mustache. "My full name is Jeffrey Clay Davis. Clay was my great-grandfather, on my mother's side. This was taken in 1890."

Zo congratulated herself. For once, her tenacity had paid off instead of landing her in trouble. She knew something was missing, and it turned out to be the link between Clay and Jeffrey. Nothing spurred passion like a family mystery, as she well understood. It was the same reason she herself was hell-bent on finding the book.

"I grew up on the legend," continued Jeffrey. "From the time I was young, my mother told me about my cowboy ancestors and what great courage they had." He scratched his nose. "I was always a sick child myself, allergies—hay fever. I couldn't be a cowboy, but I could read about them, and isn't that about the same thing?"

A smile warmed inside her. She knew that feeling. She'd immersed herself in books about make-believe families since she was old enough to read. When she was younger, she liked to pretend she was a babysitter in the Babysitter Club books. Her imaginary friends were as real as her classmates back then. "Yes, it is."

"My family knew the book existed," Jeffrey continued. "Clay was said to have bound it in his own mercantile. Little did I know Vera had it in her collection." He leaned back in his chair, as if thinking to himself. "I should have, though. She had all the books I didn't have, and when she told me this spring she was making a donation to the college, I was excited. I assume *My Journey West* was one of the books."

"She certainly had an extensive collection," agreed Zo, "and she was a respected historian. Do you think she was interested in the location of Ezra Kind's gold?"

"Vera?" He laughed. "Not at all. She despised gold diggers. She thought it was tragic how they invaded indigenous land."

Zo sympathized with the feeling. "What else of value was in the book, besides gold?"

"Oh, much." For a historian, the answer was easy. "It was a firsthand account of the pioneers of Spirit Canyon. Lots of men came to Deadwood and Lead to make their fortunes. Many of the original families would be in the book."

The comment hit a chord. "Like the Merrigans?"

"Of course. The Merrigans are still important, aren't they?" Jeffrey crossed his legs. It was then that Zo noted his boots. He really *did* want to be a cowboy. "All the old families would be mentioned."

Zo chewed over a question and then asked it before she lost the nerve. "Have you ever heard the name Hart? Associated with the town, I mean."

"It's not familiar." He stood and reached for a book about Spirit Canyon. He sat down, crossed his legs, and flipped to the index. "Nothing here, but I'd need to check other sources." He closed the book. "Why do you ask?"

"I'm adopted." It wasn't exactly the whole truth. She'd been adopted, yes, but she'd also entered the foster system when her adoptive parents couldn't care for her and their ten other children. But Jeffrey didn't need all the details. "Hart might have been my birth mother's name."

"It's different," said Jeffrey. "You might have more luck than some people." He sniffed. "It's not much to go on."

"Tell me about it," complained Zo. She stood. "But it's more than I had a year ago."

"Believe me, it can take a lifetime to unearth family mysteries," said Jeffrey. "Don't give up."

"I won't." She gave him a smile and walked toward the door. "You can count on it." He could also count on her keeping a close eye on him, but she kept that to herself.

Chapter Nine

As Zo crossed the parking lot, searching for her Kawasaki motorcycle, she noticed Professor Linwood talking to a student on the rose walk. After a second look, she realized the student was Landon. He wore a red-and-black flannel, with the sleeves torn out, and an old pair of Vans tennis shoes. Among students wearing Under Armour, Columbia, and Patagonia, he was a bit out of place, a lean in his step making him appear on the move. Zo guessed between work and school, he kept a full schedule.

She wondered if they'd heard the news about Maynard. They were in the middle of a serious discussion, and she hated interrupting it, but she wanted to tell them the news in person. A friend in their club had died, and she should be the one to tell them.

"I want this assistantship," Landon was saying when she walked up. "I *need* this assistantship. Grad school would be impossible without it."

"And you're going to get it. Hang in there." Linwood's voice was full of teacherly empathy. "Hello, Zo. What brings you to Black Mountain?"

"Hey, Professor Linwood. Hi, Landon. I'm sorry to interrupt, but I have some bad news."

Linwood tilted his head, waiting for the information. Landon quit fussing with a paper in his backpack.

"Maynard Cline passed away last night. I'm so sorry to tell you."

"Maynard?" Linwood sputtered out the question. "Oh no. What happened?"

Zo wasn't sure what to tell him. She didn't have all the information herself. But they'd known each other for a long time. Glossing over her involvement would seem like a lie. Nevertheless, she decided to leave the book out of it. Until she knew more, the fewer people who knew the specifics, the better. "I don't know all the details, but his house in Canyon Heights is built on top of the mountain, and he was found at the bottom of it this morning."

"Poor Maynard. I can't believe it. He's such a careful fellow." Linwood scratched his sparse beard. "I suppose if he heard an animal or an intruder, he might have been caught off guard.... Still, he didn't even open a door without sanitizing the handle first."

"I didn't know him that well yet, but he seemed like a nice guy," Landon sympathized. "Kind of weird, but nice."

"He could be peculiar," Zo agreed. "That's for sure. The night of our meeting, at the library, did you see anything out of the ordinary?"

"Like what?" Linwood's face grew longer with the question.

"Oh, I don't know." Zo paused. "Did Maynard say or do anything that seemed unusual?" Maybe one of them had noticed something peculiar. He wrote the name *Merrigan* on the note card for a reason. Did he have the reason before coming to the meeting? Had he done anything that would give her a clue what the reason was?

Landon smiled. "Everything the guy did seemed unusual."

Linwood put a finger to his lips, thinking. "He gave me his notes on my manuscript but passed on a cookie." He slid them a glance. "Worried about germs, I'm sure. Nothing unusual about that. He visited Hattie's display on the Gold Rush. Looked at a few books. It was the last I saw of him."

"That reminds me," added Landon. "The other librarian, the woman who wears those long skirts?" Landon pushed back a streak of brown hair from his forehead. It was damp from the hot day. "She argued with him."

"About what?" Zo remembered Agnes's apathy toward Maynard. She had no sympathy for the situation even though she would have seen him several times over the year. The group met at the library often, especially during the winter months. When she dismissed his death, Zo and Hattie briefly considered the possibility of Agnes harming Maynard, but could there be something to it?

"I'm not sure. She always seems sort of cranky, so I didn't think much of it. But now that Maynard is dead?" Landon shrugged. "Maybe it's important."

"Why would it be important? I don't see the connection." Linwood thought out loud. "Unless the librarian offended him. He *could* be overly sensitive. He snapped at me once."

"When?" she asked.

"Some time ago. I was out to his house to set up his new telescope—a fifteen-thousand-dollar piece of equipment with a triple refractor—when I

made an offhanded remark. I said the telescope was built for professionals."
Linwood cleared his throat. "I don't want to speak ill of the dead, but I've
never seen a person get so upset. He always wanted more than he needed."
No one disputed the remark.

"It's like Copperhead Mine." Landon slipped a hand in his jeans pocket.
"They keep digging and digging, no matter how high the stack of gold. It
doesn't matter if digging another hole is right or not. It only matters if it's
worth something. More is always better to some people."

Zo knew what he said was true. Greed could be all-consuming. That
was evidenced by Maynard's house, which he was still building on to,
despite being a one-person household. When would enough be enough?
Now, when he had nothing left to want. The thought was a cold one, and
despite the warm day, she shivered.

Two students rushed toward them, calling out to Professor Linwood,
and it was Zo's signal to leave. She needed to get back to Happy Camper
to close the store. Harley had a date, and she promised her she'd be back
by dinner. Plus she wanted to talk to Max. He had to have some more
information about Maynard's death by now.

Linwood gave her an apologetic look, and she assured him she needed
to leave anyway. "It's okay. You talk with your students. I need to get back
to Spirit Canyon. If I hear anything else, I'll let you guys know."

"Please do," said Linwood.

"Thanks," Landon added.

Thirty minutes later, Zo walked into Happy Camper, armed with snacks
for the night. George was waiting for her, lying in the shade of the colorful
flower box. He stood and stretched, tiptoeing ahead of her. *Good kitty.* She
would have someone to keep her company on the slow weeknight.

She put her chips, soda, and sandwich on the counter and shrugged
off her backpack. Harley was restocking a display of postcards, and
Zo called out to her. "I'm back! Have you decided what you're wearing
tonight on your date?"

Harley brought the stack of postcards over to the cash register.
"I have no idea."

"Where are you going?" she asked.

"The Presidents' Club."

Zo opened her chips. George heard the noise and decided he'd, too,
like his dinner. *What ever happened to ladies first?* She put aside the
chips and filled his food dish with kibble. "Ooh, that's a nice place. You'll
need to change."

Harley squinted. "Into what? Like, a dress?"

"Not a dress," Zo was quick to say. She knew Harley hated anything *girly*. "Maybe just a pair of capris or a sweater?"

"In this heat?" said Harley. "Hard pass. I don't know why Chance is taking me there in the first place."

"They've got great food," Zo explained. "Better than this." She indicated her mediocre supper, which now had a big fat George sitting beside it. Unimpressed with his own dinner selection, he'd jumped on the counter, deciding to annoy her as much as possible. "Maybe Chance is trying to make a good first impression."

"By taking me to a place that makes me uncomfortable? Gee, good plan." Harley pushed the postcards toward the computer monitor, and George pawed at one. "I knew this was a bad idea. I should have said no."

"Give Chance a…chance." Zo bit her lip to cover a smile.

George batted several slippery postcards to the ground.

Harley rolled her eyes. "Anything has to be better than bad jokes. I think Max is starting to rub off on you."

"Hey, that's not fair."

Harley grabbed her purse from beneath the counter.

"I can be super funny," Zo called out to her.

A wave was her only response.

She decided Max was definitely rubbing off on her. Which reminded her, she needed to call him and see if he'd found the book in Maynard's house. While she'd been at Black Mountain College, he'd been with he crime scene investigators. They wouldn't have an autopsy report back yet, but they would have completed a cursory search of the house. Maybe they'd found the book. Zo wasn't holding her breath.

After picking up the postcards and moving them out of George's reach, she pressed Max's number and hit the speakerphone button.

"Hi, Zo. What's up?"

"Just wondering if you found *My Journey West* yet." There was a pause on the line. She knew Max was in a difficult situation. As a law enforcement officer for the National Park Service, he was reluctant to reveal information that pertained to a criminal case. Brady Merrigan would see it as a breach of trust, but Brady rarely treated him with the respect he deserved. He thought Max's time was better spent in the forest, catching poachers and underage drinkers.

"I'm not the sphinx," she prodded. "It's a simple question."

He chuckled.

"So, did you find it?"

"No, we didn't," Max admitted. "And we combed through everything—his bookshelves, cabinets, and locked display cases. His safe, too. The only clue to his death is the loafer, and that you saw this morning. It's as if he walked outside and straight off the cliff."

Zo cursed under her breath.

"The guy was a neatnik," continued Max. "Nothing—and I mean nothing—was out of place. It was spotless, and when I say spotless, I mean eat-off-the-floor clean. He has no family, no girlfriend, no pets. The only motive for his murder that makes sense is the book. Plenty of people wanted it. You said the bidding was intense. One of them must've killed him for it."

"Find the book, and we find the murderer."

The statement hung between them, unchallenged. The timing was too right for it to be a coincidence. No other motives had surfaced during the search. And the book was missing. Someone—the murderer—must have taken it.

Fed up with a conversation that didn't include him, George jumped off the counter and sauntered to his other favorite area, a shelf of books.

"Who would kill for a book?" Zo thought out loud.

"Besides Hattie?" said Max with a chuckle. "A collector maybe. Perhaps one from the auction."

"Or a gold hunter." Zo relayed what Jeffrey Davis had told her about the book.

"So, wait," Max clarified. "You're telling me the book could contain the location of Ezra Kind's famed stash of loot?"

"Yes, that's what I'm saying."

Max whistled. "Someone might be mining for gold."

"Or mining for murder."

Chapter Ten

The next morning, Zo was on her deck, enjoying a silent squabble between Cunningham and his garden. He should toss in the trowel, because even from here, she could see the garden was winning. Maybe this would be the year. Like baseball, he would follow the three-strikes-you're-out rule. She sipped coffee from a colorful Happy Camper to-go mug. But if he quit, where would that leave her? Without a front-row seat to this morning's entertainment. And watching him was so much better than watching the morning news.

Wind, weeds, wilting plants—he battled them every year and lost. She'd yet to see him bring in one bountiful harvest, or even a small tomato. Still, he persisted, convinced it was what professors of a certain age did in the summer. He said it was relaxing, but he didn't look that relaxed fighting with a jammed spray bottle of insecticide. He gave it a wallop, then pulled the trigger ten or twelve times before a dismal stream of liquid started and stopped again. Looking like an angry gnome, he tossed it on the ground, and she let out a chuckle.

He looked up, adjusting his oversized straw hat. She'd been discovered. "Shouldn't you be at work by now?" he hollered.

She walked down her deck steps. "I was on my way there when I heard cursing. I know *you* don't swear, so I wanted to make sure we hadn't been invaded by *hooligans*." Cunningham had told her once that only hooligans resorted to curse words. Personally, she thought, like the occasional sentence fragment, swear words could be useful.

"Hornworms," he declared. "I've been invaded by hornworms. Do you know what those are?"

She knew she would know by the end of their conversation.

"They're exactly what they sound like. Large green worms with horns on their heads." Cunningham made pretend horns on his head with his index fingers.

Zo crinkled her nose. "They sound disgusting."

"They are." He blinked. "They're eating the leaves on my tomato plants."

"You know, Midge has a huge garden." Zo nodded toward to his neighbor on the other side of his house. "Maybe you should ask her for some tips."

"Never!" He leaned in closer. "Do you know what she said to me the last time we talked? She said I'd have a better chance growing a second head than a successful garden."

A burst of laughter escaped her lips. Cunningham and Midge were mortal neighborhood enemies. Mostly, they fought about Midge's backyard birding. Cunningham was convinced her birdseed caused weeds in his garden. He insisted the wind blew everything into his yard, including seeds. Noting an empty sack caught on the fence, she thought he might have a point. "I'm sorry. I didn't mean to laugh."

"Yes, you did," Cunningham grumbled.

Zo decided to change the subject from their contentious neighbor. She wanted to fill him in on yesterday's events before she had to open Happy Camper, and the morning was getting away from her. "I was at Black Mountain College yesterday. I met with one of your colleagues, Jeffrey Davis. Remember that book he wanted at Dalrymple's auction? Maynard Cline bought it, and now Maynard's dead."

"I heard about the accident on the news, but they didn't say anything about a book." Cunningham flicked away a weed from his shirt. "Why does the name Maynard Cline sound familiar?"

"He's in my Zodiac Club," Zo informed him. "And the news didn't mention the book because they don't know it's missing. We need to keep it that way."

"That's where I heard the name," said Cunningham. "You've said it before."

"Jeffrey was familiar with *My Journey West* but only because of his family history. Otherwise, from what I've gathered, it's only well known in scholarly circles. Have you heard of it?"

"I'm an East Coast transplant." He glared at his garden. "Which is probably why I can't get this blasted thing to grow." He faced her. "Anyway, no, I haven't. I try not to concern myself with local books and superstitions. Heaven knows there are enough of them in this town."

True. The town was raised on folklore. "Do you know anyone else who might have information?"

"Jeffrey is the expert," Cunningham affirmed. "But you might check with Sue Archer at the historical society. She's not a scholar but knows a lot about local history and folklore."

"That's a really good idea," said Zo. "See? This is why you should stick to books." She patted his arm. "You're good at them." She looked at the half-eaten tomato plants. "Gardening? Not so much."

She nodded to his garage. "Maybe you should start on the Thunderbird. It's been gathering dust for weeks." He'd bought the car on a whim, to "fix it up," but if he didn't have the patience for gardening, she didn't think he'd have the patience to repair the ancient car.

"Humph, I'm waiting for a part. It's coming all the way from Detroit." He shooed her off. "Now, get going. You're late."

But when she checked her Happy Camper wall clock, shaped like a VW van with a peace symbol, she was right on time. She flipped the store sign to OPEN and the record player to ON. Recently, she'd read an article on the Mozart Effect, which proved what she already knew to be true. Music could lower stress and improve mood. But she also learned it could help memory function and blood pressure. Music was the perfect accompaniment to her shoppers' experience.

The chimes rang out just as she was tucking her backpack under the counter. It was Harley, and she was wearing a frown.

"How was the date?" Zo asked.

"Terrible." Harley's eyes were violet with emotion. "He had a suit on."

"Aww, cute."

"Not cute," Harley refuted. "I felt like an idiot."

Zo counted out the day's money for the drawer. "Why? What did you wear?"

"Capris and a cardigan." Harley flung up her hands. "I still looked stupid."

"I highly doubt that." Zo paused to scan her outfit: black jeans, army boots, and a striped top. Even basics looked edgy and hip on her. The oversized cross earrings added a nice eighties touch. "Besides the clothes, did you have a good time?"

"It was okay." Harley wrote out WINDOW-SHOP WEDNESDAY! in curvy letters on the pop-up chalkboard. Customers saved 20 percent on all merchandise in the windows. "The conversation wasn't bad, I guess. He's an accounting student, too, and super smart. I'm going to put this outside."

"Thank you."

While Harley placed the chalkboard, Zo searched the historical society's website. What she found surprised her. Sue Archer was the president—and the woman wearing the straw hat at the auction. She'd argued with Jeffrey Davis, claiming that the book belonged in their archives. Vera Dalrymple was heavily involved in the society, and even now, her photo was still on their webpage. She was a founding member and liaison for the college. According to the page, the board members met at the Archer house, a famous Victorian beauty on Canyon Creek Road, the first Tuesday of every month. The house was open for tours every day from ten until two. Zo checked the store; it wasn't too busy. A visit could happen today. She shot off a quick text to Max, asking him if he'd like to go with her later that morning. Then she got busy.

She unpacked a new box of bird feeders that were shaped like tiki bars, complete with grass roofs, aqua windows, and pink surfboards. Over a door was a sign that read IT'S FIVE O'CLOCK SOMEWHERE. They were adorable and transported her to a beach with warm sun, salty water, and cold cocktails. It was a nice change from hills, trees, and lakes.

With the entry of a customer, George breezed in for his morning can of tuna. He walked to the counter, sat, tucked his large orange tail around his body, and stared at her. Maybe he was still upset about the hard cat food last night. But she couldn't feed him tuna twice a day! It wasn't in her budget or her vet's recommendations for a healthy lifestyle. By the miffed look on his face, however, he didn't understand the predicament.

She had just placed his tuna on the floor when two more guests arrived: Max and Scout. George's tail grew two sizes as he, foregoing his food, bounded to the bookshelf and hissed at Scout. Scout was dumbfounded by the sound, tilting her head quizzically. When the hissing continued, she grew bored and walked over to George's tuna, where she lapped up the treat in two or three bites.

Oh brother. Zo sneaked a glance at George. He was not happy. Harley, on the other hand, was laughing hysterically.

"Sorry about that," said Max, patting Scout's head. "She's normally so well-behaved."

"She's never well-behaved," Zo countered. "She never listens to you."

Zo attempted to console George, but still angry, he swatted her away. She would have picked him up, but she knew better than to tangle with his claws. They could do real damage.

Max lifted his sand-colored eyebrows. "As if you have room to talk."

Zo gave him a glare before grabbing another can of tuna beneath the counter. "Give this to George after we leave, will you, Harley? We'll be back by lunch."

Harley bowed toward George. "His majesty's wish is my command."

Scout sat between them in Max's pickup truck, and Zo had to keep nudging the dog's large head away from her face. Scout was excited for the ride, as evidenced by her long tongue. Despite the brief drive, Zo was starting to wonder if she should switch seats.

"Don't be annoyed with her," said Max. "She didn't mean to eat George's breakfast. She doesn't know any better."

Zo looked at Scout's happy brown eyes. She gave her ears a scratch, and Scout nearly climbed on her lap. "I could never be annoyed with her. Just don't tell George."

They arrived at the Archer house five minutes later. Bright teal with cream-colored trim and mauve gingerbread details, it was a traditional Victorian home, well maintained, and immediately recognizable to a local like Zo. Although the house was famous in Spirit Canyon, she couldn't remember exactly why. Opening the truck door, she knew she would soon get a refresher course. Like all tours and exhibits, most local information would come back to her within a couple minutes. "You're not bringing Scout, are you?"

"I can't leave her here in the heat," proclaimed Max.

"It's seventy degrees," Zo countered.

Max pretended not to hear the comment. "She's a service animal. She goes where I go."

Scout was a lot of things, but a service animal she was not. Unless eating George's tuna counted as a service, which perhaps it did. Zo admitted George was getting a little chubby.

Luckily, Sue Archer was a dog person and met them at the door enthusiastically. Wearing a flowered yellow dress over a white T-shirt, she looked as cheerful as her outfit. Her blond curly hair sat just above her shoulders and matched her clothing. "Two for the tour?" She patted Scout's head. "It's so good to see a doggy. I lost my schnauzer a month ago, and I've been so lonely."

"I'm so sorry for your loss," said Zo. "But we're actually here to talk to you about a book, not the tour. My neighbor, Russell Cunningham, said you might know something about it."

Sue let them in. "Of course. How is Russell? Is he staying busy this summer?"

Zo thought back to Cunningham and his hornworms. "Yes, he has a garden. Keeping it alive takes up most of his time."

Sue took a seat on a pink chair in the parlor. "Gardening is so relaxing."

Zo and Max arranged themselves on the small, tufted couch across from her.

"That's what everyone says." Zo had yet to see the appeal of it.

The room was a mixture of pastels and chintz, very Victorian and well taken care of. Vases and porcelain figurines were tastefully displayed by size, collection, and color, and some of the larger, more expensive pieces were behind glass cases, roped off from the public. Zo zeroed in on a placard in the corner, where an ornate desk with a bell stood. From what she could read, the Archer House had been the first lodging facility in Spirit Canyon.

That's right. She remembered reading that some of the West's legendary gamblers, trappers, and traders had stayed here—and still haunted it. Perhaps even Wild Bill Hickok had spent the night on his way to Deadwood, where he would eventually be shot in Saloon No. 10, holding the Deadman's Hand, a pair of aces and a pair of black eights.

Zo pulled her attention back to Max and Sue. "I'm definitely going to take the tour another day. I love old houses, and I've never been here. It's beautiful."

"Thank you, it's been in my family for years." Sue patted her leg, and Scout joined her, laying her big head on the small woman's lap. "It takes constant upkeep, and not as many people are interested in history as they are in hiking or fishing. But the historical society is always procuring new items of interest." She stood, and Scout followed her. "Like this banjo. It belonged to my great-uncle Theobald Archer, who was one of the first musicians in the area. He formed the famous barbershop quartet?" When neither of them recognized the name, she returned to the sofa. "Anyway, tell your friends about the tour. I'll give them a discount." She put her hands on her knees. "Now, what's this about a book?"

Zo noted that Sue's bookshelf, like Jeffrey Davis's, was filled with books on local history. They'd obviously come to the right place. "It's the book you were interested in at Vera Dalrymple's estate sale. *My Journey West*? I was at the sale. In fact, I know the man who bought it. He was a friend of mine."

Sue's cheerful demeanor cooled. "Charlie Clay owned Clay Mercantile and was an important businessman in Spirit Canyon. The book should have come to me."

"I'm afraid you're not the only one who thinks so." Max laced his fingers. "Several people have claimed ownership of the book."

Her brown eyes zeroed in on hm. "Like who?"

"Jeffrey Davis, for one," said Zo. "He says Charlie Clay was a relative of his."

"Jeffrey Davis." Sue sniffed. "He has enough books in his ivory tower. Most of Vera's collection went to his department. If you ask me, it's ridiculous."

Max leaned back on the delicate furniture. It creaked, and he sat up straighter. "You think they should be kept here, I presume."

"Yes, locally, where the public can enjoy them. If she were still alive, Vera would agree with me." Sue lifted her chin as if to emphasize the point. "Your friend has the book?"

"He *had* the book," Zo clarified. "It's missing. I'm hoping you might be able to tell us why."

"Well, for starters, it's a collectable. Any serious collector would be interested in the book. As you know, it's worth a small fortune."

Zo considered the idea. Maynard was an avid collector—but not of books. Hattie was the real book collector in the group. Every room in her home was piled high with books, and not just those worth money. Most of them she couldn't pass up at estate auctions. They were only gold in the reading sense. "What other reason might someone take it?"

Sue scratched Scout's ears. "Two reasons, one very obvious: gold. Purportedly, the book has a map to the Kind party's stash of gold. But let's be real. It would take more than a treasure map and a pickax to find the gold. It would take real skill and knowledge, so unless the thief had those, I think stealing the book for the treasure is highly unlikely."

There was one person Zo knew who fit that description: Landon. He was a smart, dedicated college student, but more than that, he was an employee at one of the only working mines in the area. If anyone in the Zodiac Club knew how to find gold, it was he.

Zo liked him a lot, though. Too much for him to be a liar. He'd only been in the group a few months, but already it felt as if he'd belonged forever. It would be terrible if he turned out to be the thief—or the murderer.

"What's the other reason?" prompted Max.

Sue quit petting Scout. "Like I said, Clay was a businessman. The book would contain all the stories of the founding fathers of Spirit Canyon. I would imagine any of the families mentioned would be anxious to get their hands on the book." Scout pawed her leg, and she resumed scratching Scout's ears.

The Merrigans were the first people to enter Zo's mind. If any family was mentioned, it was theirs. "For what? Bragging rights?"

A smile played on Sue's lips. "Maybe. Maybe not."

"Explain what you mean," said Max.

Sue stood and walked to her bookshelf. Zo understood she was one of those people who had lots of energy and had a hard time staying still.

"Look at these titles. They're full of legends of cowboys and gamblers and gold. They tell our history."

A narrow part of history, thought Zo. The other part wasn't told as often. The one about stealing land from indigenous people who had every right to their sacred lands—and still did.

"Nothing would be worse for a cowboy than to be portrayed as a coward," Sue continued. "If that got out, it might ruin a family's reputation or legacy."

"A family like the Merrigans?" asked Zo, thinking back to the note on Maynard's table.

"The Merrigans, the Morgans, the Matthews—any of those larger-than-life families in the area."

"The book might be of interest to a lot of people, then," Max hypothesized, thinking out loud. "Businesspeople."

But Zo was still ticking off townies' names in her head. The old families were as mythical as the spirits of Spirit Canyon. They were the cornerstones of the community and went on touting their contributions forever and ever. The idea was unfathomable and even sort of ridiculous to her, a girl with changing names. What was a name but a collection of letters? And why hadn't Sue mentioned one that was uniquely familiar—her own? *Archer* was a very important last name in town and one she'd handily forgotten. But Zo hadn't; she had tucked it away safely for later.

Chapter Eleven

That night, Zo was thumbing through a book Sue Archer had lent her. It was a comprehensive book about Spirit Canyon, penned by one of the members of the historical society. Sue said if the Harts were a known family, they would be in this book. The first thing Zo did was flip to the index and scan it thoroughly. When no mention could be found, she flipped through other chapters. Just because the book didn't mention the name didn't mean that the Harts didn't exist. *Obviously, I come from somewhere.* All it meant was they hadn't been part of the town's frontier history, which was okay by her. She didn't need to be part of that past. In fact, she'd rather not.

It was easier for her to focus on the future, which included a dinner date with Max. Lying on her couch, she glanced at the clock. She had time. Thirty minutes, to be exact.

Duncan had officially moved out, and Max was making Italian food, which he knew was her favorite. It was one meal. What was she stressing about? She scanned another page without really reading it. Finally, she closed the book and headed for the bedroom. This wasn't any different from half a dozen other times they'd spent together. Okay, there was one difference: It was at his house. Which seemed so *intimate*. Candlelit restaurants and cozy wine bars didn't bother her. Why did this?

She squared her shoulders in front of the closet. It didn't. They would enjoy dinner at his house. *No biggie.* But wine might help. She'd make a pit stop at Spirits & Spirits.

She pulled out a green cotton dress and paired it with oversized gold bangles. Though she wore little makeup and rarely fussed with her textured haircut, she adored jewelry. She loved anything that sparkled, and she selected a long pair of gold earrings to go with her bracelets. A swipe of lip gloss, and she was out the door.

Jules greeted her with a whistle as she entered Spirits & Spirits. "I guess someone has a hot date tonight. Is it special?"

Zo shrugged. "Sort of. Max is making Italian food." She scanned a display of reds. "I need a bottle of wine. What do you suggest?"

"Let's ask the cards."

Zo gave her a glance. "I thought you were the expert."

"On wine, not dates." Standing at the counter, Jules shuffled her tarot cards several times. Her fingernails were jet-black and adorned with painted spiderwebs. She flipped a card and inhaled a breath.

Curious, Zo drew closer.

Jules flashed her a card of a naked man and woman. "The Lover."

Zo chuckled. "It seems self-explanatory."

"It might look that way, but it's not. The Lover is the ultimate love card. It signifies a relationship built on respect and trust."

Zo went back to the display of reds. She wanted to avoid a lesson at all costs, even the cost of Jules's most expensive bottle of wine.

Jules joined her, pulling out a bottle of Rojo from Spain. "Respect and *trust*. They're very important in a long-term relationship."

She guessed she couldn't sidestep the topic so easily and tried switching the focus. "Because you've had so many long-term relationships."

"Hey, my clients have had plenty of success with love. Read my reviews. They speak for themselves."

Zo knew they did. It didn't hurt that Jules gave away coupons with every positive response. "By the way, how's your new roomie?"

"We're not roomies. I haven't even moved in yet." Jules's voice was all business now. "The guesthouse is in perfect condition. I don't think Vera had anyone stay in it for years. The manor, however, is another story. I need you to help me clean it this weekend if you can." She put the bottle of wine in one of her signature Spirits & Spirits bags. "That will be fifty-nine dollars."

Taking out her wallet, Zo raised her eyebrows.

"Hey, I gave you a ten percent discount. It's an excellent bottle of wine, which is what you need tonight." She put her fingertips to her temples. "Follow your destiny."

Zo returned the change to her wallet. "It's dinner, Jules, not a psychic prophecy."

"Remember the card." Jules flashed her The Lover.

Zo gave her the okay sign and walked out the door.

The evening had dipped to sixty degrees, and the cool mountain air felt good on her bare arms as she drove with the windows down. In the west, the sky was brilliant pink, streaked with stripes of red, yellow, and blue. The dark ponderosa pines were black against the light sky, creating an outline of the forest that surrounded the city. Spirit Canyon Creek babbled just beyond Main Street. Nature was never far away from the bustling tourist town. Even on the busiest days, reminders of its beauty weren't out of reach.

Max's green bungalow shone with warm yellow light as she approached the front porch, bottle of wine in hand. As she knocked on the door, she reminded herself she'd been here before—just not for dinner. She ignored the importance placed on sharing a meal with someone. The trouble was, in her heart of hearts, she knew it was true. She'd eaten enough meals alone, as a kid and as an adult, to know there was something special about eating together.

"Hey." Zo lifted up the bag from Spirits & Spirits. "I brought wine."

"Perfect," said Max. "Come in. Down, Scout." He pulled on Scout's collar. "You look great."

"Thanks." Zo handed him the bag. "She's fine. Hi, sweetie." She kneeled down to give Scout some attention. "It smells wonderful. What are you cooking?"

"Lasagna is in the oven," he called from the dining area, where he was opening the wine. "I have bread, though."

"Bread and wine are my two favorite food groups." She joined him at the table. French bread was arranged around an oil and vinegar dipping sauce.

Max handed her a goblet. He was wearing an aqua-blue, short-sleeved shirt that showed off his tan muscles and blue eyes. "*Salud.*"

She clinked his glass.

"Have some bread." Max pushed the plate toward her. "Seriously. Eat. I don't know how well the lasagna will turn out."

She chuckled. "Lasagna is kind of complicated. Have you made it before?"

"No, but I made plenty of casseroles for my mom. It's the same thing, right?"

She wasn't a chef, but she'd brought plenty of casseroles to events, and she was pretty certain they were different. "Uh, sure."

He took a drink of his wine. "This is good. I hope Jules gave you a discount."

Zo rolled her eyes. "Ten percent."

"That sounds like Jules." He took a piece of bread. "Did you find out anything about the Harts in the book Sue loaned you?"

"Nothing." She sipped her wine, agreeing it was worth the high price tag. "The Merrigans were mentioned, though. No surprise there. Do you think it's possible Maynard's death has something to do with them?" Max threw Scout a piece of bread. "I think anything's possible. The Merrigans practically run this town. Can you imagine if the book revealed something unpleasant about them?" He shook his head. "And what about the note? Maynard had a reason for writing it. I wish I knew what it was."

"There has to be a connection," Zo agreed. "Do you think we could talk to the Merrigans?"

"Ah . . . you mean, Brady's parents?" He lifted his eyebrows. "That would go over well, wouldn't it? Brady would kill me."

"They can't *not* be questioned just because of their last name, and Brady has a conflict of interest. Isn't that what it's called?" She popped a piece of bread in her mouth. If the lasagna was this good, she was in for a treat.

"Yes, but . . ." He let the thought trail off.

After she finished chewing, she continued. "So you have to be the one to ask them. Let me come with."

"No way," said Max. "He dislikes me enough the way it is, and you're his second-least-favorite person."

"Not true," Zo disagreed. "We bonded over last year's charity event. We're in a much better place." Scout barked, and she gave her one more tiny piece of bread.

"Let's forget about the investigation for tonight." He took her hand and led her to the couch. "Isn't it great being here alone, without Duncan?"

She glanced around the area that contained his living and dining areas. It did seem cozier. The wide woodwork, the beamed ceiling, the cream-colored walls. It was homey, and she'd never really noticed before. "It's nice, but don't you miss all the commotion?"

"No." Max was confident in his answer. "Duncan's a great guy, but the last thing I want to come home to at the end of the day is Creedence Clearwater Revival."

Relaxing into the moment, she tucked her feet beneath her. "I like CCR," she teased him.

"But you don't live here." He gave her a lopsided smile. "Not yet, anyway."

An awkward silence fell, and Scout underscored it by looking between them, waiting for someone to say something. Zo decided dogs were so much better at reading people than cats were, or at least caring about them. If George were here, he would be perfectly fine with the odd silence.

Max took their wineglasses and set them down on the coffee table. He gave her a brief kiss on the cheek and added, "Of course, that could easily change."

Wow. Had she just heard him right? It was their first dinner at his house, and here he was extending an invitation for her to move in. Was he crazy? He knew how much her store meant to her, not to mention her home. Didn't he? Why would he even suggest such a thing? She pulled back.

He blinked, his blue eyes softened by his sandy eyelashes. "I'm not saying tonight or anything. I'm just saying one day it could be possible. Couldn't it?"

"I don't think so." She picked up her wineglass to put some space between them. "I've wanted a house like Happy Camper my whole life. What makes you think I would ever leave it?"

"I'm sorry—I didn't mean." He stopped and sniffed. "Oh no! The lasagna." He tore off toward the kitchen, and she followed.

Smoke poured from the pan. The top was a layer of charred cheese. "What the heck?" she asked.

"The directions said to set the oven to broil to 'brown the top.'" He threw his hands up. "I did exactly that."

"The oven was on broil?" She wasn't a cook by any means, but even she knew never to leave a kitchen when the oven was on broil, a setting that took seconds, not minutes, to do its job.

"Yes, just like the directions said." Max fanned a potholder over the pan. "What are we going to do?"

Zo could see he was disappointed. The time, energy, and thoughtfulness that went into the meal was apparent by the downhearted look on his face. She gave him a smile. "Come on. I know a way to fix this."

Max was puzzled.

"How?"

She grabbed his hand. "Takeout from Lotsa Pasta."

Chapter Twelve

The next morning, Zo ran errands. It was easier to keep busy than think about last night's awkward dinner. *Actually,* she thought as she entered the bank, *dinner at Lotsa Pasta was great.* It was the timid discussion that was weird. She and Max had been out several times, and because they'd been friends for a while, conversation was always easy. She handed Happy Camper's deposit to the bank teller. Last night was anything but easy. The minutes dragged by until their food arrived, and when it did, the chitchat was still guarded. Forty-five minutes later, she practically ran home to hug George, who gave her a welcoming growl. When the sun hit her shades eight hours later, she popped out of bed like a jack-in-the-box and had been on the move ever since.

Leaving the bank, she saw Vera Dalrymple's niece, Cora, enjoying breakfast on the veranda of the Waterfall Inn. Zo approved of the lodging choice, which had a wraparound deck wide enough to dine on while enjoying Spirit Canyon's celebrated waterfall. Although she'd never stayed at the inn, she'd eaten there several times. The food was really good.

It'd been almost a week since the auction, so Cora would be leaving soon. The thought gave Zo pause. This might be her last chance to ask Cora about the missing book. She and the Tracey brothers had access to the house much sooner than the general public. Heck, Cora spent much of her childhood there with her great-aunt and might even have personal knowledge of the story. Why hadn't Zo asked before? *No time like the present.*

Zo greeted her with a wave, and Cora waved back. *Good. She recognizes me from the estate sale.*

"Jules said she's cleaning out your aunt's house this weekend," said Zo. "You must be wrapping things up."

"Trying to," Cora admitted. "I need to make a stop at Tracey Auctions today. I still can't find my aunt's necklace, and I'm running out of places to look." Cora's freckles, as well as the skin under her eyes, were made darker by the shade of the table umbrella. Or maybe the week had worn her out. Going through this all alone must be taking a toll on her.

Zo gave her a sympathetic look. "It wasn't with her things?"

Cora shook her head. "Cedric thought it might be in her safety-deposit box, but it wasn't. I finally got the key yesterday, but it wasn't there."

"If it shows up at the house, I'll let you know." Zo rested her hands on the back of a chair. "I'm helping Jules this weekend."

"Would you?" A flicker of hope flashed in Cora's warm brown eyes. "Thank you so much."

"No problem at all," said Zo. "Just remind me to get your number in case we find something."

Cora quickly scratched her phone number on a corner of the receipt and slid it across the table. Zo tucked it in her purse. "I suppose you'll be glad to go home."

Cora sighed. "Sort of. I know I'll probably never be back, so it's a double-edged sword." She looked up and down the street. "It's such a trendy little town. I don't remember thinking that when I was young."

"It wasn't always trendy," Zo affirmed. "It's become more popular over the years."

Cora nodded, sipping her soda.

Zo used the lull in conversation to ask her about the book. "Can I ask you a question? Do you remember seeing, or better yet—reading—*My Journey West*? It's missing, and I need to know what's in it."

Cora squinted. "Missing? It sold for sixteen thousand dollars. Even the Tracey brothers were surprised at the amount."

"Right, the man who bought it was my friend," explained Zo. "But he had an accident, and the book is nowhere to be found."

"That's terrible," Cora said. "My aunt would be so disappointed."

Your aunt? What about my friend?

"Vera showed me so many books over the years, it's hard to know if I ever saw it," continued Cora. "I'd like to say it seems familiar." She let out a small laugh. "But that would be a lie. When the Tracey brothers told me its value, I was stunned. Vera thought all her books were valuable and treated them like treasures. Every one of them."

Zo smiled. She really wished she would have known Vera better, especially after hearing her niece describe her. Stories like Cora's pulled on the heartstrings, and it was hard not to wonder if she had a great-aunt or -uncle whom she might feel the same way about if only given the chance.

"She'd been everywhere and studied everything." Cora brushed her strawberry-blond hair back from her forehead. "Honestly, I just liked hearing her talk. It didn't even matter about what."

"She sounds like a great person."

Cora nodded, but it was obvious her mind was on the past.

"You don't remember anything particular about the book, then?" prodded Zo. "Or a treasure map? Or gold?"

Cora's eyes lit up on the word *gold*. "Oh my gosh, yes. Aunt Vera said she knew where all Spirit Canyon's gold was buried. I told her we should dig it up, but she said some secrets were meant to be kept hidden." Cora resituated the straw in her cola. "She thought money was the root of all evil, which is funny, considering she had a ton of it."

"Did she give any specifics?" asked Zo. "About the location of the gold?"

Cora's eyes snapped to Zo's with new skepticism. "No, and frankly, even if she had, I wouldn't tell anyone. I would never betray her trust."

The last thing Zo wanted was to offend her. "I'm sorry. That came out wrong. I'm not searching for the treasure myself. The friend that I mentioned, Maynard Cline? He was killed in the accident. He was the last person seen with the book. That's why I'm asking."

"I'm so sorry," Cora quickly apologized. "I didn't realize. What happened?"

Zo decided to gloss over the particulars, just in case Cora was somehow involved or knew someone who was. "He had a fall, and the book is gone."

Cora's gaze turned outward: to the trees, waterfall, and canyon beyond the town's edge. Her face was placid, introspective.

"Cora?"

Cora came back to the moment. "Sorry. I was just thinking about how Aunt Vera was right. About everything, but especially the important things."

Zo waited for the advice Vera had imparted to her niece.

"The past is never really the past, is it?"

It was an interesting notion and one Zo agreed with in this situation. The past was somehow connected to the future and finding Maynard's murderer. She just needed to figure out how. "No, maybe not."

Cora pushed back her chair.

Zo let go of hers. "Thanks for taking the time to visit, and if you do remember anything about the book, please give me a call. I own Happy Camper. I'm usually there."

"I will," Cora promised.

Zo had just returned to her car and buckled her seat belt when she received a text from Harriet, her editor at *Canyon Views*. As Harriet rarely texted (she didn't trust technology), Zo paused and read it right away. It said that Brady Merrigan was holding a press briefing—in five minutes. He must have information about Maynard Cline's death. Harriet wondered if Zo should attend.

Heck yes, I should! Rummaging through her backpack, she dug for her *Canyon Views* name badge. As a weekly columnist, she didn't have much use for it. Press briefings were a thing of the past. She hadn't been to one in almost three years.

She found the lanyard at the bottom of the bag and slipped it on. The action brought back memories, and her heartbeat increased as she took her Outback out of PARK. She couldn't beat the exhilaration that came with chasing a story. The truth was in short order these days, so finding it was even more important. Even if Maynard hadn't been a member of the Zodiac Club, he deserved justice. If she could help, she would feel she'd done her duty.

She pulled up to the police station, a newer building among older structures. It had a little pine tree on the sign, however, that fit with the charm of the area. The old police station, the one where she had been left as a baby, didn't exist anymore. Like any other organization, Spirit Canyon Police was trying to keep up with the changing times, which included more technology.

Zo kept her head down and her badge up as she entered, avoiding eye contact with the clerk. Spirit Canyon was a small community, and everyone knew everyone. Plus Zo had been here on more than one occasion, and not as a member of the press. Someone might recognize her.

"Second floor," said the officer stationed at the front desk. "You'd better hurry."

Zo did just that, pushing the elevator button twice. After a short ride to the second floor, the door opened to a conference room, where she saw Max positioned near the back. She tapped lightly on the floor-to-ceiling windows, and he turned around.

He opened the door a crack. "What are you doing here?"

"My editor told me about it," whispered Zo.

He leaned on the door. "Are you on the crime beat now?"

"You know I'm not." She squeezed past him, wriggling into an open space at the back wall. He stood next to her, both of them waiting for Brady to enter the room. He did so by an interior door, accessible only to officers. As he walked to the podium, the reporters grew silent, waiting for him to begin.

Brady flashed them a big Merrigan smile.

Zo rolled her eyes. Now wasn't the time for charm; now was the time for information. Someone must have agreed with her, because they coughed.

Brady began.

He went over what she knew already: Maynard Cline had been found dead at the bottom of a ravine Tuesday morning. He was last seen alive Monday evening by members of the Zodiac Club, to which he belonged. Brady didn't mention the book, nor did he mention his own surname being found on a note in the victim's house. *How handy.* Then came the new details she was waiting for.

"The initial autopsy report is back, thanks to my brother Morgan, and Mr. Cline's death will be investigated as a homicide," Brady informed them.

The room buzzed with whispers.

Zo leaned close to Max. "Morgan Merrigan is the medical examiner?"

"Convenient, right?" Max said out of the side of his mouth.

She could think of more colorful words, but *convenient* also described it.

"So wait, you're saying Maynard Cline was pushed off the mountain?" The interruption was Justin Castle's. He was at the front of the room, his chin up like a fish waiting to be fed.

"That's correct," Brady confirmed.

"How do you know?" pressed Justin.

"There is evidence of a struggle, including scratches and abrasions. Eventually, they will provide us with DNA and help us identify the other participant in the altercation."

"Has suicide been ruled out?" Justin pressed.

"Mr. Cline was found in the anterior position." Brady straightened his notes on the podium. "Suicides don't walk backward off cliffs."

"But—"

Brady held up his hand. "I'm not going to get into technical jargon like velocity, etcetera. That's not my job. The main thing you need to know is that there's a killer in Spirit Canyon, and I'm going to find them, or my name isn't Brady Merrigan."

If only there were a sunset he could ride into. Still, she'd found out what she wanted to know. Maynard was dead, and an accidental fall had been ruled out. Now all she needed was to get to work, finding the book that was mixed up in his death.

"Questions?" Brady asked.

"You said the Zodiacs were the last people to see Maynard alive," said Justin. "If Maynard was murdered, they must be your main suspects. Correct?"

"You're putting words in his mouth," Zo shouted out. "He didn't say that." The entire room turned to see her at the back. Max covered his eyes. Brady squinted. "Zo Jones?"

"What are you doing here?" hissed Justin. He spun around and addressed Brady. "She can't be in here."

Zo flashed her *Canyon Views* badge. "My press badge says otherwise." As if watching a tennis match, the attendees turned to Brady for a response.

"She writes the Curious Camper column!" huffed Justin. "That's not even journalism. That's creative writing."

Zo was so tired of compartmentalizing. A writer was a writer was a writer. Period.

"If there are no other questions about Mr. Cline's death?" Brady waited a heartbeat. "That's it for today, folks. Thanks for coming. Ms. Jones, a moment, please."

"Great," Zo muttered under her breath.

"Don't worry," said Max. "I got your back."

Reporters gave her looks as they walked past. One said, "Good luck."

Justin came to a full stop. In his slim-fit Oxford shirt and pointy loafers, he reminded Zo of a well-preened duck. "I wouldn't put it past someone in your little voodoo group to do something like this, and maybe that someone is you. You're the one here. In fact, you've been every place this story has been." He tapped his chin, which had just the right amount of whiskers popular in men's magazines. "Why is that? What's in it for you?"

"Unlike you, I actually try to *do* good, not just look good," Zo answered.

Justin clasped his hands together. "Oh, the happy camper and her can-do attitude!" He rolled his eyes. "Spare me. You weren't close to Maynard Cline. He was an uptight mega-millionaire. What are you really looking for?"

Zo opened her mouth and shut it. He didn't deserve a reply.

He crossed his arms and leaned in. She could smell his expensive ocean breeze cologne. "Ah, see? There's something. I'll find it, you know. You're not the only person who was taught how to chase a lead."

She tried to keep her face open and calm, but she was so close to bopping him in the nose that she had to clench her fists at her sides.

"Why don't you do us all a favor and head over to the Cut Hut?" Max interrupted. "I hear they're having a sale on pomade, and it looks like you missed a spot right above your ear."

"As if I go to the Cut Hut." Still, Justin smoothed the hair above his ears.
"Excuse me," said Brady, though he didn't have to say anything. His clunky gun belt and two-way radio had already announced his arrival. "Do you need something?" He aimed the question at Justin.

Justin looked from Brady to Max to Zo, memorizing their faces. "Not yet." He twisted his pen closed and slid it into his leather binder. "But soon."

Brady watched him walk out. When the door was closed, and they were the only ones left in the room, he said, "That was weird, wasn't it?"

Max nodded. "You said it."

Brady's gaze turned to Zo. "You know you're not with the press. Why are you here?"

Zo didn't see any reason to lie. In fact, she thought it was obvious. "I needed to know that Maynard's fall wasn't accidental. I needed to know he was killed because of the book."

"Now *you're* putting words in my mouth," said Brady. "We don't know the motive yet, and we won't know it until we've completed a thorough investigation. There could be any number of reasons he was killed. You need to let me do my job."

"Whatever is in that book is worth killing for," Zo continued. "That's why Vera Dalrymple kept it hidden. It could be land. It could be gold. It could be—" She stopped herself from revealing too much. If the Merrigans were involved, Brady would be partial. They needed an uninterested party involved in the case. They needed Max. If only Brady saw it that way.

"It could be nothing," finished Brady. "We're still combing Canyon Heights for clues. It's a big area."

His comment gave Zo an idea. She hadn't been back to the mountain since Maynard's death, and she knew the Merrigans lived just down the hill. Maybe Max needed to take another look. A smile crossed her lips. Maybe she needed to keep him company.

"Bottom line, I can't have you pull another stunt like today's." Brady's square jaw softened. "You're a good kid, and I know you're trying to help, but this is official police business."

Zo blinked. Had she just heard him right? Did he say she was a "good kid"? First of all, she was thirty-four years old. Second, they'd tangled many times in her teens, when she was picked up for truancy and curfew violations. Rules changed from house to house, and after a while, she quit caring about them. She did her own thing, planning for a future that didn't include courtrooms or cops. Funny how she'd found herself talking to one a lot the last few years. "Okay."

"Okay?" Brady pretended to clean his ears. "Just okay? Now I *know* you're up to something." He put a hand on her elbow. "Look, I haven't forgotten about the book. I promise. If I find it, you'll be the first person to know."

Max quirked a brow at him.

Brady cleared his throat. "The second."

Chapter Thirteen

After much arm-twisting, which included a reminder of Zo springing for their recent dinner at Lotsa Pasta, Max agreed to go to Canyon Heights. As they left the police station, she convinced him he needed to oversee the investigation, or at least get involved as an unbiased observer. How could they trust Merrigan to do the right thing when his family was involved? Family complicated everything, at least that's what she'd been told. What could it possibly hurt to take a peek, and on such a beautiful day?

His reputation, he'd answered, but climbed into her Subaru Outback anyway.

It *was* a beautiful day, and a day off for Zo, who loved nothing better than taking a drive on a free afternoon. Happy tourists lined Main Street in cars and campers, ready to explore the area. Traditional activities like hiking, kayaking, and fishing awaited them, but so did untraditional pursuits such as hang gliding, wine tasting, and outdoor theater performances. It was too much to do in one vacation, which was why they often came back.

After a few miles, the traffic subsided, and she and Max were alone on the road, settling in to the comfortable quiet that nature provided. The white cottony clouds were magical against the cobalt-blue sky, and the shade of the deep woods provided respite from the warm afternoon sun. They snaked higher and higher up the mountain, her car changing gears to make the climb.

"Do you think the book was tossed off the mountain?" asked Max. "Is that why we're here?"

Like her, Max must have used the quiet time to consider the problems surrounding Maynard's murder. The missing book was definitely a question that needed answering. She'd figured out what was *in* the book. Now she just needed to figure out *where* the book was. "Maybe," she answered. "It's possible it went over the edge with Maynard."

"I didn't see a book anywhere near the body, and we searched the house."

A slice of sun crept up her windshield, and she slipped on her Ray-Ban sunglasses. "Where else could it be?"

"The Zodiac Club met the night before Maynard's death." Max flipped down his visor. "Did he fight with anyone?"

"Agnes," she answered. "Landon saw him arguing with her but didn't know the context of the argument. Then, when Hattie told her Maynard was dead, she had zero empathy. Her only concern was taking her medication on time."

Max shook his head. "I've heard of strict librarians, but that's taking it a bit too far." He put out his hand to shield his face from the sun. "Can you really see her pushing Maynard off a cliff in her gray cardigan, though? And over what? An argument?"

Zo shrugged. "Maybe she knew him in some other capacity."

"Brady interviewed her…" Max's attention was out the window. His eyes were following a disturbance up ahead. "I'll mention it to him. Hey, slow up."

She decreased her speed. An older man and woman were near the tree line, and the woman was making a commotion with her hands. Soon Zo understood why. A whitetail deer was caught in the barbed-wire fence.

She pulled over to the side of the road, realizing it was the Merrigans' property. In the distance, a large Merrigan nameplate hung over a gate to a house set back from the road.

Max sprang into action as soon as the car was stopped. "That deer is hung up. I need to help."

His voice was as steady as his movements, and Zo was glad for his cool head. Seeing an animal in such peril, she felt as frantic as the older woman. But she kept her emotions in check as she followed him to the fence. The couple was on the other side of it.

"Oh, thank goodness!" The woman clasped her hands together. "Thank you for stopping, Ranger."

"He's caught in the fence." The man held up a pair of wire cutters. "Whenever I try to get near him to cut him out, he bucks and makes it worse for himself."

"Zo, why don't you take a walk with these folks?" Max took the wire cutters from the man. "Whitetails can be skittish, and I don't think he likes all these eyes on him."

"We'll meet you at the turn-in, dear," the woman said to Zo. "By the sign."

Zo walked to the gravel path, meeting the couple at the entrance. In their late sixties, they still held hands, which she thought was cute. The woman was short and stout, her arms round and soft like bread dough. The man was slim and average sized, but his cowboy boots made him seem taller. He had an old-fashioned mustache that was a twirl of black and gray and a smile that matched his wife's.

"What did the ranger say your name was?" asked the woman.

"Zo—short for Zoelle," she answered.

"Oh, I love that." She turned to her husband. "Don't you love that, Peter?"

"Very nice," Peter agreed.

"I'm Katie Merrigan." She looked down the hill, showing off a perfect gray bun at the nape of her neck. "I sure hope that boy can work some magic."

Katie Merrigan! They must be Brady's parents.

"He can." Zo followed her gaze. "He got my cat off the ledge of a waterfall once. He's amazing with animals."

"I don't know why we still have that silly fence up anyway," Katie huffed.

"The deer were eating your garden, remember?" Peter turned to Zo. "Katie grows tomatoes the size of my fist." He doubled up his hand in demonstration. He wore a beautiful gold timepiece with a Celtic cross that looked as if it had been handed down through the generations. "I have pictures of them."

"Impressive," said Zo. "My neighbor can't even get little cherry tomatoes to grow."

"It's all in the soil." Katie stood on her tiptoes, angling for a better position to see how Max was doing. "I don't see the ranger. He's disappeared. Something's happened. I just know it. Go look, Peter."

"All done," announced Max, coming up behind them.

Zo jumped. "Is the deer okay?"

"Yep." Max returned the wire cutters to Peter. "I had to cut a small piece of your fence. Sorry about that."

"The important thing is the deer is free," exclaimed Katie. Her pretty green eyes were highlighted by long, black eyelashes. "I can't bear to see any animal hurting." She grabbed Max's arm. "Let me give you a piece of cake for your trouble."

"It was no trouble at all." Max smiled.

"She won't let you leave without eating something," Peter mused. "It might as well be cake."

"You, too, dear," Katie said to Zo. "Come on."

They walked around the curved gravel drive to the front of the property. The instant they walked under the swinging Merrigan sign, Zo felt like she was entering another world, a private world. A huge apple grove grew at one corner of the property, and when Katie quit talking, which wasn't often, Zo could hear a brook in the distance. The garden Peter had mentioned must have grown most of their food and then some. It was that big. How the couple managed the place on their own was a mystery. Then she remembered the couple had three sons. They must have helped with the property.

"This is gorgeous," Zo said to Peter, who walked beside her. "Have you always lived here?" No reason she couldn't talk and do a little investigative work, too.

"Yes, my granddad was one of the first prospectors in the area." Peter pointed to a creek, which came into view. "He and Nesbitt found a little gold in that creek there, but it didn't amount to much." He nodded to the house. "The land, however, amounted to a good deal when the Canyon Heights development came to town. They added a community pool, a gym, a guesthouse." A chuckle moved his mustache. "A little fancy for my taste, but it keeps property values up. I'm practically sitting on a gold mine."

Zo recognized the name he mentioned. "Nesbitt. He has a daughter, Olivia?"

Peter took her elbow as they stepped over a tree root. "Yes, they're our neighbors and have been since the beginning. Carl's great-granddad came West with mine to stake a claim. His place is even nicer."

"Nicer?" Zo shook her head. "I don't believe it."

Peter laughed. "Okay, then, bigger." They walked toward the house, a large two-story with a wraparound porch, complete with a swing and comfy pillows. "This was built new fifty years ago. The original property was no more than a shack."

"It's beautiful." Zo meant it. She'd seen a lot of fancy houses built in the Black Hills. This wasn't that. It was a traditional family home. It didn't have the soaring drop-off or the towering A-frame of some expensive houses, but it had something they didn't have: a homey, welcoming feeling. It settled over her the moment she stepped inside.

"Come into the kitchen." Katie was several steps ahead of them and walked flat-footed, a little like a penguin. "I made an apple cake this morning. You like apples, right?" She shook her head, not waiting for an answer. "What am I saying? Everybody likes apples." She picked up a knife and pointed it at the heavy, round table. "Sit there. Peter, get the kids some coffee. Do you drink coffee?"

"Yes, thank you," said Zo.

Max took a chair next to hers, shooting her a smile.

She tried to remember all the questions she had for the Merrigans but had a hard time focusing on anything but the cheerful yellow kitchen, the crisp white curtains, and the delicious scent of apples and cinnamon that filled the room. Katie served the apple cake on beautiful milk glass plates. Zo admired the antique pattern—and the treat.

After pouring the coffee, Peter placed the carafe on the table. He raised his coffee cup. "I bet this young man would rather have a beer after tangling with that buck."

"The cake is great," said Max. "I didn't eat lunch, so this hits the spot."

"You shouldn't have said that," Peter whispered.

"Said what?" asked Max.

"You didn't eat lunch?" exclaimed Katie, who was about to sit down. "A big, strapping man like you..." She popped back up and cut another huge slice of cake. It balanced precariously on the spatula on the way to table, then hit Max's plate.

Zo bit her lip to keep from laughing. If she had to guess, a third of the cake was on Max's plate. He was going to go into a sugar coma if he ate it all. But the cake was a nice mix of cinnamon, sugar, and tart Granny Smith apples, not overly sweet and quite filling. He wouldn't walk away from the table hungry; that was for sure.

After a few bites, Zo brought up Maynard's death. "One of your neighbors passed away this week, Maynard Cline. He and I belonged to the same astronomy club."

Katie put down her fork. "Isn't it awful? Peter and I were just talking about it this morning. Brady says he was *murdered.* Pushed right off the cliff. I can't believe it."

"Brady stopped by to make sure our security system was working." Peter sipped his coffee. "It is. I might be old, but I can still take care of my property. I think he forgets sometimes I was the chief of police."

"I'm sorry," said Katie. "You said Mr. Cline was in your club. Was he a friend?"

Zo shook her head. "More an acquaintance than friend. He was smart and knew a lot about architecture. But he kept to himself. He could be obsessive, especially about germs."

"Maybe that explains it," mused Katie. "When he moved to the area, I brought him a pound cake. He *refused* to take it." Her nostrils flared. "It wasn't good enough for the likes of him."

"I'm sure it wasn't the cake," explained Zo. "He had a hard time interacting with others."

"Still, he didn't have to be rude." Finished with his cake, Peter crossed his arms. "Some folks have no manners. He thought a lot of himself—and his mansion."

"I didn't like the looks of it," Katie admitted. "It was very showy." She gave a curt bob of her head, satisfied with the description. "He was a show-off."

After seeing the house, Zo couldn't disagree, but she wasn't going to disparage an acquaintance, and a deceased one at that. She switched topics. "You guys have been here a long time. Have you ever heard the rumor of a buried treasure, maybe in the area? The reason I ask is because it might have something to do with Maynard's death. Recently, he'd bought a book that might have given the location of the treasure."

"You're talking about Ezra Kind's gold, I assume," said Peter. "My granddad was looking for it when he came here. He was an adventurer." A twinkle sparkled in his eye. "The trait runs in the family."

Katie rolled her eyes. "Everyone's grandad was looking for it." She topped off her own coffee. "More?"

"No thanks," Zo said.

Max also passed on the refill. "I take it your granddad didn't find gold?"

"Heavens, no," said Katie.

Peter held up his cup to the outstretched thermos. "It's out here, though. Buried somewhere deep in these Hills. I'd bet my pension on it."

The twinkle in his eye told Zo if Peter had time and permission from his wife, he'd be combing the hills right now with a metal detector. Katie, however, was the more practical—and bossy—of the pair. It was a wonder *she* hadn't been the chief of police.

"Pish. There's no such thing. It was an excuse they told their wives to come West." Katie put down the carafe with a plunk. "And it worked."

"What about the book?" asked Max. "Do you think it might really include the location of the gold?"

"Maybe," said Peter. "Maybe the writer wanted to hand down man's greatest adventure: treasure hunting. But why would someone reveal such a prize?"

"For the greater good." Katie tipped her chin. "Greed is a dangerous sin, perhaps the most dangerous of the cardinal sins. I've seen it destroy people and families." She gestured toward the window. "Look at Mr. Cline. The kids seem to be saying his death has something to do with the gold." She clicked her teeth. "If you ask me, I hope it stays buried forever."

"The book or the treasure?" asked Zo.

"Both," she answered definitively.

The belief exposed another dimension of Katie, one that revealed her deep distaste for greed. Zo questioned how far the older woman would go to keep secrets buried, especially if they involved her family or loved ones. She was motherly, kind, and opinionated. Although the possibility of her killing Maynard was far-fetched, Zo couldn't dismiss it yet.

"I thought I recognized that voice."

Zo turned to see Brady in the kitchen doorway. Her stomach fell and all the cake with it. "This isn't what it looks like."

"It's exactly what it looks like, and give your mom a kiss before you say another word." Katie pointed to her cheek.

Brady walked over to his mom, but his eyes never left Zo's. "And Maxwell. You're here, too."

"I said not another word!"

Brady kissed her cheek. It would have been cute if he wasn't shooting daggers in Zo's direction.

"We had a buck stuck in the fence," said Peter. "This nice ranger stopped to get him out."

"Nice, indeed."

"If you don't start using your manners right now, Brady Merrigan, you can just hightail it out of here," Katie scolded.

Zo looked between the mother and son. Brady was as tall as she was stout, but they shared the same gleam in their eyes, the one that indicated spirit and stubbornness. Who was the more stubborn? That was the question soon to be answered.

"Cake?" asked Katie.

Brady Merrigan took off his hat and sat down. "Yes, please."

"Good boy."

Chapter Fourteen

Waving good-bye to the Merrigan clan from the front seat of her Subaru, Zo felt her heart shift. It was a nice family. Brady wasn't just a cop she clashed with now; he was a son with a mother he loved and respected. His parents were adorable, really. It seemed possible they were just as good as everyone said they were. The cake was certainly good. She glanced at Max, who sat in the passenger seat. He'd definitely enjoyed it.

"What?" Max stretched out his seat belt. "Has my stomach grown two sizes?"

Zo laughed. "You did eat a lot of cake."

"I couldn't *not* finish it."

She pulled onto the main road. "Katie would have been totally offended."

"They were nice." After a moment, he added, "I liked them."

"Me, too."

They continued on the road in silence. Zo was tucking away the new information into the Merrigan file in her head. They might be nice, but they were also possible suspects in Maynard's murder. She admitted the idea seemed unlikely. It wasn't that they weren't strong enough to push a body off the mountain. Maynard wasn't a big man or an athletic man. Anyone might have shoved him to his demise, even the fussy Agnes. It was that they seemed genuinely good. However, theirs was a lineage that stretched back a century. It was hard to fathom what that kind of history felt like or what one would do to protect it. And she had to face it: Their name *was* on a note on Maynard's hall table. It seemed like a pretty big clue to dismiss for a smile and a piece of cake.

A pop and a tug at her wheel pulled her thoughts from the Merrigans. "What the heck?"

She cranked the car to the side of the road, hearing a familiar *wub, wub, wub.* "I think I have a flat tire."

"Shoot." Max undid his seat belt.

She turned off the car, and Max followed her to the rear wheel. It wasn't completely flat—yet—but it was well on its way. She flung up her hands. "First a deer, now a nail? It's as if someone doesn't want us here."

"It seems that way, doesn't it?" He kneeled down for a look. "You have a spare?"

"Of course I have a spare." Zo had lived in the Black Hills her entire life and never went into the woods without being prepared. A spare tire, a blanket, and an emergency kit always went with her. But as she popped open the trunk, an image of white-haired Cunningham crept into her mind. In the picture, he was standing under the hood of the ancient Thunderbird, smiling. *No, no, no,* she thought, lifting the cover. The tire was in place, but the wrench was missing.

Cunningham, the least mechanical man in the entire world, had borrowed it for the classic Thunderbird he'd purchased a few weeks ago. The funny thing was, Cunningham didn't drive. He told her East Coast traffic was the reason he'd moved West in the first place. But he was "inspired" to fix up the old car, which reminded him of the one his father used to drive. Personally, Zo thought it was a substitute for his failed gardening hobby, but she hadn't said so. She didn't think someone who didn't own a lug wrench should be purchasing, let alone repairing, classic cars in the first place.

She recounted the situation to Max. They were too far from the Merrigan place to go back. A tow truck seemed like the only viable option. She pulled out her phone. No signal. A common problem in the forest or the canyon.

"It's okay." Max glanced up the hill. "There's a turnoff to the right." He squinted. "It looks like a private drive. We might be able to borrow a tool there."

It was worth a try, so they started walking.

"You must think I'm a real idiot," she said.

He put his arm around her. "I think *Cunningham's* a real idiot for not getting it back to you. What is he doing buying an old car, anyway? I didn't think he drove."

"He doesn't, but it seems it's a requirement for collecting classic cars." When they came to the private drive, she read the sign on the mailbox: Nesbitt, Merrigan's neighbor and Olivia's dad.

"At least we don't have to worry about a tow truck," he said. "They will have something."

And Max was in his park ranger uniform, so the Nesbitts would be more than willing to loan him the tools. At least she thought they would until she and Max reached the large iron fence. They shared a look. Peter Merrigan wasn't kidding when he said the Nesbitts' place was bigger than his. It was also fancier. Could they simply ask to borrow the tools? And how?

Max studied the intercom box. "What do I do? Push the button?"

"May I help you?" came a man's voice from the speaker.

Zo jumped. "Oh, hi. My car has a flat tire just down the road." She pointed behind her, despite not knowing whether the person on the speaker could see her or not. "We were wondering if we could borrow a lug wrench?" A beat of silence passed, and she pushed Max in front of the speaker. "He's a forest ranger."

"I'll be right there," said the voice.

The gate opened, and they inched forward. A sprawling ranch met their view. It, like Maynard's house, had an amazing drop-off that captured the mountain view. But that's where their similarities ended. The Nesbitt house was older and more carefully crafted with a hand-placed stone front. While Maynard's house was modern, this historical home was a testament to care and workmanship. When a middle-aged man met them inside the gate, Zo was not surprised. It must be Olivia's dad.

He stuck out his hand. "Carl Nesbitt." He wore a short-sleeved plaid shirt with a mint green vest and gray shorts. His glasses were square, black, and thick, but not unattractive. He was a tall man with long tan legs and could get by with wearing large accessories, like his platinum wedding ring. As most of her jewelry consisted of beads and bangles, Zo didn't know anything about rings, but if she had to guess, this one cost as much as her motorcycle.

Max shook his hand. "Max Harrington, and this is Zo Jones. We ran into a little problem down the road. A nail from somewhere popped the back tire."

"I know where," said Carl. "That monstrosity up the hill." When he pointed, the sunlight bounced off his ring. "My neighbor never quit building. I think it was a gazebo this month. The trucks went up and down the hill all day long."

Zo zeroed in on the comment. "You mean Maynard Cline, don't you?"

"Yes. He's been in the papers. They say he fell right off the mountain." Carl started walking and motioned for them to follow him. "I believe it, too. He worked on that place night and day. Like he was obsessed with it. I have a wrench in the garage."

"Brady Merrigan released a statement today, just a few hours ago." Max easily kept pace with Carl's long strides. "He said Maynard was murdered." They stopped in front of the four-stall garage.

"Maynard Cline murdered?" Carl shook his head. "Why?"

"That's the question," said Max.

Carl entered the garage. He didn't just have a tool chest; he had an entire system of shelves and drawers. He scanned the back wall. "I suppose it's possible, but I can't fathom who would do that. Maynard kept to himself. I don't think I said two words to him, and he's lived here for a while." He pulled open a red drawer full of wrenches and stepped aside.

Max moved forward to select one.

"Did he talk to any other neighbors?" Zo asked. "I know the Merrigans live down the road."

A bright white smile crept over Carl's face. "The Merrigans didn't care for him. Peter said the house was an *abomination*." He imitated Peter's voice. "He himself was a victim of the constant construction, like you. It affected his photography. Peter takes nature stills—or did. The animals stayed away because of the constant noise."

Zo remembered seeing a collection of photos in the entryway, including several owl photos shot at dusk. She didn't realize Peter had taken them himself, although he had mentioned pictures of Katie's tomatoes. Was it possible he was out the night Maynard died? She tucked away the idea.

Max held up the wrench he needed.

"Old families," continued Carl. "They have ideas about how the area should look and be. My dad was the same way. Personally, I thought Maynard's house had value. The architect was well known; the lines were clean." He made for the garage door, and they followed. "Granted, it didn't fit in. I'll give Merrigan that. But I didn't think it had to, either. Things are changing. This isn't the Wild West anymore."

No, it wasn't the Wild West, and no one would confuse Carl Nesbitt for a cowboy. He was as preppy as a private school boy. Zo bet he was the cool dad in Olivia's friend group, the one who sprung for ice cream or whatever rich dads sprung for, maybe spring break trips to Miami.

"It's a nice house," Max agreed. "Someone will pay a lot of money for it."

"Unless someone inherits it." Zo wondered if Maynard had family. Max said he hadn't found a next of kin, and she'd never heard Maynard speak about them, nor a significant other, at the Zodiac meetings. Carl was right about Maynard keeping to himself. He was on an island of his own making.

Carl stopped at the gate. "You think? I never saw a soul go in or out of the place. Just construction trucks."

Maybe Carl saw something the night of his death. She decided to ask. "Did you see anyone go in or out Monday night?"

"No," Carl said. "I can't say that I did. The police asked me the same thing."

"Maybe your daughter saw something?" Zo tried.

He shook his head. "She was with her boyfriend, at some meeting. She stayed in town."

That's right. Olivia was at the Zodiac meeting with Landon.

A whisper of wind curved through the trees, and the ponderosas swayed back and forth. In the distance, a woodpecker worked on a tree trunk. Like the town, the forest had its own pulse. If something out of the ordinary had happened, Carl would have noticed.

"Your wife?" tried Max. "Did she notice anything?"

"She passed away of cancer five years ago." He gazed at his house. "But she's always close, in my heart."

"I'm sorry," Zo said.

"Me, too," Max added.

"It's okay." His thick glasses magnified blinking lashes. "I have Olivia, and she reminds me a lot of her mother."

A beat passed, and with nothing left to say, Max held up the wrench. "Thank you for this. We'll bring it right back."

Carl smiled. "Keep it. I have more, and no one should be in the forest unprepared."

Feeling the embarrassment of the situation all over again, Zo silently scolded herself as they walked back down the hill.

Chapter Fifteen

The first thing Zo did Friday morning was to retrieve her wrench from Cunningham's badly organized garage. The second was to make an appointment at the local repair shop. She couldn't drive around on a spare tire. Luckily, no one had the Kawasaki reserved. Would the weather hold out? She checked her phone. The ten-day forecast looked decent. *Nice.* She would be able to deliver her Curious Camper column to Harriet without the threat of it getting wet. As long as the wind didn't blow it away, she would be fine.

George put a stop to her productive morning by placing his large orange rear end on the open rental schedule. Pausing to enjoy his company, she scratched his chin, and a purr began to rumble in his throat. The town was waking up, and she was forgetting to notice. *Shame on me.* She heard the cowbell from the O.K. Coffee Corral signaling someone's order was up, the tinny radio from Buffalo Bill's, the whiz of a fat-tire bike racing by, and now the crunch of footsteps on gravel.

The footsteps were followed by a knock at the door. Startled, Zo glanced out the window. *Harriet!* Zo checked the clock. It was still an hour from opening. She wasn't late with her column, so what was Harriet doing here?

"I need a gift for my niece," Harriet explained when Zo unlocked the front door. A spicy mix of cinnamon and floral perfume trailed behind her. "Two birds with one stone and all that. I hope you don't mind my coming early. I was on my way to the office."

Zo couldn't smell cinnamon without thinking kindly of the fifty-one-year-old woman. Her professional demeanor—smart, critical, and efficient—belied the depth of her generosity. Though she demanded excellence at the paper, she was quietly compassionate, always thinking of others. It was Harriet, in fact, who came to Zo with the idea for the Curious Camper column in the first place. Zo had just opened Happy Camper after being laid off by the *Black Hills Star*. Harriet said the column would be the perfect fit, and it was. Once a week, Zo handed in a short article about new places or trends. It gave not only tourists, but locals, the opportunity to keep abreast of happenings in the area. It also kept Zo in the information business.

"Not at all." Zo flipped the sign to OPEN. She might as well open the store since she no longer needed to take a trip to *Canyon Views*. "How old is your niece?"

"Twenty." Wearing fitted black slacks and a black-and-white-striped blouse, Harriet checked out the FIRESIDE FRIDAYS display. During the summer, Zo offered a discount on books that were perfect to read aloud around a campfire. This week's display included a book of poems by Joy Harjo, the U.S. Poet Laureate. Harriet picked it up. "This is perfect. She loves poetry. I'll take it."

"Are you sure you don't want to look around?" Zo asked.

"No." Harriet was resolute. "I hate shopping, no offense to your store."

Zo laughed as she walked to the cash register. "None taken." George jumped off the counter, and she shut her bike rental schedule and placed it on the shelf below, retrieving her column. "Here's this week's column. Would you like the book gift-wrapped?"

"Is it free?"

Zo rang up the purchase. "For my favorite editor? Of course."

Harriet pointed to the plaque that said COMPLIMENTARY GIFT WRAPPING. Like her lipstick, her fingernail was bright red. "I see I get all the perks. What's your topic this week?"

Zo zipped the debit card through the machine. "Gold Rush Days."

Harriet scanned the printout. "I heard Max is dressing up as Smokey the Bear and taking pictures with kids."

"He's so sweet," Zo gushed.

Harriet hiked a dark eyebrow. "That's not what you used to say about our Smokey the Bear."

Zo handed back the card. "People change."

"*She said with great affection.*" Harriet returned her attention to proofreading the column.

"We've been working together a lot," Zo defended. "This situation with Maynard is so confusing. The deeper I look, the more clues I find. Maybe it's the book that's got me off track."

"The book about Spirit Canyon?"

Zo nodded as she selected a funky giftwrap. Since Harriet's niece was young, she thought she would appreciate the colorful peace signs.

Harriet tucked the column in her purse with her credit card. "The column is fine. And I think you're right to focus on the book. Maynard was an interesting guy and all, but hardly worth murdering."

"Harriet!" Zo snagged a piece of tape.

"I'm just saying, the book has something to do with his murder. He's dead, and it's missing. There has to be a connection." Her brown eyes narrowed, considering the dilemma. Not finding an immediate answer, she continued. "This town has its spirits—but it also has its secrets. Find the book, and you could solve the mystery."

Including the mystery of my birth mom. After placing a Happy Camper sticker on the package, she handed Harriet the gift.

"You think of everything, don't you?"

Zo smiled. "I try."

Harriet tugged her purse over her shoulder. It was large and shaped like a doctor's medicine bag. She was a sort-of doctor—with words. "Except where to place a hyphen."

"Except that."

Harriet gave her a wave over her shoulder. "See you next week at Gold Rush Days."

"See you."

Zo finished preparing the store to open, which included selecting a record—she decided on the Beatles' *Abbey Road*—and cleaning the front window. She was tucking away her cleaning cloth when she received a text reminder that her sky-gazing book was overdue. *Shoot!* Because it was brand-new, she had promised to bring it back on time, and here it was two days late.

As soon as Harley arrived, Zo took off for the library on the motorcycle, the book safely tucked in her jacket. She entered the little brick building spouting profuse apologies. When it came to books, Hattie was like Harriet with punctuation: merciless. "I'm sorry, Hattie." She put the beautiful hardcover book on the reference desk. "As you know, my mind has been elsewhere."

"Like murder?" No longer in her gold attire, Hattie was back to her jeans and sweatshirt. Her red reading glasses dangled from two strands of colorful beads.

"Like murder," Zo repeated. At least Harriet understood.

"Shhh!" Agnes paused next to them. "People are trying to read."

Hattie waited for her to continue walking by. Then she crooked a finger at Zo, indicating she should come closer. "Reading isn't the only reason she wants me to stop talking about murder." She opened a drawer and flashed a library card. "I found this by her desk."

Zo focused on the name. "Maynard Cline! Why does she have Maynard's library card?"

"That's what I asked her," Hattie continued. "She said the argument they had Monday night was over a damaged book. She claims he spilled something on it, so she *revoked* his privileges until he paid the fine."

Zo had a hard time believing Maynard spilled anything anywhere. He was careful to a fault. And he, like Hattie, appreciated books. Heck, he'd just bought one for over ten thousand dollars. "Can she do that? Take away his library card?"

"Technically, yes." Hattie tucked the card away. "Practically, no. Maynard had plenty of money. If he ruined a book, he would have no trouble reimbursing the library. I think there's another reason she took it." She peeked over her desk toward the shelves, where Agnes had disappeared with the cart. "A reason she's not telling me."

"But what?" asked Zo. Agnes was a prim woman who adored rules. Although…Maynard was a bit of a stiff himself. He could be compulsive and unapproachable. Zo could see similar personality traits. Maybe they knew each other in some capacity.

"That's for you to find out," said Hattie. "When I questioned her, she clammed up. Maybe you and Max can be less obvious."

Hattie could be blunt. When it came to her civic space, she had a no-holds-barred policy. Anything but total transparency was an offense to the public's right to information. "I'll see what I can do," Zo promised. "Even if she did know him, it doesn't mean she killed him. I have a hard time seeing her push someone off a mountain."

At that moment, a patron let out a yelp, and Agnes said, "Excuse me. Your toe was in the aisle." She continued pushing the reshelving cart with velocity toward the nonfiction section.

Hattie lifted her silver eyebrows in Zo's direction.

"Okay, maybe so."

Two patrons sidled up to the reference desk, and Zo recognized one as Jeffrey Davis. He was with a young man dressed in jeans and a Pink Floyd T-shirt. "Hi, Professor Davis."

"Zo, right?" Jeffrey asked.

"Yes, good to see you again."

He gave her a brief smile. Though his face was thin and wan, his eyes were intelligent. They turned to Hattie. "We need a few books from the Special Collections room."

Library patrons always came first, so Hattie put aside their conversation, standing up from the desk. "I'll get my keys. Be right back." She hurried off toward the Employees Only sign.

The Special Collections room was a place where patrons and scholars could read and study rare books that were stored in the room's locked bookshelves. Most of the tomes were, in some way, related to South Dakota history. That must be why Jeffrey was here. Black Mountain College's library was larger and contained more books, but none as specific to the area. "What are you researching?" Zo asked.

"Not me." Jeffrey pointed to the man with him. "Thomas is one of my brightest graduate students. He's researching the first settlers of Lawrence County."

Humbled by the compliment, the student gave her a shy wave. Like his mentor, he was thin with a jaunty frame and long arms. "Tom Lancaster."

"Lancaster?" Zo asked. "Like the Lancasters who own the casino in Deadwood?"

Tom smiled, showing off a scruffy, pointed goatee. "You know your history."

"Not really," Zo admitted. "I've lived here my entire life. I heard they opened a hotel in town. I haven't been there myself, but tourists say it's really nice."

"A nice place to lose a lot of money. They run a shuttle to the casino in Deadwood twice a day. That way people can gamble *and* drink."

The smile didn't leave his face, and it was hard to tell if he was joking. When he continued, Zo realized he wasn't.

"My family has been stealing money from people since the beginning of time," said Tom. "Great-Great Grandpa stole his first dollar from a gambler down on his luck. The gambler shot himself later that day in Saloon No. 10. The family's lived off people's misery ever since."

"Thomas has specific opinions about gambling," explained Jeffrey.

That was one way to put it. "I bet they don't make you popular at holiday gatherings."

Tom cuffed his upper arms with his hands. He was all angles, hungry for justice. "I'm no longer invited, so that makes it easy to avoid the conversation."

Zo frowned. "So why study the history of Lawrence County, then? Doesn't your family play a prominent role?"

"We can't learn from history by burying it. Professor Davis taught me that." Tom's voice was thick with emotion. "I plan to expose my family and all the other crooks who came to the Wild West. They're not heroes— they're thieves. It's time somebody rights the wrongs."

She looked between Jeffrey and Tom. Here were two men on different sides of history, both scholars. One considered it his duty to preserve it, the other his duty to expose it. It was fascinating to her that they could collaborate while holding such opposing viewpoints. If only more people did that today. "Charlie Clay's memoir might make your job easier. Too bad it's missing."

"That book was supposed to go to Professor Davis," Tom insisted. "But like so many important pieces of history, it's been sold to the highest bidder."

Jeffrey held up his hand. "It's okay. We'll find what you need elsewhere. Here comes the librarian."

Hattie avoided chairs, computers, and cubicles as she walked toward them, her spectacles bumping up and down on her sweatshirt. "I'm sorry it took so long. The keys were buried under my new book order."

Jeffrey Davis pulled out a piece of paper with a list of titles. "These are the books we need to borrow."

Hattie slid her glasses onto her nose, reading the list. "You can't check out books from the Special Collections room."

"I'm the *chair* of the history department," stated Jeffrey. "That's why I'm here. I want to make sure Thomas gets what he needs. He's an important scholar."

Hattie glanced up from the list. "I don't care who you are. Nothing leaves the Special Collections room. Period."

Jeffrey bristled. Tom flinched. The statement was a blow to their egos, but Zo enjoyed seeing Hattie set them straight. This wasn't the first time Jeffrey had dropped his title to try to get what he wanted. He should know better than to try to use his position for special favors, especially in Hattie's public library.

With Hattie's point firmly made, they had nothing to do but follow her back to the Special Collections room like two scolded dogs. Zo wondered if they were dogs enough to steal something they couldn't borrow. For all Tom's high and mighty talk, it might be a hard family tradition to break.

Chapter Sixteen

"Careful!" cautioned Jules. "That's a real crystal ball."

Gritting her teeth, Zo covered the purple orb in bubble wrap before placing it into the open box. It was Friday night, and they'd been packing for hours. Her back was killing her, and she was growing weary of Jules's very specific directions. After carefully tucking away its stand—because what was a crystal ball without a stand?—Zo stretched her legs. "How about a glass of that wine before all the glasses are packed away?"

From the kitchen, Jules held the bottle in midair. "A 2001 Bordeaux? You have good taste." She admired the label. "Oh, what the heck. It's my last night in this house. *If* we finish packing."

Zo gestured to the room, piled high with boxes. Except for the oversized picture of Medusa, which Jules wouldn't let her touch, they were almost finished. "This is the last of it, isn't it?"

Jules reached for the wine opener. "We still have the mood stones to pack. None of them can touch each other."

Zo ticked off the seconds until her first sip of wine. She loved Jules, she really did, but her friend could be super finicky. Zo had been subjected to all sorts of voodoo rules the entire night. If the stuff was so sensitive, Jules should have packed it herself and left Zo to the dishes or something that didn't have an aura. "How does Duncan like the guesthouse?"

The cork came out with a *pop*. "He loves it, and to be honest, I like having him there, to keep an eye on the place." Jules filled two stemless glasses. The sound was music to Zo's ears.

Jules liked having Duncan there now, but what would happen when she moved into the manor? Zo took the glass of ruby liquid, and they clinked glasses. She guessed they would soon find out. "To your new house."

"And to a new chapter," Jules added. "For both of us."

Zo swirled the wine, then sipped. Jules might be pretending when it came to predicting the future, but she wasn't pretending when it came to wine. *This stuff is good.* "Does that mean you and Duncan are—"

"I don't know why everyone thinks just because you let a guy move onto your property that you're dating." Jules plopped cross-legged on the floor beside her, her pink bun flopping to one side. "Max asked me the same thing."

Zo knew Jules well enough to let the remark slide. In Jules's mind, it was a business proposition, nothing more. She obviously didn't see the budding relationship that others did.

"What about you and Max?" asked Jules. "You never told me how dinner went. I know the wine was good, because I sold it to you. How was everything else?"

Everything else was the dilemma. "He burned the lasagna, so we had dinner at Lotsa Pasta." Zo brought her wine to her lips to avoid saying anything else.

"And?" Jules's brown eyes did that thing they did when she wanted to know something. It was almost as if they turned another color, melting away secrets.

Zo pulled her sweater tight. "And he mentioned my moving in with him."

"Oh, Max." Jules shook her head. "That's terrible."

"Right?" Zo took a sip of her wine. "What was he thinking? I love Happy Camper. I would never move in with him, with anyone."

"Did you tell him about your trust issues?" asked Jules.

"Sure, I slid it in right after passing the Parmesan." Zo set down her glass. "I don't have trust issues. I have issues with people I just started dating asking me to move in with them. It took us months to have dinner, and out of the blue, he drops that bomb? It's crazy train."

Jules tapped her long purple fingernails on her wineglass, waiting.

Sure, Zo's voice had risen two octaves in the last few minutes, but really, Max's remark was out of bounds. Dinner at his place was a stretch. Moving in together? Even mentioning it was pure lunacy. She polished off her wine with one big gulp. "Let's get back to it. We don't have all night. Where are the mood stones?"

Jules leveled a look at her. "If you ever treat a 2001 Bordeaux like that again, I'll serve you screw-top wine for the rest of your life."

"Sorry. It was a long day at Happy Camper, and I'm just tired." She put on her best happy face. "So, what's next?"

"You finish the kitchen," instructed Jules. "*I'll* do the mood stones."

It was well after midnight when they taped the last box shut. If Zo thought Jules had a lot of wine, she had even more wineglasses. Stemless, long-stemmed, flutes. While Zo packed a dozen cupboards, Jules had secured six mood stones for transport. But Zo didn't mind. She was just glad to be finished.

She stared into the quietness. Devoid of pictures, candles, music—it was weird. Maybe Jules was right about energy. Every ounce of it seemed drained from the place. The ring of Jules's phone interrupted the silence. Zo jumped. "Who in the world?"

Jules frowned at the screen. "It's Duncan." She answered the call. "Hello?" A few moments passed. "No, it's not me. Go see who it is."

"Someone's in your new house?" whispered Zo, though there was no reason to whisper.

Jules covered the mouthpiece. "He's checking."

"Don't let him go in there alone. If it's a burglar, he could get hurt." Zo took out her phone. "I'm calling Max."

"Duncan's outside, walking around the perimeter. Tell Max we'll meet him."

Zo woke a tired-sounding Max. He promised to be right there. She hung up the phone on the way to the car. "He's coming."

A few minutes later, they pulled up to Mountain View Manor. In the shadows of the streetlight, it didn't look as friendly as it did the day of the auction. It was tall, dark, and foreboding, perhaps even haunted. Zo checked Jules's reaction. Her eyes were sparkling. Yep, this was the perfect place for her to live.

Wearing lounge pants and nothing else, Duncan met them in the driveway. It was hard not to stare at his rock-solid abs, but Zo made an attempt to avert her eyes.

"*Dang…*" Jules threw the car in PARK and shut off the ignition. "I don't know why I'm being tested like this."

"With abs like that, it might be a test worth failing."

Jules threw her a look before getting out of the car.

"Hey, guys." Duncan ran a hand through his jet-black hair. "I thought I saw someone climb over the fence, but when I checked, nothing."

"Was someone inside?" asked Zo.

He glanced back at the house. "I don't know. I saw a flashlight. At least that's what I thought it was. I was taking out the garbage, and I saw a flicker through the windows, like someone was walking around. I was in my boxers, so I had to get some pants on. And call you. By the time I did, the light was gone."

Jules retrieved the house key from her purse. It still had the Tracey Auctions key chain attached. "What about the fence? Where did they get through?"

"In the back, near the carriage house," said Duncan. "I'll show you."

"I want to go inside first." Jules started for the front door. "I need to make sure nothing was damaged."

"Wait. Here comes Max." Zo knew it was Max by the rumble of his pickup truck. That thing really needed a new muffler.

Jules squinted into the inky night. "Is that Scout?"

"Of course it's Scout. He brings that dog everywhere." Duncan turned to Zo. "You should hear him baby-talk to her."

As soon as Max parked, Scout spotted Zo and gave her two loud barks. The two loud barks were followed by a run, a jump, and a dazed Max, dressed in a sweatshirt and athletic shorts. His sandy blond hair stuck up on one side, showing Zo on which side he'd been lying when she called. A dark outline of whiskers deepened his jawline.

"Hey, sleepyhead," Duncan greeted.

"What's going on?" asked Max.

While petting Scout, Zo filled him in on the details.

"Let me go in first." Max signaled for Scout, and she moved next to him. Zo was impressed. It was almost like Scout was Max's partner, not just his sidekick.

Jules opened the door and stood aside. "By all means."

The house was so quiet Zo could hear the sound of her own breath—and Scout's. Their footsteps echoed on the cherrywood floors as they entered the foyer. Max looked upstairs while they hung back in the living room. A car drove by, the shadows from the headlights dancing on the walls.

Spirit Canyon was, by nature, a quiet place to live. Not much happened after dark, except campfires and a little country music at Buffalo Bill's. When something out of the ordinary happened, people noticed. Zo wondered if anyone else besides Duncan had seen the intruder near Jules's home.

The click of Scout's nails on the stairwell made her turn. Max followed with heavy footsteps and a shrug. She noticed he had on hiking boots with his athletic shorts. She smiled. Duncan might be hot, but Max was cute.

"Nothing upstairs," Max said. "I wonder who was here."

Jules flipped on the lights. "There's nothing to steal. I don't move in until tomorrow."

"People steal copper, appliances, building materials." Duncan peeked into the kitchen. "Nothing out of place here." He returned to the living room, leaning against the door frame. "What are you going to do with all this space, Jules? Throw extravagant parties and invite me, I hope." Jules crossed her arms. "Throw extravagant parties and not invite you." "How about throwing on a shirt for starters?" asked Max.

Duncan gave Max a once-over. "Your style has declined since I left." "You've been gone a week." Max threw up his hands. "Give me a break."

"Seriously, why would anyone bust into an empty house?" Jules scanned the group for answers, but they had none to give. It didn't make sense. Why this house, and why now?

Zo had an idea. "Maybe it has something to do with *My Journey West.* We know it belonged to Vera."

Max nodded. "It's possible."

"It's something," Jules agreed. "Let's check the library."

The library looked a lot bigger without floor-to-ceiling books covering the walls, but the smell was the same. Musty, worn, academic tomes had filled the room for years, and there was no replacing the distinctive—and Zo thought comfortable—smell. She inhaled deeply, noticing an open glass door of an empty bookshelf. She poked her head in. "Was this open when you left?"

"I don't remember it being open the day of the walk-through," said Jules. "It's hard to say for certain, though. I had a lot going on, and it's been a week."

"No one's been in or out of here since?" asked Max.

Jules shook her head, checking the other cabinets.

Scout sniffed the corners of the room. Following the dog's nose, Zo noticed a sparkle in the moonlight near the window. She bent down to see what it was. An expensive gold barrette with three princess diamonds lay on the floor. Only a very wealthy woman could afford a piece of jewelry such as this, and Zo guessed whom.

"What is it?" Max joined her. So did Duncan and Jules.

She held it up in the light. "A barrette."

"It looks antique," said Duncan. "Maybe it belonged to the old woman who lived here."

Except that it didn't. Zo admired the clear, square diamonds, evenly spaced. She'd recognize the jewelry anywhere. "This isn't Vera's." She looked up at the three faces staring back at her. "It's Olivia Nesbitt's."

Chapter Seventeen

"Olivia Nesbitt, Landon's girlfriend?" asked Jules. "What would she be doing in my house?"

Duncan, Max, Scout, Jules, and Zo were in the kitchen, studying the barrette like a bar of gold. The kitchen was the place people congregated even when there wasn't food—or furniture. Zo loved that about kitchens. They were so comfortable. "Was Olivia at the estate sale? Maybe she lost it then."

Scout's panting filled the silence, and Jules cut the dog a look. "I don't think so, but it's hard to concentrate with that...smell in the air."

Max patted Scout's head. "It was hamburger night. She likes pickles."

"I don't remember seeing Olivia, but a lot of people were here." Zo's last few days, in fact, were a whir of people. The Zodiac meeting, the auction, the library event. She focused on the occasions that involved Olivia. "Max and I met her dad, Carl, when I blew a tire out by his place. He's really nice. He lent me a lug wrench." She turned the barrette over in her hand. "But this is hers. I know it. She has two of them."

"Right," added Jules. "She wears her hair pulled back."

"But why would she break in?" Max asked. "She has all the money in the world. You've seen her house."

"Like Zo said, maybe it has something to do with that missing book." Duncan sniffed. "Scout really does need her teeth brushed."

"We need to get some more mint snacks, don't we, girl?" Max patted her head. "Yes, we do."

They stared at Max's voice change.

"What? They're shaped like little toothbrushes. She loves them." Max cleared his throat before continuing. "The book is the only clue we have to go on, and the barrette *was* found in the library. The evidence connects her to the crime."

The statement hung in the air unchallenged. It was true, but it didn't explain the hair pin. Olivia must have been here sometime, but if not tonight, when and why? "If only we had the book," Zo muttered.

"I'll ask her about it when I return the barrette," said Max. "There's nothing more we can do tonight."

Zo held up the shiny gold object. "Except I'm the one who found it. We both need to return it."

"Fine." Max hooked Scout's leash.

Duncan *tsk*ed. "You're not going to argue about her coming with us for the next ten minutes?"

"Or recite police protocol?" added Jules.

"Or quote the handbook?" Duncan waggled his finger. "You're not just losing your style; you're losing your edge. What kind of ranger are you?"

"The kind who's falling for a girl," said Jules said in a singsong voice. She and Duncan shared a fist bump, congratulating themselves on the exchange.

"Neither of you have room to talk," said Zo. "You're *literally* living on the same property."

Their smiles faded, but Max's grew. "Yeah. What she said."

Zo followed Max out, and Jules locked the door behind them. After bidding the guys good night, they climbed into Jules's VW Bug. "Does this mean I'm done for the night?" Zo asked.

"I suppose," Jules said with an exaggerated sigh. "Seriously, thanks for all the help. I couldn't have done it without you."

"No problem." Zo rolled down the window, taking in the cool night air. She needed to relax if she was going to get some rest. The night had been a bustle of physical and mental activity. She focused on the quiet outside her window.

The town whirled by like scenes from her favorite movie. The new, the old, the older. The pretty brick buildings and ornate lampposts told her she was close to home. "Will you need help tomorrow?"

Jules turned into Zo's driveway. "No, the movers will be hauling furniture and boxes most of the day, and I don't want to be in their way. But I could use your help on Sunday, if you have time."

"I'll make time." Zo smiled. "You're not afraid to be at the house alone after this?"

Jules shifted the car to PARK. "What do you think?"

She sneaked a peek in her friend's direction. Her witch T-shirt said no.

Jules smiled. "Look, we're not even sure someone was *in* the house. I'm not going to stress about it until it's time to stress. A lot of energy is wasted that way."

Though she knew what Jules said was true, Zo stressed about the break-in most of the night. Oliva Nesbitt was the least scary person she knew. Pretty, smart, and fashionable, she was hardly a criminal, so it wasn't that. It was the fact that someone was in Jules's house, looking for something. Was it the missing book or not related to the book at all? *If only I had that book...*

When the first hints of daylight hit her shade, Zo was up, too wired to stay in bed. Or too hot. George was curled up next to her in a ball. When she tossed off the covers, he blinked, surprised that, for once, she was up before he was. Then again, he'd just come to bed at four o'clock. She knew because he'd announced his arrival with a long, relaxing bath.

After a quick cup of coffee, she hit a walking trail not far from her house. The mountain air instantly cooled her off as the scent of pine trees surrounded her. It felt good to be outdoors, especially on a morning like this, with the sunlight just beginning to sweep over the trees in the distance. Spirit Canyon was coming alive, and soon tourists and travelers would fill the tiny town with happy laughter. Like her, they thought the town was a marvel. But for now, it was hers alone, the crunch of her shoes on the trail the only sound, except for Spirit Canyon Creek, which followed the trail all the way to the iconic waterfall.

On the way home, she grabbed a second cup of coffee at the O.K. Coffee Corral. The geraniums in Happy Camper's window boxes greeted her with popping pink blooms, and she watered them and the pots of white and yellow daisies, which just screamed *happy* to her, before going in for a shower.

Trekking up her deck stairs, she noticed Justin Castle leaving Cunningham's house. She almost didn't recognize him because he was there alone, no KRSO van in sight. Had he made a personal call? Zo doubted it, but she couldn't ask right now. She had to open the store in one hour.

After she was dressed, George was fed, and the Happy Camper sign was flipped to OPEN, she called Cunningham. He wasn't the easiest person to talk to on the phone and enjoyed face-to-face interactions better. Texts were altogether out of the question.

"Hello?" he answered.

"Hey, I saw Justin Castle leaving your house this morning. Everything okay?"

"Believe it or not, he was asking about the Zodiac Club. He thought I was a member." Cunningham chuckled. "I told him he was confusing me with Linwood. Common professor problem."

Zo doubted Justin was confused. He knew everything that went on in town, and he'd crashed one of their Zodiac meetings before. She wondered if he had other motives for dropping by. "Did he ask any questions about me?"

Cunningham's white whiskers scratched against the mouthpiece, and with a wince, Zo pushed her speaker button and laid the phone on the counter.

"He did," answered Cunningham. "You weren't home, and he wanted to know more about Maynard. He's covering the homicide."

"You didn't tell him anything, did you?"

"I didn't know the man," said Cunningham matter-of-factly. "I have nothing to tell."

"But about the missing book?"

"Of course not."

"Justin is digging for dirt." The bell on the door chimed, and Max entered. She waved him forward, pointing to her phone. "He's trying to figure out why I care so much. He knows Maynard was just an acquaintance."

"So, why not tell him?" asked Cunningham. "You're both journalists. The truth is important in your line of work."

It was important to her; it didn't seem important to Justin. He cared more about popularity and ratings than facts. Likes, retweets, and shares were what mattered to him.

"Imagine what could happen if you collaborated, instead of arguing," Cunningham continued. "You'd find the book in a jiffy. I know you would."

"That may be true, but collaboration isn't in Justin's vocabulary," said Zo. "He's too self-centered to share the spotlight with someone."

"Is that Max's pickup truck over there?" asked Cunningham.

"Hi, Cunningham," Max said. "I just got here."

"See what good things can happen when people collaborate? Like you and Max. To be honest, I never thought you'd get a serious boyfriend," he added. "That deck was a spinning door."

"Thanks for repeating that out loud," grouched Zo. "Gotta go. Bye."

Max smirked, crossing his arms. "Was it really spinning?"

"Like a top."

Chapter Eighteen

Max helped Zo hang a new print of Badlands National Park, which was located about an hour east of Spirit Canyon. Drenched in rose, gold, and brown, the print was a beautiful depiction of the rugged terrain by a local artist. She would have a hard time parting with the stunning painting. That was the only drawback to owning Happy Camper. Some of the items she bought for resale ended up being permanent fixtures in the store or house. The 1940s radio, the Remington typewriter, the bison print by her favorite Lakota artist—they were all part of her décor now, which was okay. Tourists bought less-expensive items, like the durable plastic dinnerware, perfect for camping, homemade postcards, and of course, her Happy Camper merchandise.

Harley stomped through the door without saying hello to her or Max. Instead, she marched over to the garbage can, pressed the foot pedal, and threw a bouquet of pink carnations in the trash.

"Hey!" Zo retrieved the flowers. "At Happy Camper, we don't throw away perfectly good flowers. What's the matter with you?"

"Chance, that's what's the matter." Harley tucked her bag under the counter.

Seconds later, Chance rushed through the door calling her name. At least that's who Zo assumed he was. He was the same age as Harley, but their similarities ended there. While Harley was dressed in army pants and combat boots, Chance wore khaki shorts and a blue polo. Zo squinted. *Wow.* Was Chance a golfer? From his outfit, he was on his way to play right now.

"Harley, I'm sorry," Chance said. "Please believe me."

Zo and Max took a step back from the counter to give the couple some privacy. Trying to look busy, Zo seized the opportunity to put the flowers into a vase. Max studied a nearby knickknack. Chance must have done something really awful.

Ignoring him, Harley turned to Zo and Max. "He said roller derby wasn't a sport."

Zo winced. Harley took her participation in the local roller derby league very seriously. She was committed and incredibly talented, and Zo loved watching her tournaments. To question it being a sport was a bad move. A very bad move.

"I didn't say it wasn't a sport," Chance explained. "I said it wasn't a *classic* sport."

You're not helping yourself, dude.

Max tried to disappear into the corner.

"In the sense that it's not played on campus, that's all I meant!" Chance touched Harley's elbow. "I loved watching you skate. It was exhilarating. Much more exciting than golf."

Ah, so he is a golfer. Zo sort of felt bad for him. He had on a lopsided grin that begged for forgiveness.

The look didn't escape Harley, who didn't exactly return the smile but blinked in a way that said she might speak to him again.

Chance glanced at Zo. "You must be Zo." He stuck out a hand. "Harley has told me all about you. It's nice to meet you."

Zo shook it. "You, too."

"And you're...a forest ranger?" he asked Max.

"Correct," Max said, swallowing a chuckle.

"He's Zo's boyfriend, Max." Harley's voice still held a hint of irritation. "You guys must be on your way somewhere."

"The Nesbitt house," Max said.

"Hey, they belong to the country club." Chance relaxed his stance. He was relieved the topic was off him. "I know them."

Zo grabbed her backpack.

"I caddied for the dad once," Chance added. "He wears these big glasses." He made binoculars with his hands. "But he's a pretty good golfer."

Harley must have known the conversation was a desperate attempt to get the topic off himself. Ignoring his comments, she turned to Zo. "Go ahead. I can take it from here."

Zo threw her sack over one shoulder. "Thanks, Harley, and it was really nice to meet you, Chance."

When Max and Zo were in Max's pickup truck, Max asked, "You don't play any unconventional sports I should know about, do you?"

Zo laughed. "No, unless you call chase-the-cat a sport."

Max headed down Main Street, out of town. "I thought George was getting better at staying home."

"Better—but not good." She rolled down the manual window. The truck didn't have air-conditioning, which wasn't a problem for their area. Spirit Canyon had an arid climate that rarely called for cooling systems. Heaters, on the other hand, were an absolute necessity. Winters could be cold, not to mention snowy. Mother Nature dumped over fifty inches of snow per year in the canyon.

"You can't expect a guy to change overnight," said Max. "It takes time. Be patient."

She checked his face. "We *are* talking about George, right?"

His lips turned up. "Right."

Zo was happy to see Olivia's car parked in the Nesbitt driveway. At least she thought it was Olivia's car. It was a red Mustang convertible with the top down. She couldn't imagine Carl driving a car like that.

Max hung his arm out the window and pushed the intercom button. He told the voice on the other end the reason for their visit and was buzzed in.

"You brought the barrette?" Max opened the truck door.

"Of course I brought the barrette." They didn't get all the way up the path before the front door opened.

"Oh, hey." Olivia was surprised to see them. Her straight blond hair was pulled to one side with the matching pin Zo had in her backpack, and she wore a pink sleeveless button-up and jean shorts. "What's up?"

"Hi, Olivia." Zo gestured to Max. "This is Max, by the way. He's a forest ranger for the National Park Service."

"Cool," said Olivia.

"We're here to return something we believe belongs to you." Max nodded at Zo, and she retrieved the barrette from her sack.

Oliva grabbed the gold and diamond pin from Zo's hands. Her fingernails sported a perfect French manicure. "I've been looking all over for this! Where did you find it?"

"Funny you should ask," said Max. "We found it in Julia Parker's new house. Mountain View Manor?"

"Oh." Oliva didn't sound surprised or alarmed.

"There was a break-in last night," explained Zo. "This was found in the house."

She looked over her shoulder, then closed the door. They were alone on the front porch. Two rocking chairs and a table sat neatly to one side of the door. "I had nothing to do with a break-in, if that's what you're implying. I was at Vera Dalrymple's estate sale. That must have been when I lost it."

"Okay, but I was at the estate sale." Zo shook her head. "I didn't see you there."

Carl opened the front door. He wore khaki shorts, displaying tan legs from afternoons spent at the club. His face was tan also, showing the resemblance between him and his daughter. Only the hint of gray above the ears and thick glasses betrayed his age. "Hello there. I hope you didn't drive all the way out here to bring back my wrench."

"We didn't." Zo opened her backpack. "But I brought it with me. We were returning a barrette to Olivia."

Olivia flashed him a cautious smile as she showed him the jewelry. Like her dad, she had fair hair that was made lighter by the warm coloring of her face and a distinguished cleft chin.

"That was your mother's, Olivia. How could you be so careless?" Carl angrily snatched the barrette from her hand. "Where did you find it?"

"What's important is that it's back," Olivia said. "I promise I'll be more careful."

Max ignored Olivia's interruption. "Mountain View Manor."

Carl crinkled his nose, his glasses inching up his face. He looked at her critically. "Why were you there? And you'd better not say Landon."

They all waited on an answer.

"I was there..." Olivia started, but her dad cut her off with a scoff. "Fine, I was there for Landon, but that's not a crime. The sale had a lot of stuff from the mines, and I thought he might like something."

Carl lodged his complaint with Max. "If you can do anything about that boy, you should. He's a thief and a liar. He stole my cuff links, and when I confronted him, he lied right to my face."

"He is not a thief or a liar!" Olivia insisted. "He works all the time. He works every weekend. He's working right now." The defense came as fast as she could spit it out, her face flushed with emotion. "Just because he's poor doesn't mean he's a thief or a bad person."

"I never said that." The discomfort in Carl's voice was palpable. Perhaps he was embarrassed that she'd uttered the suggestion in mixed company. Obviously, a ranger and a small business owner didn't live in the same world he did, but that was all right with Zo. She wasn't interested in the high life.

"What I said is that he's no longer welcome in this house, Olivia," Carl added. "I don't trust him."

"*No one's* welcome in this house," she muttered.

Carl turned his ear to her. "What did you say?"

Olivia stood taller, looking more like an adult. Her voice was stronger, too. "Look, Dad, I'm sorry, but Mom's been gone five years, and you still can't leave. The place is like a...a tomb." Her lips quivered, and she blinked back tears. "I can't live that way, and you can't keep me here forever. I'm moving on—with Landon. You should, too." Not waiting for an answer, Olivia hurried to her car.

"Olivia, wait!" But she was gone. Carl turned to Max and Zo, shaking his head. "I apologize for her behavior. She doesn't know what she's saying. I've spoiled her more than I like to admit. Someday she'll realize the value of a home. I hope." Then he held up the pin to the light. "Thank you for returning this. She loves the set, or used to, before she became so reckless. I know it's because of Landon. He's a bad influence."

Although Zo had only known Landon for six months, she felt the need to defend him. "He's in my astronomy club, and he's really not a bad person."

"I know what I know." Carl crossed his arms. "Ever since Olivia met him, she's changed. She's doing things she would have never done before. Staying out late. Going to parties, protests—estate sales." He raised his hands in frustration. "What was she doing there? Looking for some old junk to buy for him? He's using her for her money. I know it."

"Zo says he's really smart," Max said.

"He is," she seconded. "He's applying for a graduate assistantship next fall. He wants to be a scientist."

"Maybe so, but look around." Carl motioned to the oversized entryway. It was a stone masterpiece of black, brown, and green. "The kid can see we have a lot to offer. The only way for him to get ahead is through Olivia."

Zo didn't agree with that but kept quiet. She knew how sensitive dads could be about their daughters, and Olivia was his only family. It made sense that he was overly protective. "We'd better be going. Thank you for your time."

"Thank you again for bringing this back." Carl glanced at the jewelry. "I'll see you out."

They walked to Max's truck, which looked even older in the upscale surroundings. Waving good-bye, they jumped into the cab, agreeing to pay Landon a visit before leaving the driveway. Copperhead Mine, where he worked, was only five miles away.

As they inched down the private drive, Max asked, "Do you really think Olivia was at the estate sale, like she said?"

"I didn't see her." She turned to Max. "But there *were* some items from the Homestake Mine for sale. I saw them while browsing the tables."

Max rounded a curvy corner. "She doesn't seem like the kind of girl who shops estate sales. No offense."

"None taken." Zo loved estate sales, all the mementos and stories that made up a person's life. She also liked the idea of repurposing items and furniture instead of taking them to the local dump. "Her dad says she's changed. Maybe Landon is rubbing off on her, in a good way."

"Like you're rubbing off on me?" Max flashed her a smile before refocusing on the next turn.

"Exactly like that."

"Anyway, I hope we find the book, and when we do that, it sheds some light on your story."

Zo watched the trees fly by like the pages of a glossy magazine. They seemed to go on forever and ever. "It's a long shot."

"I believe in long shots."

She glanced at him, sharing his smile. "Me, too."

Chapter Nineteen

Like many gold mines, Copperhead Mine was an ugly scar on an otherwise beautiful landscape. The giant crater in the earth was the ultimate sign of greed, in Zo's opinion. People traded the environment for money, or gold that would turn into money. Scanning the area, layers of smooth rock where trees had been, Zo felt her stomach turn. She didn't like seeing nature used this way. From the furrow of Max's brow, he didn't, either.

Heavy equipment loaders lined the hillside, as well as workers in orange helmets and yellow vests who operated them. In the dock area, containers were in various stages of being loaded, and the large doors stood open, showing the activity that went on inside. Men and women alike were busy hauling, separating, and measuring minerals from dirt. In the hot summer sun, with no trees to provide shade, the work had to be daunting.

Max drove through the parking lot, filled with cars, and pulled into an open visitor's spot near the small office building.

A man in a protective jumpsuit gave them a nod as they got out of the truck. "Can I help you with something, Ranger?"

"Actually, you can," said Max. "I'm looking for Landon Hess. Do you know him?"

"Sure," said the employee. "But you won't find him in the office. Follow me."

Max and Zo did as he said, following him to a metal building with large dock doors. Like the other workers, Landon wore a protective jumpsuit covered in dust, an orange hard hat, and goggles. He was busily sifting a sluice box over a large receptacle.

"You got visitors."

Landon looked up from his work. Even with goggles on, his brown eyes were focused and intelligent. "Hey, Zo. What are you doing here? Please tell me nothing else is wrong at the Zodiac Club. We're meeting at the observatory tonight, right?"

Zo assured him the club members were fine and the meeting was still on. "Believe it or not, we were kind of in the area, and Olivia said you were working today. I've never been out here, so we thought we'd drop by. I hope that's okay."

"Sure, it's okay," said Landon.

She touched Max's elbow. "This is Max."

They exchanged hellos.

Landon set down his box and wiped his calloused hands on his jumpsuit. "Someone in the office might be able to give you guys a tour, if you're interested."

"Maybe another day." Zo tried to keep her voice neutral. It was great that the mine employed so many people. Work could be hard to find in town. But the last thing she wanted was a tour. "Last night someone broke into Jules's new house, the old Dalrymple place on Mountain View Road."

"You're kidding," said Landon. "Jules must be fuming. The person had better watch out. She'll put a spell on them." He took a step closer to Max, lowering his voice. "You know she's a witch?"

Max smiled. "I've heard that rumor."

"What did they take?" A pile of rock pummeled an oversized bucket behind them, and Landon motioned outside the work shed. It was too noisy inside to have a conversation.

They followed him to the cool shade of the building, where he took off his hard hat, wiping damp hair from his forehead before returning the head covering. Mining was daunting, sweaty work, especially in the July South Dakota sun, and he looked older than college-age.

Zo understood the toil work could take on the body and mind. From the time she was very young, she worked one odd job or another, paying for essentials that might have been provided by a stable family or parents. Seeing Landon here reminded her of the additional obstacles he faced that other students didn't and admired him all the more.

Returning to his comment, she realized she hadn't considered the possibility of two thieves. Maybe Duncan had seen only one person of a pair. She tucked away the idea. "Nothing was taken that we know of, but something *was* left behind."

"We found Olivia's gold barrette at Jules's house," said Max. "That's why we were at the Nesbitts. We returned it to her."

"Wait." Confusion crossed Landon's brow. "Olivia's? That doesn't make sense. Why would she be in Jules's house?"

"That's what we were hoping you might be able to tell us," Zo explained. Landon took a moment to consider the question. He was a smart guy. Zo knew that from the short time he'd been in the club. He could rattle off constellations she hadn't even heard of or find a star in the professional telescope in a matter of minutes. She hoped he was awarded the assistantship for grad school. Next to Harley, he was the hardest-working and most dedicated young person she knew. Hopefully, the awards committee saw it the same way.

Not coming up with an answer, he let out a breath. "It doesn't make any sense. I can't think of any reason for her being there. Did you ask her?"

"She said she went to Dalrymple's estate sale," explained Max. "She claimed to be shopping for you."

"Dalrymple owned some relics from old mines, including Homestake," added Zo. "She thought you might be interested."

Landon's face cleared. "That explains it. I've worked this mine since we were sophomores, and I've read a lot on the subject." His lips curled into a smile. "That's kind of cool that she went. I bet it's the first sale like that she's been to."

"So, what did she buy you?" Max asked.

Landon squinted. "What?"

"From the auction?" Max reiterated. "What did you get?"

"I don't know." He shook his head. "She hasn't given me anything—yet. Maybe she's saving it for a special occasion."

Or maybe she's lying, Zo silently added.

"Olivia's dad said something about cuff links..." Max approached the conversation cautiously. "They went missing after you were there. Do you know anything about them?"

"Ah. I get it." Landon huffed a breath of disgust. "*That* explains why you're here." He pulled down his work goggles from atop his hat. "I might be poor, but I'm no thief. I've worked every weekend for the last two years. Ask any guy here."

Zo felt the sting of his words. "Max isn't saying you are. We're just trying to figure out why Carl thinks so."

"That guy is a jerk. He accused me of taking the cuff links one day when I was there with Olivia. She was grabbing some of her things, and I was on the deck—nowhere near his bedroom, where he claimed they were. Supposedly he'd laid them out for a black-tie event." Landon pulled on his zippered jumpsuit, his hands covered with dirty and grime. "What would I do with them? Wear them to work?"

"He thinks you sold them," Zo explained. "For the cash."

Looking into the distance, Landon shook his head. "I'll never change his mind. I don't know why I even try. I'll never be good enough for his daughter."

The comment pulled on Zo's heartstrings. She knew what it meant to be underprivileged. As a teen, people teased her hand-me-down clothes and outdated ten-speed bicycle. When other kids were driving cars to school, she was still biking or walking. And if something went missing at school, a backpack or lunch money, her locker was always the first one searched. Landon wasn't a teen, but the accusation still hurt. The blank look on his face said it all.

Max must have sensed his discomfort, and perhaps hers, as well. "Let's forget about the cuff links. Let's get back to last night. Where was Olivia? Do you know?"

"She was with me." Landon's attention returned to the conversation. "We went to the drive-in movie."

"Yeah?" Max asked casually. "What was playing?"

Landon didn't skip a beat. "*Godzilla.*"

Zo considered the timeline. The Stars and Screen Drive-In had one show, and it started at eight o'clock. It would have ended well before midnight. Still, a date, movie, and burglary in one night? Maybe Olivia was telling the truth.

She noticed the determined set of Landon's jaw.

Or maybe they were both lying.

Chapter Twenty

On the way back from Copperhead Mine, Zo and Max stopped at Canyon Vines for a drink. The wine bar had an early happy hour that included their signature charcuterie plate and two beverages for a bargain price. With the sun no longer overhead, the late afternoon air was warm but pleasant, and Zo was happy they snagged an outdoor table. The bar was on the small side, and only four outdoor seating options were available. Two tables were situated on either side of the front door, under the vine-and-grape awnings. She and Max grabbed the last one.

As Zo sipped her sauvignon blanc, she noted Main Street was winding down for the day. Shoppers hurried out of stores with their packages, sightseers sped by with their full camera rolls, and the busy two-way street was dotted with fewer and fewer cars. The downtown would come alive again when people became hungry and returned for dinner, drinks, dancing, and theater, which was always popular but especially on Saturday nights. Canyon Vines would be filled with the after-theater crowd, and no one would be able to get a seat.

"We got lucky," said Max.

Zo smiled. "I was just thinking the same thing."

He set down his glass of beer. "The other night, I said something that upset you."

She tried not to tense but felt her muscles tighten. Did they have to talk about it? The date had ended on a positive note. (Lasagna at Lotsa Pasta was always an affirmative experience.) Why couldn't they leave it at that? "I wasn't upset. How could I be after that awesome meal?"

Crossing his arms, he leaned back in his chair. "This isn't about the lasagna, and you know it."

"The bread sticks were good, too..."

"Come on. Level with me." A ray of sunlight dusted his thick lashes, turning his eyes sky-blue. "I mentioned living together. It upset you."

With his eyes intently on hers, she couldn't lie. "You're right."

Max reached for his beer. "It wasn't like I meant today or anything. I just meant someday, in the future."

"I know."

"So, why were you upset?"

The waiter placed the charcuterie plate on the table, and Zo popped a candied almond in her mouth so she could think over her response. It wasn't the idea of living with him that bothered her. It was leaving Happy Camper. She dabbed her lips with her napkin. "Happy Camper means a lot. It's not just a store. It's a real home, and that's a first for me."

Max nodded. "I think I understand, but help me."

She busied her hands with a cracker and cheese. It helped the words come easier. "Even when I worked at the *Black Hills Star* and lived in my apartment on Spruce, I felt...disconnected. The commute didn't help. I was bouncing here and there, like always. When I was younger, it was a way of life." She added a sweet pepper to the top of her cheese and took a bite. *Delicious.* After swallowing, she continued. "Things are different now. I have my store, my cat, Cunningham. It just feels like I'm finally in the right place."

"And me," he added. "You forgot to mention me."

She reached across the table for his hand. "And you."

Max's other hand tried to sneak the last almond, and she swatted it away. He laughed.

"See?" She joined in the laughter. "This is why I don't trust you."

Now he took both her hands, his eyes losing their playfulness. "But you do trust me, don't you, Zo?"

Such an easy question, but one that made her want to flee. Run for the Hills. Sure, she trusted him, but for how long, before he did something to betray her trust? It was so much easier to be the one to leave than to be the one left behind. She gave him the easy answer. "Yes..."

"I feel a *but* coming."

It didn't have time to surface before they were interrupted by a noise a few stores down. Zo squinted at the scene. It was Tom Lancaster, Professor Davis's grad student. He was with a merry band of protesters—three to be exact—exiting Dawn's Dimes and Nickels. It was a little casino on the corner, hardly worth the money the group spent on poster boards and markers. The signs read SPIRIT CANYON SAYS NO TO GAMBLING.

She didn't disagree with the sentiment and certainly didn't want gambling to become a form of revenue for their tiny town. Plenty of gambling was to be had in Deadwood, just twenty miles away, for the entire state. But Dawn's Dimes and Nickels was just that: a place to gamble away dimes and nickels. Maybe people lost thousands of dollars that way, but Zo doubted it. Most times, she saw patrons sixty-five and older enter the casino. They met up as much to drink coffee and talk as to gamble.

Max looked over his shoulder. "You think that's going to need my attention?"

She checked his half-full beer. "I don't think so. Tom Lancaster is a grad student, and you're off duty. It looks like they're moving on."

He turned back to her. "How do you know him?"

Zo told him about meeting him and Jeffrey Davis at the library.

Max's forehead wrinkled in confusion. "The Lancasters own that big casino in Deadwood."

"Yep, but Tom is vehemently opposed to gambling—as you can see."

He plucked a grape from the dwindling plate of food. "You think it's possible he murdered Maynard for the book?"

"Why? For his research?"

"To keep it out of the wrong hands." Seeing her question, he continued. "If the guy feels that strongly about gambling, he might want the gold to remain hidden—forever."

It was a possibility, and one she hadn't considered. Actually, it was the opposite of the other ideas she'd considered. Gold and gambling weren't the same thing, but plenty of people had lost their lives because of them. Maybe Tom didn't steal the book for money; maybe he stole it so that no one else got hurt. Watching him and his group march toward her, she didn't discount the notion. In fact, he might be just the kind of concerned citizen to take action.

"Hey, Tom," Zo called out.

"Hold up, guys," Tom said to his friends. One friend had long dark hair, braided perfectly. The other had blond hair, pulled into a half ponytail, that showed off a wide forehead and pale blue eyes. They all wore black T-shirts that read, STOP PREDATORY GAMBLING, in white print. "Zo, right?"

She nodded. "And this is Max. What's going on at Dawn's Dimes and Nickels?"

"A sit-in." Tom stood with one foot in front of the other, ready to move at any moment.

"A sit-in?" repeated Max. "How does that work?"

"The idea is to go into a casino, put a dollar in or whatever, and then read a book, talk to a friend, etcetera," Tom explained. "Then you cash out for a refund when you're done. A bunch of students did it in Reno not that long ago. We thought it was a good idea."

"I get it," said Max. "To show patrons there are better ways to spend their time."

"Right." Tom flashed his sign to a puzzled passerby. "We'll have better turnout in Deadwood. More of us from the college are meeting up there."

The light-haired man twirled his sign. "We can't let the gambling in Spirit Canyon go unchecked."

"This is how it starts," agreed the other man.

"Will you go to your family's casino?" asked Zo.

Tom laughed. "We're starting there."

Max raised a brow. "That's going to be awkward."

"Not really," Tom clarified. "But your comment highlights the problem—perception." His eyes left the gawkers and focused on Zo and Max. His face was narrow and his chin pointed, highlighted by the shape of his goatee. "A town thinks of the casino owner as a saloon keeper—an old man, pouring drinks, wiping the counter, keeping the peace with his customers."

In Deadwood, the idea wasn't far from her mind.

"But it isn't true." Tom emphasized each word. "My dad doesn't even live in Deadwood. He spends most of his time in his LA mansion, lounging by the pool, sipping mojitos. It's the same thing for the other bloodsuckers. Do you think Kevin Costner ever spent a minute in the Midnight Star before it closed?" He didn't give them a chance to answer. "No. And neither do any of the other millionaires who make money off other people's addictions."

"Exactly," ground out one friend.

"Truth," agreed the other.

With his friends sounding agitated, it seemed like a good time to pivot topics. Zo asked about their recent library experience. "Did you and Professor Davis find what you needed at the library?"

"Except for that missing book." Tom blinked. "Professor Davis said you knew the guy who bought it. Why did he want it in the first place? From what Davis told me, he wasn't a scholar."

"That's what I'm trying to find out," Zo admitted.

"Do you have any ideas?" asked Max.

Tom scanned the street crowd. It was dwindling, and fewer people noticed him. "Money. Isn't it always? It was probably worth a lot of it."

"Easy for you to say." Zo shrugged. "You've got quite a bit of it."

Tom's eyes snapped back to hers. "What does that mean?"

"It means it's easy for people with money to disparage it." Zo tried a smile. "It's a universal truth. Don't take it personally."

Tom jerked a thumb at her, talking to his friends. "Do you hear this?" When he returned to her, his voice had lost a little of its edge. "Look, I don't take blood money from my father. I pay my own way. I don't know why your friend wanted the book, but if I find it, I will expose every rotten cowboy in its pages. You can bet on it."

His friends were poised to go, and he turned also.

"Good luck in Deadwood," she said.

"It isn't about luck."

"Drive carefully," added Max as the group moved on down the street. When they were out of earshot, he leaned over the table. "Did you hear what he said?"

"I don't see how I couldn't."

"He said if he *found* the book." Max's eyes widened with excitement. "Which could mean he's looking for it."

"That would also mean he didn't take it from Maynard." Zo handed the empty charcuterie board to the server. "Do you think he could have been the person in Jules's house?"

Max finished his beer as he considered the question. "I can't think of any other reason for a break-in besides the book. Brady hasn't mentioned it to the press. Still, it doesn't make sense. Anyone interested in the book would know Maynard purchased it at the auction. Wouldn't *his* house be the one to break in to?"

"Not with cops climbing all over the place." She had to admit he had a point, though. Maynard's house would hold more clues to the book than Dalrymple's did. They had found one: the note with Merrigan's name on it. Still, they must be missing an important link between the book and the break-in. Unless a link didn't exist. Then they were spinning their wheels.

Max held up his empty glass. "Do you want to have another drink?"

"I'd love to, but the Zodiacs are meeting at the observatory. We're viewing Sagittarius, so I'm excited." She didn't know her official birth date (she was left at the police station right before Christmas), but she knew her zodiac sign, and that meant a lot. It was the reason an archer tattoo graced her shoulder. "Do you want to come?"

"I promised Scout a long walk before I left. She'd be bummed if I skipped out. Rain check?"

There was something endearing about being passed up for a dog, especially one as sweet as Scout. "No problem. I'll see you tomorrow."

Chapter Twenty-One

Saturday night, the parking lot of Black Mountain Observatory was dotted with cars, including Jules's and Hattie's. Hattie never missed a meeting, but Jules had a house to move, so Zo was surprised she was there. Also present was Professor Linwood, who was tinkering with the telescope. He always got it just right, so the group didn't have to spend time searching for a constellation. Landon hovered nearby, watching him make adjustments. Olivia was nowhere in sight, but Hunter was there, wearing black jeans and a white T-shirt.

He was quick to greet her as she walked in. "Where's your ranger?"

"He's not *my* ranger." She unzipped her jacket. "And he's with another girl."

"That's terrible news." Hunter's deep dimple contradicted his words.

Jules and Hattie stopped talking, and seeing their concerned faces, Zo let them in on the joke. "He's walking Scout."

She joined them near the open-air portion of the observatory, where the ceiling opened like a vault to the night sky. This was one of her favorite places in the entire world. Its immensity made her feel like a small, but important, part of the picture. "I thought you'd be unpacking, Jules."

"Not until we clean." Jules had her head wrapped in a turban and looked a little like a genie. A quick nod added to the effect. "The place is a mess."

"I can imagine," mused Hattie. She wore a cap with a large gold buckle. "With all that ancient furniture gone, you have your work cut out for you."

"I'll bring my scrub brush…" promised Zo, but scrubbing was the last thing on her mind. She was staring into the inky night, looking for the sign, *her* sign. It was silly, she supposed, but it was the one thing that felt definite. She didn't have a birth date, time, or mother, but she had Sagittarius.

Classic depictions of the constellation identified a centaur with a bow. Another way to find it was to imagine the shape of a teapot, which, being a tea lover, was easy for Zo. When stargazers looked at Sagittarius, they were looking at the heart of the Milky Way. Located in the galactic center, it was easy for even novices like her to identify. With the help of Professor Linwood and his telescope, it would be not only easy, but informative.

As the group gathered around, Linwood informed them he would be pointing out the stars in the constellation, including Kaus Australis, the brightest star located at the southern tip of the centaur's bow.

"The interesting point is that centaurs didn't use bows in Greek mythology," pondered Linwood. "So, where does the reference come from?" Like a good professor, he didn't wait for them to figure it out. "Perhaps the satyr Crotus, an accomplished hunter, athlete, and artist who grew up under the inspiration of the Muses. For those of you who don't know, satyrs are the offspring of Pan, half-man and half-goat. Lustful creatures, but in Crotus's case, highly skilled and a great contributor to the arts. Zeus complied with the Muses' requests by placing his image in the sky."

"You hear that, Zo?" whispered Hunter. "*Lustful* creatures."

Zo slid him a look. With his beachy blond hair and five-o'clock shadow, it was hard not to keep looking.

"It explains your passion." He touched her chin. "Doesn't it?"

She jerked away. Typical Hunter. He always asked questions to which he never really wanted answers.

"Shh," Hattie scolded. "I'm trying to learn something."

He leaned in closer. "And I'm a Scorpio, the most passionate of all the signs."

She took a step back. And there you had it, the reason she'd broken it off in the first place. He could turn any topic into a conversation about him in less than thirty seconds.

"Did you have a question, Hunter?" Linwood asked.

Zo smiled at Linwood's professorly intrusion.

"I'm good," Hunter answered.

"I've been talking long enough." Linwood took the hint from the side conversations cropping up. "Let's look at this thing, shall we?" He kindly stepped aside. Hunter was the first one to seize the telescope. The rest of them gathered around.

"How is the manuscript coming?" Zo asked while they were waiting.

"Much better because of you all." Linwood smiled at the semicircle of group members. "Your feedback was invaluable. I don't know how I'll thank you."

"Do a book signing at Happy Camper when it's published," suggested Zo. "I'd love to have a star talk at the store."

Linwood gave her a thumbs-up. "You got it."

"We'll all come—as long as Zo makes cupcakes," said Jules.

Hunter looked up from the telescope. "I'll come even if there aren't cupcakes."

Zo rolled her eyes. What was she thinking when she dated that guy? *I couldn't have been thinking at all.* Maybe she was the lustful creature Hunter said she was.

"Zo has the best book signings," Jules explained to Landon. "You weren't here last fall, but she made the cutest witch cupcakes for Marianne Moore's book talk. They were to die for."

Zo and Hattie stared at her.

She shrugged. "Sorry. Bad choice of words."

"If you host the event, let me know," said Landon. "I'll share some pics I took last Saturday at the astronomy equipment fund-raiser. We raised over ten thousand dollars."

Linwood's lips twitched with a smile. "They were *out of sight.*" His was the only laughter in the observatory. "Hey, if Jules can make puns, so can I."

Landon snorted a laugh, and Zo was glad to see he was back to his usual good humor. The tension from the mine had faded. "Okay, so the department is kind of geeky." He flashed her a picture of one of the cookies, shaped like Saturn. Orange, red, and yellow, it was a swirl of sugary beauty. He swiped through a few more. The earth, the moon—Olivia.

Zo felt a prickle of adrenaline shoot through her spine. It was the break she'd been looking for. "Can you send me those?"

"Right now?"

Zo tried to remain casual. "Sure. I like being prepared, and I host all sorts of events. These are perfect for campers. They stargaze all the time."

"And you have that event next month—Camping with the Stars." Jules's smile reached across her face. "I love the play on words, by the way."

Landon selected several photos and airdropped them to her phone.

As Hunter finished and Hattie moved forward, Zo moved a step closer to the telescope, but what she was really looking at were the pictures of Olivia with Landon, Saturday afternoon, the day of Dalrymple's estate sale. In one photograph, Olivia was taking a big bite of a Mars cookie. Behind her was a perfunctory wall clock that read 2:45. The estate sale was limited in time, from noon until three. Zo had assumed Olivia arrived after she and Hattie left, but now she understood that wasn't the case. Olivia wasn't at Dalrymple's estate sale after all. She'd lied about being at the sale and had probably lost the barrette at Jules's house last night, during the break-in. Now Zo had proof of it on her phone.

When it was her turn to view Sagittarius, she let go of thoughts about the photos and savored the moment. Thanks to Linwood, she knew the names of the major stars. Now it was time to see them. The southernmost point of the bow, or the southeast corner of the teapot, depending on how one looked at it, Kaus Australis was the brightest and easiest to recognize. In the telescope, it appeared so close she could almost touch it although she knew it was thousands of miles away.

So many things seemed that way lately. Her relationship with Max, her birth mother—Maynard's murderer. The last had a definite resolution, and she knew she would find it, eventually. But the others? Would she ever really know where she came from? Would she ever experience the feeling of family? And was the lost book just another excuse to keep searching for something she might never find?

Zo traced the other stars with her eye. She cared about Maynard. Of course she did. He'd been with the Zodiacs for a while. But in her heart, she knew one of the reasons she was desperate to find the book was entirely selfish. No one came and went in a little town like Spirit Canyon without a trace. Let alone leave a baby. A reason had to exist, and she was determined to find it. The book about Spirit Canyon was a last resort in a long line of failed attempts. Would this one fail, too? The second-brightest star, Nunki, twinkled a little brighter, giving her a glimmer of hope. She would keep going. She had to follow her star.

After everyone had viewed the constellation, Zo, Hattie, and Jules had a sidebar in the parking lot. Zo was parked next to Jules's VW Bug. Linwood and Landon were still inside, putting away the equipment, and Hunter and the others had left after their turns at the telescope. Alone in the parking lot, Zo told them about the pictures.

"Are you sure it was her?" asked Hattie.

Zo showed them the picture of Olivia eating a cookie.

"That's her, all right," Jules huffed. "I can't believe that twerp might have been in my house last night. But why?"

"I wish I knew." Zo didn't meet Olivia until the Zodiac meeting. Since then, they'd talked only a few times. She thought back to their conversation the day of the library event. Allison Scott had told them both about *My Journey West* and what was purportedly in the book. In fact, Allison was the first person who had mentioned Ezra Kind's stash of gold and his friend Charlie Clay's attempt to find it. Could the information have anything to do with the break-in? Did Olivia, perhaps, catch gold fever, and go looking for clues to the loot?

Hattie lowered her voice. "What about Landon? Do you think he could be in on it? He doesn't have a lot of money, and I know he really wants to attend grad school. The college has more applicants than assistantships. You know how competitive they are."

Zo knew Hattie was right. Everyone wanted to attend grad school in the hip mountain town. The campus was perfect for nature lovers looking for that granola vibe. Landon was smart, but sometimes it took more than intellect to land an assistantship at Black Mountain College.

Jules put her fingers to her temples, closing her eyes. A moment passed before she spoke. "I can't see Landon committing murder." When her eyes reopened, they looked almost black in the moonlight. She not only resembled a genie but a witch.

"Me, neither," Zo said. "But if he is in on it, he just made a huge mistake by showing us that picture. We can't rule him out—yet." Zo tucked away her phone. "What time should I be at your house tomorrow? Harley's working all day, so I can be there any time."

"How about noon?" asked Jules. "Duncan likes to sleep in, and he promised to help."

Zo blinked. Hattie cleared her throat.

"What?" asked Jules. "Everybody has their sleep preferences, and you know I'm more of a night owl, too. Don't read anything into it."

Hattie adjusted her cap, pulling the brim low on her forehead. Her short gray hair poked out at the sides, and a smart remark bubbled to her lips. "Librarians read. That's what we do."

Zo chuckled as Hattie and Jules got into their respective cars and proceeded down the hill that led to Spirit Canyon. Alone in the dark, she gazed up at the stars. They hugged the earth in a jeweled embrace. Each constellation told a story of different times or beliefs. The Lakota believed the stars gave each baby a spirit at birth called a *wanagi*. When a person died, the spirit traveled back to the cup of the Big Dipper of the Milky Way. Looking at the sky, Zo thought it was a nice idea.

A *click* in the night brought her back to the parking lot. She checked the observatory. Landon and Linwood were still inside. She scanned the lot, noting a black sedan in the far corner. She wouldn't have even noticed it except someone was getting inside. A younger man, dark hair—*are you kidding me?* Zo stomped over to the car. "What are you doing here?"

"You don't know?" Justin Castle flashed a set of glowing white teeth at her. "Maybe you're not the journalist I thought you were."

"*Former* journalist," Zo corrected. "And answer the question."

He leaned an arm over his open car door. "Writing a weekly column doesn't exactly scream retirement to me. Not to mention chasing leads and busting up press conferences. Admit it: You want back in the business."

Zo gritted her teeth. "I didn't bust up anything, and I don't want back into the business. I *own* a business, and I want to keep it that way. Maynard was my friend."

Justin nodded toward the observatory. "And so are the others. How does it feel to be on friendly terms with a murderer?" He took a step closer. "You know one of them did it. The group met the night before Maynard was killed. Hunter said Maynard was about to lend your favorite librarian a very expensive book." He raised his eyebrows. "Maybe she wanted to borrow it—permanently."

"You talked to Hunter?" Zo was incredulous.

"Um-hum," Justin confirmed. "Before tonight's meeting. He was incredibly eager to talk about the group, and himself. Well, mainly himself, but I got what I needed."

That's why Justin had talked to Cunningham earlier. He *did* believe he was part of the Zodiacs. Now he'd talked to Hunter. He was trying to pin the murder on one of them, and from the sounds of it, Hattie was his immediate target. Zo wouldn't allow that to happen.

"What *do* you need? To discredit me? Is that it?" Her questions came in rapid-fire succession. She had no idea what he had against her. Harriet said it was professional jealousy, but she didn't believe it. They were in different leagues, and that was fine with her. She wrote a small weekly column, and he basically ran KRSO news. No similarities in the two whatsoever.

"Don't play innocent with me," he spat. "You know the entire town flocks to your column and your store. They trust you. But not for long. When they find out the group had something to do with Maynard's murder, they'll see you in a new light."

"This is the reason they can't trust *you*," spat Zo. "You put professional gains above everything else—the town, the truth, the people. It has nothing to do with me."

"I'll be the judge of that." He got in the car and slammed the door.

Zo watched him speed down the hill, hoping he didn't hit a deer—for the deer's sake.

Chapter Twenty-Two

Sunday morning dawned like a prayer, and Zo was there for it. Red streaks stretched across the sky followed by orange and gold. In the east, the sun was a new yellow globe of light, carrying with it a brilliant blue sky. Soon the myriad colors would be replaced with solid blue, so she didn't waste a moment, grabbing her shoes and unlocking the mountain bike from the rack outside Happy Camper.

Fastening her helmet, she headed out of town, toward the canyon. Crossing under the granite arch near the entrance, she entered a world where Mother Nature ruled. Luckily, the old woman was in a good mood this morning, providing Zo with calm winds and heavenly skies.

In the distance, a campfire burned, and Zo imagined a family cooking breakfast on an open flame. Something they'd done a hundred times was new and exciting because it was performed outside. Maybe the kids had helped, or at least watched, since cell phones rarely caught a signal outside of Spirit Canyon.

Or maybe the family wasn't a family, but a woman like Zo, traveling solo. More and more women opted for weekends alone, testing their autonomy one trip at a time. Setting up camp, gathering firewood, and cooking meals were just some of the activities they could try. The forest was the perfect place to explore the limitless options provided free of charge by nature.

Zo imagined several scenarios—a hard habit to break from her journalism days—before turning around at a pull-off, her legs burning for a break. After letting her limbs rest while drinking in a rugged view of the canyon, she started for home with an increased heart rate and a new appreciation for the day. Nothing beat fresh air for motivation, and by the time she returned to Happy Camper, she was ready to take on the world—or at least Mountain View Manor.

She met Harley outside the store. "You're here early. It's not even ten o'clock."

"I know." Harley turned the key. She was dressed in dark blue jeans and a black T-shirt. Around her neck were several short silver necklaces and a long one with a pendant that read COURAGE. "I was starting to get grouchy. Coming here always makes me feel better."

Zo locked up the bike and followed her inside. "Same, but I thought it was because I owned it." George wandered in behind her, ready for breakfast.

"Nope, it's this place."

"Any reason for the grouchiness, or just life in general?" Zo fed George while Harley counted out the day's cash.

"I couldn't sleep," said Harley.

"That's so frustrating." Zo noted the shadows under her Harley's violet-blue eyes. She *did* look tired. "But I have something that will help."

Harley stopped counting coins. "What?"

"I'll be right back." She went to the storage room and returned with a large pitcher and clear, disposable wineglasses. "Sangria Sundays! Nonalcoholic, of course, but customers can add wine at home. The infusion kit includes a recipe card." She pulled out her surprise, a bottle of iced coffee. "And caffeine for you."

"You're a lifesaver." Harley opened the beverage and took a swig, turning over the recipe card with a picture of an iced sangria on it. "These are so cute. Everyone will love them."

"I have a table in the back. I decked it out in a lemon-and-orange tablecloth. If it stays nice, bring it outside, next to the pop-up tent. Everything else is in the fridge." Zo nodded to Harley's lunch bag. "Do you want me to put this in there, too?"

"Yeah, thanks." She flashed Zo a smile. "I really do feel better."

After putting Harley's lunch in the fridge, Zo dashed upstairs for a quick shower before heading to Jules's house. She didn't spend much time getting ready because she knew most of her work would entail cleaning. Jeans and a T-shirt would do. Thirty minutes later, she jumped on the Kawasaki, letting the motorcycle do the work her hair dryer hadn't.

Jules greeted her at the door wearing a baseball cap, the pink ends of her hair looped through the hole in the back of the hat. Gold star earrings dangled from her ears. "Messy looks good on you."

"Thank you?" Zo ran her fingers through her hair.

"I'm telling the truth." Jules motioned to the kitchen. "I have sandwiches."

"Great!" Zo followed her into the room, where Duncan was seated at the small white table. "I'm starving, but I didn't want to be late. I setup Sangria Sundays before I left. It's new."

"Sounds like someone's invading our turf," said Duncan, tossing a pickle off his half-eaten sandwich. He wore gray joggers, a Def Leppard T-shirt, and a lazy smile.

Zo noted his use of the word *our*. Harley did the same thing sometimes. To Zo, it meant he had a personal stake in the business, and that was a good thing in her book. "Not at all. You know I can't sell alcohol. It's an infusion kit. In fact, it might drive up business if customers need a bottle of wine or brandy to go with it."

Jules handed her a paper plate. "Make sure you send them my way."

"I always do." Zo selected a turkey sub sandwich. "Thanks for lunch."

"Don't thank me yet," Jules cautioned, taking a sip of diet soda. "This place is bigger than it looks. Cleaning the kitchen took all day yesterday."

Zo scanned the gleaming countertops, appliances, and floors. "It looks great. What are we cleaning today?"

"The upstairs." Jules handed her a miniature bag of chips. "We'll start at the top and work our way down."

"What's up there?" asked Zo after swallowing a bite of sandwich. "Just bedrooms?"

"Three of them and a dormer." Jules returned to her plate, which was almost empty. Only a few chips remained. "I think Dalrymple used it as an office. Honestly, I didn't even know it existed until after I bought the house. You can only access it by a pull-down ladder."

"You do the dormer." Duncan pointed to Zo. "You're the shortest. I don't want to hurt my back. I have a gig tonight."

"Cool," said Zo. "Where?"

Jules's lip quivered with a smirk. "Split Rock Retirement Home."

Zo covered her smile with a napkin.

"Hey, they pay really well, so don't judge." Duncan's dark eyes narrowed beneath his matching sweep of hair. "Despite being reasonable, rent is a lot higher here than my last place." He popped the last bite of sandwich in his mouth.

Which was free, Zo added to herself while munching a pickle. Jules and Duncan debated the word *reasonable* while she finished her sandwich and chips. By the time they headed upstairs with the cleaning buckets, scrub brushes, and rags, a consensus was determined. Reasonable was whatever Jules deemed it to be.

In the hallway, Jules reached for a loop on a string, and a ceiling door opened, revealing a ladder to the dormer of the house. The ladder squeaked as Jules extended it to the floor.

"Uh…that will hold me, right?" Zo squinted at the worn wood. By the scuff marks on the middle of the old steps, the ladder had been used repeatedly.

Jules handed her a rag and a dust mop. "Don't worry. I've been up there. If it can hold me, it can hold you."

Tentatively, Zo climbed the ladder, pausing with each crack and creak. When she reached the top, she slid the mop and rag on the floor and jumped inside. It wasn't as bad as she thought it'd be. In fact, with the two arched windows, it was much taller and kind of pretty. She walked around, admiring the wide-plank oak floors. They weren't as decorative as the floors downstairs, but with a fresh coat of polish, they would be just as nice.

She pushed the curtains open, enjoying the view of Spirit Canyon. Noting the cloud of dust, she slid them off the rods. It must have been a while since Vera Dalrymple had been up here. Then again, she was in her late eighties when she passed. She wouldn't have wanted to chance breaking a bone by climbing the rickety ladder.

Zo tackled the windows first so she could enjoy the sun while she cleaned the rest of the room. Behind a dark green hill, a storm cloud hovered. Summer storms came and went frequently in the area. First, they hit the canyon, creating a spectacle of light with electricity, then the town, with a quick rain burst. It was definitely heading their way.

Near the windows, the floor was faded, the shape of a wide rectangle. It must be where Dalrymple had her desk. *It's where I would put my desk if it were my house.* She could see the entire town from here, not to mention the waterfall in the distance. She imagined the professor doing all her professorial work from here: reading, writing, grading. Would Jules keep her office up here? Maybe that's why she wanted it cleaned. But Zo couldn't see it. For some reason, a dormer was not a place she imagined Jules working. The wine cellar, however, was another story. She frowned. *Hey, that was the area I wanted to clean.* Yet here she was, stuck with cobwebs.

Pushing the complaint out of her mind, she attacked the small ceiling fan and vents, using her disposable duster to get all the crevices. Next she wiped off the white, built-in bookshelf, angled to fit the slanted ceiling. She supposed this was where Dalrymple kept her history books. The white finish didn't fit with the rest of the woodwork, and Zo guessed it was added later. The house had been in the family for generations. She wondered if Vera had known she would be the last Dalrymple to own it.

Swiping the inner corner with her dust rag, she heard a spring, or something being stretched. She tossed aside the cloth and moved her fingers over the wood. It was a lever. She'd pushed it by accident. Stepping back with a blink, she surveyed the shelf. Then she pressed it with both hands. The bookshelf creaked open, revealing a sliver of darkness behind it. Zo's stomach did a flip-flop. *You're kidding me.* Could this house be any better? An attic office and now a secret compartment? She peeked inside.

The area was small, but that didn't make it any less intriguing. It exposed the inner workings of the house: the wood, boards, and insulation. And what else? Zo pressed the flashlight on her phone. If anyone had a secret kept under lock and key, it was the town historian.

She peeked around the corner, hoping a bat didn't fly out from the blackness. It looked empty. Maybe the Tracey brothers had been up here and cleaned it out, but if that were true, why all the dust? No. No one had been up here in years. Zo was certain of it.

She scooted inside, flashing her phone light in the corners, and that's when she saw it. A gold nugget the size of her fist. Was it real? Like a paperweight, it was placed on a piece of paper—no, a page of a book. It had a page number. She set down her phone and picked up the shiny rock, holding it over the light. It was surprisingly heavy. She set it aside and shined the phone light on the yellowed piece of paper. Mountains, hills, valleys—an *X*. It wasn't just *any* sheet of paper. It was the treasure map to the gold of Ezra Kind.

Chapter Twenty-Three

Zo raced down the ladder as fast as she could without dropping the gold nugget, or, more importantly, the treasure map. This was what the entire town had been searching for—the famed clue that would lead to Ezra Kind's stash of gold. It was taken from the pages of a book, and if Zo had to guess, that book was *My Journey West*. Maynard might have purchased the collector's volume, but the key page was missing. The auctioneer had mentioned a few missing pages, as well as creased and damaged spots. But this page was removed and hidden on purpose, perhaps many years ago. Dalrymple didn't want anyone to find the location of the gold, which she might have found herself if the gold nugget was any indication. Or if not Dalrymple, one of her family members.

Zo jumped from the ladder to the floor with a single leap, and Jules came running out of the bathroom, her yellow rubber gloves still on. "Are you okay?"

Zo held up the nugget. "Better than okay."

"Is that real?" asked Jules, taking the piece of gold.

"I don't know. I found it behind a bookshelf. It opened when I pressed on it, and look." Zo showed Jules the map. "I think this is the location of Ezra Kind's gold."

Duncan was leaning against a bedroom doorway, a light cobweb stuck in his dark hair. "I knew I should have called dibs on that room."

"What should we do?" asked Jules.

"I'm going to call Max and ask him to go with me and check this out." She scanned the map. "I have a general idea where this is, but I'll need his help for specifics."

"Good idea," said Duncan. "We'll come, too."

Jules handed him her gloves. "You're going to stay here and clean. I'm taking this to the jewelers to see if it's real."

"Come on," Duncan pleaded. "Don't make me stay here alone."

Jules fisted her hands on her hips. "You're kidding, right?"

"It's a big house."

"Fine, you can come with me, but not a word about where we found it or Ezra Kind." Jules pointed her index finger at him. "Deal?"

Duncan agreed, and Zo dialed Max's number and relayed the discovery. He was in the middle of bathing Scout and said to pick him up in ten minutes.

"I have the key to Spirit Canyon's biggest mystery, and he wants to finish bathing his dog." Zo rolled her eyes. "Incredible."

"It's so like him," added Jules.

"What else is the guy to do?" defended Duncan. "Leave the soap in her fur?"

"True," agreed Zo. "I just thought he'd be more excited."

Jules slid the gold nugget in her carpenter pants pocket. "It's not time to get excited—yet."

But on the way to Max's house, Zo could feel the excitement start to thrum through her body, and it was hard to stay under the speed limit. She eased up on the throttle, not wanting Brady Merrigan to give her a ticket before they ever left town.

Max and Scout met her in the driveway, Scout with a very wet body and Max with a very wet shirt. Scout put her paws on Zo's chest, despite Max's repeated requests to stay down.

Zo held the big dog's face in her hands. "You look so pretty, Scout. You're a pretty girl."

He smiled. "She cleans up nice. Let's see the map."

She glanced at his neighbors' houses: neat, tidy ranches with lots of windows and lots of curious eyes. "Inside."

"Good idea," Max agreed. "I need to change before we leave, anyway."

She followed him into his bungalow, where he promptly pulled off his wet T-shirt and rummaged through the laundry basket on his couch, looking for another. Staring was unavoidable. First, he was right in front of her, and second, his chest was broad, muscular, and well-defined. She shouldn't have been surprised. He worked outdoors. Still, the intake of her breath was audible.

He looked up from the laundry basket and smiled, the warm smile that made his blue eyes smolder, like clouds filling with rain.

She swallowed.

He pulled on a shirt, and she remembered to blink.

The map was tucked inside her jacket, and she reached for it carefully. It was old yet incredibly well-preserved. Spanning two pages, it must have been carefully taken from the pages of Charlie Clay's memoir. Who knew what other secrets were inside Dalrymple's house? The family had owned Mountain View Manor for over a century.

Max moved the laundry basket off the couch, and Zo sat down with him, handing over the map. He studied it closely. "It looks like it points to a spot near Crow Peak. Or at least I think that's Crow Peak." He brought the map closer to his face.

"Let's assume it's Crow Peak. The Thoen Stone was found near Lookout Mountain, which isn't far from there."

Max glanced up from the pages. "You found this in Dalrymple's office, right?"

Zo nodded. "Right. In the attic, behind a secret bookshelf."

He rubbed his light whiskers.

"What is it?"

"The break-in the other night at Jules's house." He held up the map. "I wonder if the intruder was looking for this, not the book."

The idea made sense, but how would anyone know about the map, unless they heard stories of it or knew Dalrymple's house, intimately. Zo's mind landed on Dalrymple's niece. She possessed knowledge of both. "Cora stayed at her aunt's house many times when she was younger. Maybe Dalrymple told her the story of Ezra Kind's gold or mentioned the map. We talked about the subject just the other day. Maybe it jogged her memory, and she came back to retrieve it."

"It fits," agreed Max. "We need to talk to her—*after* we check out the location on the map."

Zo stood. "So you know where we're going?"

"I think so. I'll grab my backpack."

Ten minutes later, they were cruising toward Crow Peak, Zo with her hands around Max's waist. She'd agreed to let him drive since he knew the best way to get there. The map pointed toward the far side of the mountain, deep in the forest. Tall pines shaded the road, and she was glad for her windbreaker, pulling it tighter as they went farther into the woods. The sun had disappeared behind the ominous cloud hanging over the mountain. She hoped they reached their destination before the rain hit.

Max pulled over near a small gravel path. "This is as far as we can go on the bike. We'll have to hike the rest of the way. Can I see the map again?"

She handed it to him, and he pointed in the direction of an outcrop of rock. "Over there."

"That far?" she asked.

"I think so." He checked her tennis shoes. "At least you have proper footwear."

They started up the path. "I would have worn hiking boots if I'd known I was going treasure hunting."

"We could have stopped and changed."

"I'm fine. These are comfortable." But thirty minutes later, she chided herself for being in a hurry. Time had always been a problem for her because she had a dread of things ending. A school counselor told her it was from her experiences with foster homes, and maybe the counselor was right. Even as an adult, it was a trait she couldn't always overcome.

Just when things were going well, life would change, and although Zo didn't have proof, change always seemed to happen before an event or occasion. She'd be excited for Thanksgiving, and boom, she'd be placed with another family who didn't celebrate the holiday. It happened over and over, fueling a seize-the-day attitude. But the characteristic wasn't all bad. After all, it had brought her here, searching for a lost treasure from over a hundred years ago.

Stepping over a large tree root, she stumbled, catching herself before she fell. *Yep, life did have a habit of repeating itself.*

Max spun around. "Are you okay?"

She waved away his concern, bending to rub her ankle. "I'm fine. We're almost there." But her ankle hurt like the devil.

"Let's take a break." He turned toward a shallow stream they'd been following. Scanning their surroundings, his eyes landed on a large rock nearby, and he held out his hand, guiding her to it. They sat for a moment, listening to the babbling waters. She inhaled a breath.

Nowhere else did she feel the peace the Hills brought her. Sitting on the rock with Max, her worries seemed to float away with the water. Even her ankle felt better. In the distance, a warbler sang, carrying away her aches on the notes of a carefree tune.

The first drop of rain on her cheek was invigorating. The hike had been rigorous, and the water felt good on her skin. The second and third, however, were a warning of what was to come. Summer thunderstorms and lightning strikes were common in the Black Hills and came on as quickly as they dissipated. They would need to move on.

Max gave her a look, and she knew he was thinking the same thing. But they were only half a mile from their destination and couldn't stop now. A little rain never hurt anyone. A low rumble from the sky loudly disagreed.

"Wait here." Max left, scanning the area for shelter. A few minutes later, he returned with good news. "We're in luck. There's a cave ahead. We can wait there until the storm passes."

"But we're so close," she pleaded.

He shrugged. "Nothing we can do except obey Mother Nature's warning."

Spoken like a true forest ranger. She trudged behind him, her shoes turning muddy from the deluge of rain, making her ankle feel worse than it already did, the thick clumps of dirt making it hard to walk.

Max stopped by a tall mound of rock. The Black Hills had many beautiful caves, including Wind Cave and Jewel Cave. This wasn't one of them. It was a crack in the side of a hill, more shelf than cave. She wasn't sure it was even safe.

They ducked inside. The downpour continued, like a curtain between them and the forest. Zo turned around, scanning the interior of cave. It wasn't as bad as it first appeared. Its width gave it the illusion of space. But deep in the mountain, it narrowed into a tunnel. She wouldn't be going that far. She would be staying right here, where the open air was steps away.

A shiver shook her shoulders, and she pulled her jacket tighter. The cave was cold and damp, like her skin, making it hard to remember it was the middle of July. The weather in South Dakota was anything but temperate.

Max took her hands in his. "Are you cold?"

"Just a chill."

He peeked out the cave, looking left and right. "I'll be right back." Five minutes later, he returned with a small stack of kindling.

Zo couldn't believe her luck. "Are you going to do your forest ranger thing and build a fire?"

Smiling, he arranged the wood and kindling like a teepee. "Every good forest ranger knows how to build a fire—and brings waterproof matches." He pulled them from his backpack and within minutes, had a fire started near the entrance of the cave.

Removing her wet jacket, Zo sat on it with her knees up, close to the fire. Although small, it was warm and dried her limbs instantly. Max joined her, putting an arm around her shoulders.

She decided she could get used to the feeling of his embrace. It brought with it a sense of security, something that had evaded her in the past. Her store and home had given her refuge, but never another person. Before she could wonder whether or not she should trust it, he turned her face toward his and kissed her gently. A droplet of rain fell from his short, wet hair, melting into her skin like his warm lips. The question flew out of her head, and she simply enjoyed the moment.

They sat quietly by the fire, waiting for the rain to pass. When it continued, Max stood and looked outside. Without explanation, he dashed out of the cave, staring back at her from a distance. He returned with a puzzled look on his face.

"What's the matter?" she asked.

"Let me see the map."

She unfolded the paper.

He pointed to the stream on the map, or what she thought was a stream. It was the curvy line they'd been following. Now she wasn't sure what it was.

His eyes flickered with excitement. "Just as I thought. This line isn't a creek. It's a cave."

She blinked, not understanding what it meant.

"Which means we could be on top of Ezra Kind's gold!"

Chapter Twenty-Four

Max had to be kidding. Could they have really stumbled onto Ezra Kind's stash of gold by accident? Zo didn't believe in accidents; she believed in fate. Had the latter brought them here?

She touched the sun and moon necklaces that always hung around her neck. The moon, engraved with the name *Zo*, had been left with her at the police station. The sun, which read *Elle*, was found in the theater last fall, a happy twist of fate propelling her forward. They fit together, forming her full name: *Zoelle*. It was a piece of a puzzle she put together one day at a time.

But this puzzle needed to be solved soon. Maynard's murderer needed to be brought to justice, and the only way to do that was to follow the clues that led them here.

Max dug through his backpack and pulled out a flashlight. "I'm going deeper into the cave." He gave her a tentative look. "I'd like you to stay here, in case the rock's unstable."

She was happy he'd asked and didn't tell her what to do, but the truth was, she was claustrophobic. Although she wanted to go with him, in case he found the gold or another clue, she couldn't get her mind over the mental impasse. Wide-open spaces were her thing. Small, enclosed spaces were not. "Okay."

He blinked, his blue eyes relaying his relief. "Great. I won't be long."

"Don't go too far," Zo cautioned. "You don't know where the tunnels lead. It might be dangerous."

"I won't. I promise."

She watched him walk deeper into the cave, until the light from his flashlight disappeared. With each step, her heart sank further into her stomach. When he first made the announcement, she'd been thrilled. The idea of discovering one of history's most famous treasures was exciting. But now, excitement changed to fear. What if something happened to him? What if the cave caved in? All the gold in the world wasn't worth losing him.

The feeling terrified her. She didn't know when he'd become so important to her. They'd only been dating a few months and not seriously. She'd kept it light and fun. The pit in her stomach was anything but light and fun. She shook it off, telling herself it was the cave, her claustrophobia, and the storm.

Lightning cracked outside, and the dark sky flashed white. A few loose rocks tumbled to the ground, and her limbs went numb. She knelt by the fire, hoping to return to its coziness, but it had disappeared, like Max, into the cave.

She stared into the rain, a gray downpour between the cave and the rest of the forest. It created a fast-moving river, washing away pine needles, dirt, and any chance of leaving safely. How and when would they ever get out of here?

The minutes ticked by, and she felt like a patient waiting for test results. Max hadn't been gone long, yet it felt like centuries. She checked her watch. It'd been exactly five minutes. Taking a deep breath, she tried to relax, but her head wouldn't have it. Her ears were attuned to every snap and crackle in the distance.

She heard a sound—a sniff. Definitely not human. Definitely not Max. The noise came from behind her and brought with it a prickle of fear.

Slowly, she twisted her head. In the corner of the cave, she saw two glowing eyes and a sharp, angular face. She didn't need to see the rest of the body to know it was a mountain lion.

Like the pages of a book, facts about mountain lions whirled through her brain. Sometimes called pumas or cougars, they were North America's largest cat. They weighed up to two hundred pounds, yet they ran as fast as a car, around fifty miles per hour. Their population in the Black Hills had dwindled, but obviously not completely. Three hundred big cats lived in the area, last she'd heard.

None of this helped or made her feel better. What she really needed to know was what to do if she encountered one. Run? Tiptoe? Cry? A thrumming noise began in her ears as she tried to recall and failed. *Move, move—move!* But she didn't. Even her eyes didn't obey. She stood still, not blinking. The yellow eyes of the cat, however, got larger and larger. Was he creeping closer?

Her feet stirred then, awakened by sheer preservation. She started backing out of the cave, but the cat followed, his tan body low, sleek, and muscular. His dense tail was high, poised to pounce. She stopped. Fleeing felt like the wrong choice, but what else could she do? If she stayed put, the cat would attack her. Its teeth were bared.

The cat's attention snapped, and she followed its gaze. It had spotted something behind her.

Brady Merrigan! He was just a few feet outside the cave. Never had she been happier to see that black-hatted cowboy in all her life.

Until he raised his hands above his head and hollered.

Then she decided he really did hate her and was okay with the idea of her being attacked by a wild animal, one of the creatures for which she was always fund-raising. It would be the perfect accident—and ironic, too. The cat would tear her apart, Brady would be a few minutes too late, and then *he'd* do a fund-raiser for *her.*

"Get out of here." Brady stepped under the threshold of the cave, puffing up his chest. "I said *move!*"

Squeezing her eyes shut, Zo braced for impact. The cat would have its jaws on her any second.

She felt Brady's hand on her shoulder. "Are you okay, Zo?"

She flicked open her eyes. He was staring at her with concern. She spun around. The mountain lion was gone. She blinked. Had he shot him? No. She would have heard the gun.

"He ran out of the cave," explained Brady.

She turned back.

"See, if you crouch down or back away, the cat thinks you're prey. It will hunt and chase you down. But if you maintain eye contact and stand your ground, it will get scared and run away."

He didn't hate her. He'd *saved* her. He'd risked his life to save a woman who generally made his life harder. Choking back a cry, she threw her arms around him.

He awkwardly patted her back. "It's okay."

The words reassured her, and she felt the breath reenter her lungs. "Thank you."

Hurried footsteps echoed through the cave. Max appeared from the tunnel, his T-shirt and jeans smeared with earthy grime. He squinted, adjusting to the new light.

A gulp escaped her throat. He was a little dirty but safe.

"What happened—Brady?"

"It was a mountain lion," answered Brady. "Everyone's fine. And before you get your feathers ruffled, that includes the mountain lion. He ran away."

"Are you all right?" she asked.

"I'm fine." Max ran his hand through his hair, brushing away rock dust. "A mountain lion?"

She nodded. "It had me cornered. Officer Merrigan showed up just in time. I froze."

Brady cleared his throat. "I know Zo. She would have come to her senses eventually. Those big cats are scary. No other way to put it."

She shook her head. "I don't think so. I couldn't move. I couldn't blink. I couldn't breathe." Thinking back, she shivered. "I don't know how to thank you. You saved my life."

Brady made a noise. It might have been *you're welcome*, but Zo couldn't tell because he adjusted his hat at the same time. He changed the subject, talking to Max. "What were you doing back there, in the tunnels?"

Max looked at Zo.

He was silently asking her approval. If Brady could be trusted to save her life, he could be trusted with Ezra Kind's gold. She nodded.

"Zo found a map," explained Max. "She was helping Jules clean Mountain View Manor when she found it stashed in the attic. We think it's the location of Ezra Kind's gold."

Brady crossed his arms. "A *treasure* map?"

This was the skeptical cop she knew how to talk to. She was back on familiar ground. "Yes," she answered, retrieving the map from her jacket. "We think it was taken from the pages of *My Journey West*."

Brady examined the paper while Max looked on. Brady touched the bound edge. "It does look like it comes from a book." He scanned the drawing. "And you think this is here?"

Max shrugged. "I *did*, but I didn't find anything in the tunnel." He looked at Zo. "Sorry."

"No need to be sorry." It would be really great to find the gold. It would be even better to find the book and another key to her past. But finding Maynard's murderer was the most important thing right now. He deserved justice, and she was determined to find out the truth behind his death.

"There are other tunnels," Brady suggested. "I wouldn't give up the idea just yet." He lowered the map. "You say you found this at Mountain View Manor?"

Zo knew she had to tell him about the break-in at Jules's house. Although they didn't have any physical evidence, he needed to know her theories, even if he didn't agree. "Yes, and that's not all. Friday night, someone broke into Jules's house. I think they were looking for it."

Brady let out a breath. "Since I'm hearing this for the first time, I assume you didn't call Spirit Canyon Police."

"They called me," explained Max. "I checked out the house. I didn't find any signs of a break-in."

"Except the barrette," added Zo.

"Right, but we don't know when it was left. My buddy Duncan—he's renting Jules's guesthouse—thought he saw someone jump over the fence."

Brady held up his hand, which grazed the roof of the cave. "Whoa, partner. Tell me everything, from the beginning."

Max described the sequence of events, step by step. He ended by telling Brady they suspected Olivia Nesbitt, because of the barrette in the library.

"And we know she wasn't at the estate sale, like she says she was. Landon—he's in my Zodiac Club—said they were together at a fundraiser for the astrology department. I have a picture of them on my phone."

Brady brought his fingertips together. "What about Dalrymple's niece? She would know the house better than anyone. If someone went back looking for something, it might have been her."

"Max said the same thing earlier," Zo added. Still, shouldn't have Cora taken the map with her when she left? It wasn't the kind of thing to be forgotten. Unless she didn't know about it when she auctioned off the house.

Zo recalled the conversation with her on the hotel veranda. Cora had just finished clearing out her great-aunt's safe-deposit boxes. It was possible she'd found out about the gold then. "I think you're both right," Zo concluded. "It could have very well been Cora in Jules's house that night. Could you ask her?"

Max pretended to rub his ears. "Did you just say you thought we were *both* right?"

Brady cupped his hand like a horn to his ear, leaning into one leg. "Say it again. I'm not sure I heard you the first time."

Zo wasn't above groveling if it meant finding the key to this murder. "Fine. You're both right. Now, please go interrogate her."

"I think that's a good idea." Brady peeked out of the cave. The rain had stopped as quickly as it started. Not a drop fell on his cowboy hat. "You need a ride back to town? Or do you think that little red motorcycle of yours can make it?"

They followed him out. A rainbow started to spread across the sky, chasing away the dark gray clouds.

"*That's* how you found us," said Max.

"Yep, I saw Zo's bike parked on the side of the road and worried she was in trouble."

"Thanks for stopping," said Zo.

He touched his hat. "Anytime—just not anytime soon."

Chapter Twenty-Five

Zo's clothes dried quickly on the ride back to Spirit Canyon. However, the chill of the rainstorm and incident with the mountain lion had soaked through to her core. There was no drying away her feelings. She was disappointed they hadn't found Ezra Kind's gold; it would have been nice to know that some Wild West legends were actually true. But she was more disappointed they hadn't found clues to the book or to Maynard's murderer. Each step forward brought with it another step back, and she was no closer to solving the mystery than walking George on a leash.

On a more promising note, the lights were on at Jules's house, and that meant Jules had returned from the jewelers and would know whether the gold nugget was real. Zo looked forward to hearing what she had to say. And the search for Ezra Kind's gold wasn't over—yet. Max vowed to keep looking for the stash. But next time, he would be more prepared, and so would she. For tigers, bears—and mountain lions.

"You look terrible," Jules declared when she met them at the door. Still in carpenter overalls, she had taken off her hat and twisted her long hair into a floppy bun at the nape of her neck. "What happened?"

"Ditto for you." Duncan's eyes flicked over Max's dirt-smeared T-shirt.

"Thanks," said Zo as she and Max entered the house. "We got caught in the storm."

"Huh." Despite his chores, Duncan looked the same as he did at lunch, his retro T-shirt and joggers still dry and fairly clean. "It hardly rained here."

"You're cold." Jules frowned. "I'll grab you a sweatshirt. Duncan, start the fire."

They followed Duncan to the living room, where he heaped logs into the oversized stone fireplace. Max did the lighting, and within minutes, Zo was wrapped in a warm sweatshirt, two sizes too big, and the coziness of the fire. Max snuggled in beside her on the rug, and she felt better.

After checking the fire, Jules returned with a tray and four glasses of wine. She placed the tray on a large box in the middle of the floor. The room was lined with boxes and furniture that hadn't been put away yet. It would take days, if not weeks, to get the house in order, and Jules was not the kind of person to rush.

It's what made them great friends. While Zo was often in a hurry, Jules advised caution and careful thinking. *Methodical* was a word that described her. Zo would never forget the instance she quit a job at the ice cream shop because of a rude employee. At the time, Jules told her to wait it out, that the mean girl wouldn't last a week. Despite liking the job, Zo quit after another heated argument. The next week, the girl was fired for treating a customer badly. Ever since, Zo promised to take Jules's advice to heart before acting rashly.

"Red for everyone." Jules handed Zo a glass, interrupting her reverie. "I hope you don't mind. I thought it would warm us up."

"Not at all." Zo inhaled the cherry and blackberry notes mingled with smoky oak spice. "Thank you."

"What did the jeweler say about the gold nugget?" asked Max, taking the next glass.

Jules handed Duncan a glass, then took the last one for herself. "You first. I have to know what happened out there in the woods. It looks as if you were attacked by a bear."

"Close," Zo said. "A mountain lion."

"Shut the front door." Jules sat crisscross. "Like, a *real* mountain lion?"

"As real as real can be." Zo thought back to the moment and shuddered. "With sharp teeth and everything."

"How did you get rid of it?" Jules aimed the question at Max.

He held up his hands. "I had nothing to do with it. Brady Merrigan found us and chased it away. So we did evade a mountain lion, but we didn't find the gold."

"I assume you came up empty-handed, too?" asked Zo. By Jules's cool demeanor, she could only assume the gold was fake. Who knows? Maybe the map was also.

"This is why you're a shop owner." Jules winked at Duncan. "She'd never make it in the psychic biz."

"Never," Duncan seconded.

Zo sat up straighter. "Wait—it was real?"

Jules flashed her a wide smile. "As real as real can be."

"Did you take it to Glitz and Gold?" asked Max.

"Is there another jeweler in town?" Jules swirled her wine. "Of course I took it to Glitz and Gold. Mac has been in town fifty years." She took a sip and swished it around in her mouth. "He confirmed what I already knew—through my abilities."

Abilities that included business savvy. "That's great news," Zo congratulated. "Did he give you any idea what it was worth?"

"Around ten thousand dollars."

Max let out a whistle.

"Incredible," added Zo. "I wonder if it came from Ezra Kind's stash..." Her mind started to drift to the possibilities. "Merrigan thinks Cora might have been the one who broke into your house, looking for the map. Maybe she was looking for the gold."

"Or both," added Max.

"You need to tell her about it," said Zo.

Jules's eyes narrowed. "No way."

Zo blinked. "You're kidding, right?"

"No," said Jules. "I'm completely serious." She gestured to their historic surroundings. "I paid a lot of money for this house. It's mine, and so is everything in it."

"I agree," Duncan said.

Zo checked Max's expression to see if he agreed with them. He lifted his brow in question, and she knew, he, too, had concerns. She returned to Jules. "But her aunt was Vera Dalrymple."

"And mine was a witch in Salem."

"Is that true?" Max asked out of the side of his mouth.

"Partly," Zo murmured. "It was her great-aunt."

"Look." Jules held up her wine goblet. "If I told you this is from a bottle of 1951 vintage Penfolds Grange I found stashed in the corner of the wine cellar, what would you say?"

"Nothing," Zo answered tentatively, mainly because she had no idea what it was.

"I'd say it's wasted on Max." Duncan pointed in his direction. "He's more of a beer drinker."

"And when did you become a wine snob?" Max countered. "Last week?"

Duncan leveled a look at him. "I've been working at Spirits & Spirits for six months, genius."

Jules ignored the bickering. "Right. You'd say nothing. Or you'd applaud my good fortune. The same principle applies to the gold nugget."

Zo understood the point and agreed with it to some extent. But the Dalrymples had been in Spirit Canyon for years. Vera was the town's historian. An important piece of history couldn't be lost after a lifetime of keeping it secret. If it was from Ezra Kind's stash, it should be placed in a museum or something. It would be evidence to a story widely deemed a myth. Even today they were searching for a book, a clue to what had actually happened. If the golden nugget could prove it, they needed to protect it. "At least let me ask Cora about it. I want her to know before she leaves town."

"What if she wants it back?" asked Jules.

They all turned to Max. He tossed up his hands. "That's a good question for Brady Merrigan. He didn't ask Zo to return the map."

Zo nodded. "With all the commotion of the mountain lion, I thought he forgot."

"I doubt it," said Max. "But we can ask him."

Zo noted the stubborn point of Jules's chin. "At least let me question Cora about it. All I need is her reaction. You can come, too. I could use your *psychic* powers."

Jules lowered her lids. "Now you're just trying to butter me up."

Zo smiled. "Is it working?"

"You know I could never say no to you," Jules said.

"You say no to me all the time," murmured Duncan.

Zo let loose a laugh. Did he mean what she thought he meant? She didn't have time to find out before Jules whirled at pillow at him, preventing further discussion of the topic.

On the ride home, Max told her he'd like a redo of dinner the other night. As the eldest son of a single mom, he knew how to cook and wanted to prove it to her. "I can't have burned lasagna be your impression of my cooking skills," Max insisted. "Let me make it up to you."

She turned onto his street, and a blast of wind hit, making it harder to hear. "You don't have to make it up to me," she shouted behind her. "Dinner was great."

"Because I didn't cook it," he shouted back. "Admit it. You're scared."

Laughing, she pulled into his driveway and waited for him to jump off the back of the bike. She took off her helmet. "After today, I don't see how a burnt piece of lasagna could be scary."

He crossed his arms. "That's not a yes."

"Okay, okay," she surrendered. "I'll come for dinner."

He stuck out his hand. "Shake on it."

She took his hand, and he pulled her close. The heady scent of pine enveloped her as he kissed her softly. She leaned in, enjoying the warmth of his body and the feeling of his lips. Their friendship had blossomed into a special closeness. Deep down, she said a secret prayer, hoping it would last.

When their eyes met again, it felt as if he'd heard her prayer. "Do you want to come in?" he asked.

She glanced at her helmet. "I'd better go. I need to get started on my Curious Camper column. It's about the first prospectors in Spirit Canyon."

"Timely topic, but I know your schedule. It's not due until Friday."

She cleared her throat. "It includes history, so it will take more time. Research."

He nodded, but she could tell he was unconvinced. "Are you sure Justin Castle will approve?"

"I don't care whether he approves or not." She pulled on her helmet, flipping open her visor. "This is my town, my column, and it fits in perfectly with Gold Rush Days." She started her bike. "Besides, I'm out of events until August. I have nothing else to write about."

He chuckled, waving good-bye, and she backed down the driveway, turning on Main Street. It was back to Happy Camper, where a hanging lamp she'd purchased at a thrift store glowed in the miniature window above the door. With George on the doorstep, it made a happy homecoming.

She parked her bike, and George scooted away. *So much for the welcome home.* But as she turned the key to her deck door, she heard the jangle of his cat collar and waited. He was coming up the deck steps. *He knows who fills his kitty dish.* He shoved past her.

Tossing her keys on the counter, she turned on the light. A hot cup of tea would be the perfect writing companion. She opened her cupboard, selecting a Happy Camper mug. George meowed loudly, swerving against her legs.

"Excuse me, your majesty." She gave him a bow. "How rude of me. How may I assist you?"

Now that he had her attention, he sauntered to the sink cupboard, where she kept his cat food. He looked at her with half-closed amber eyes.

"One dish of signature seafood medley coming right up." She scooped the food onto his plate and returned to making her tea, a mint-orange blend perfect for a summer's evening. Then she settled into her office chair to work on her column, looking out to the forest of trees beyond her window.

She brought the mug to her lips, inhaling the sweet orange scent. The moon was as large and as white as a saucer of milk. Only the jagged branch of a tree, close to her house, kept it in perspective. Otherwise she could've believed it was hung at her window to shine a light on her desk.

All that glittered was not gold. But was real gold worth killing for? Past experience said yes. Men had killed for it and lost their lives for it. The map, still in her jacket pocket, burned in her memory. Men would *still* kill for it, if Maynard's death was any indication. The town had been founded, in part, by greedy gold diggers willing to tear up the Hills to see what was inside. Something told her they wouldn't hesitate to do it again. She needed to protect the location of the gold at all costs. Until they brought Maynard's killer to justice, no person—or Hill—was safe.

Chapter Twenty-Six

The next morning, Jules strolled into Happy Camper with two coffees from the O.K. Coffee Corral. She held the Styrofoam cups out at her sides, showing off a black T-shirt with a skull and the words Spirits & Spirits. "What do you think of my new merch?"

Combined with tight jeans and untied tennis shoes, the outfit was pure Jules. "Nice. I love it."

Jules set the coffee on the counter. "I thought you would. You're the one who gave me the idea, with your Happy Camper line." She gestured to a table of colorful mugs, coasters, and notepads. "Of course, mine is black and has a skull."

"Of course. What would your merch be without a skull?" Zo laid down the history book on Spirit Canyon she'd been perusing for her Curious Camper column. "Why the coffee?"

Jules popped off the lid. "I thought it might have been a late night, with Max."

Zo grinned. "Ah. Thank you."

Jules raised her eyebrows. "Was it?"

"Actually, it was." Zo sipped her coffee.

Jules paused.

"I was up late working on my column."

Jules blew on her coffee. "Bor-ing. I thought the two of you looked pretty comfortable on my rug. They say a near-death experience can bring people together."

"I don't know if I'd call it near-death, but it was the closest I've ever been to a mountain lion. That's for sure." She switched topics. "How about you and Duncan? It's almost like you live together or something." She batted her eyelashes innocently.

Jules's eyes were masked by the steam of her coffee. "I'm not going to lie. He's growing on me. Or at least his muscles are. He's got a bad habit of walking around shirtless, and I'm getting a bad habit of staring." She blinked. "It's addicting."

Zo let out a laugh. "At least you admit it."

She shrugged. "Why wouldn't I? I'm a woman with needs, same as everyone else."

A jingle at the door announced Harley's arrival. Putting away her book, Zo grabbed her purse beneath the counter. "Did you bring the *thing*? To show to Cora?" she asked Jules.

Jules retrieved the gold nugget from her purse and held it in the sunlight. "By 'thing,' do you mean large hunk of gold?"

Harley skidded to a stop. "Wow. Is that real?"

"It's not a hologram," said Jules, twisting it in the sunlight. It shot gold flecks all over the store. "I'm thinking of turning it into a mood ring. What do you think?"

"I think we'd better see Cora first." Zo turned to Harley. "Please don't tell anyone about that." She pointed to the gold nugget.

Nodding, Harley lifted her bag over her pixie cut. "This is why I like working here. I never know what's going to happen next. Or to whom."

Zo chuckled. "By the way, I filled the cooler with water bottles, but I should be back in time to help pass them out at the Fun Run." The Fun Run, a five-mile jaunt around Spirit Canyon, was the official start of Gold Rush Days, kicking off three days of festivities. Runners, joggers, walkers, and plain-old strollers took part in the activity.

Jules tucked the nugget back into her purse. "Unless she isn't. In that case, call Officer Merrigan and tell him Cora killed us."

"Will do," agreed Harley, not missing a beat. "Have fun."

Monday morning traffic was busier than usual because of Gold Rush Days. Event goers were enjoying the summer day, occasionally ducking inside for water or ice cream, waiting for the carnival to kick off. Located in the center of town at Cascade Park, the carnival was one of Zo's favorite parts of the festival. Adults and children alike came for the carousel and cotton candy, not to mention the funnel cakes. Topped with powdered sugar and strawberries, they could persuade even the most avid dieter to try one bite.

Zo sighed. The smells of summer would fill her days and nights for the next three days, and the store would be busy. But she, like the tourists, wanted to be outside, reliving a few blissful moments of childhood.

"You're thinking about the carnival," said Jules.

"How'd you know?"

"I'm thinking about it, too." Jules nodded toward the park as they sped past in her VW Beetle. "I can hear them setting up." She flipped on her blinker. "Remember the time we broke in after dark and stole those pink bears?"

Zo scrunched up her nose. "Can you really call it stealing if we spent twenty dollars apiece on that game?"

"My mom marched me to the police station the next morning and made me confess." Jules rolled her eyes. "I can still see the disapproval in Officer Merrigan's face. Though he was decent about it and said he wouldn't file charges and would take the bear back himself."

Not file charges. That sounded like Brady Merrigan. "I still have mine," Zo admitted.

Jules shot her a look. "You're kidding."

"Nope." Zo twisted toward Jules. "Did you know they started adding stuffed animals in the duffel bags I donate to? For the younger kids? I think it's a great idea." She donated to an organization that gave out duffel bags to foster kids so they didn't have to haul their belongings in garbage bags. She remembered the black plastic bags vividly. If she could prevent even a handful of kids from going through that experience, the donation was worth it.

"That's awesome." Jules looked left and right before turning onto Main Street.

"I hope Cora's still at the hotel."

"She is." Jules turned into the parking lot, on a side street behind the Waterfall Inn.

"Intuition?"

Jules put the car in PARK. "Nope. I talked to the Tracey brothers this morning. They asked me to stop by and sign a paper they'd missed. They needed Cora to do the same."

"That's perfect." Zo hopped out of the car. "Now we have an excuse for being here." When they reached the front door, Zo was relieved to see Cora in the lobby with the Tracey brothers. They were bent over an ornately carved table, signing papers.

Jules strode over to the area. "Hey, Cedric."

Cedric looked up. His round glasses were low on his nose, and he pushed them up with a well-manicured finger. "I'm confused. Did I ask you to meet us here?"

"No," answered Jules. "We're here to talk to Cora, but I thought I could take care of the paperwork at the same time."

Cora paused, pen in hand. "Hi, Jules. Hi, Zo."

Zo took note of the large emerald on her finger. "That's a beautiful ring."

"It was my aunt's." Cora smiled at the gem. "We found all sorts of treasures in Aunt Vera's house—but not my necklace." A wrinkle appeared between her light-blue eyes. "I can't believe she gave it away."

Cedric kept his eyes on the paper. "It happens."

Jules pulled up a chair. "I'm finding things, too."

"Oh?" Cedric's eyes flicked to Jules. "Anything interesting?"

Jules pressed her lips into a mischievous smile. "Mostly dust bunnies."

Cora chuckled. "I'm sorry. I should have had it cleaned. Vera wasn't known for her tidiness."

"Not necessary with an auction," interjected Sean. Like his brother, he was small, but he had a gaunt face and pointy cheekbones. He was in a hurry to finish the paperwork and looked irritated with the chitchat. He gripped the knees of his crossed legs.

Zo was determined not to let him rush the conversation. "I guess when you're the town historian, you don't have to worry so much about a clean house. History is more important."

"Some might say the *most* important." Cora brushed back a fringe of light red hair. "Aunt Vera would have. She didn't let the little things, like cleaning, weigh her down. I'm going to miss her."

"So will the historical society," added Zo. "She organized a lot of events for them."

Jules adjusted her black pearl earring. "The entire town will."

Sean cleared his throat, reminding Cora of the task at hand. She resumed signing and dating the sheet in front of her. It was the last on a pile of copies.

When she was finished, Cedric pointed to the paper. "Ms. Parker, if you'd sign here, we'll be all set."

Cora stood, and she and Zo moved a few steps away to give them privacy. The hotel lobby was all windows, and they took up a sunny spot near the newspapers. "You mentioned the historical society, but did you know Aunt Vera argued with them?"

"Really?" asked Zo.

Cora nodded. "She and the president butted heads several times."

"Sue Archer?"

Cora snapped her fingers. "That's her name. Aunt Vera didn't like the way she squandered her donations."

"What donations?" pressed Zo.

"Aunt Vera donated thousands of dollars, yet the foundation was in jeopardy because of ongoing debt." Cora lowered her voice. "The day before the auction, Sue came to me and said Aunt Vera had promised her the book about Spirit Canyon. But my lawyer didn't find anything about it in her will. When I asked her to leave, she made quite a production, insisting I was ruining my aunt's good name." Cora sniffed. "I hope that's not true."

Zo tried to ease Cora's fears. "You could never ruin her good name. If Sue wasn't mentioned in the papers, you were right not to give away the book. I just wonder if she tried to get it some other way…"

The Tracey brothers stood. Sean put on the suit jacket that hung over the chair. "We're all finished, unless you need anything else."

"Not at all," said Cora. "Thanks for everything."

They put the copies in a folder and shook Cora's and Jules's hands before leaving.

Once the door had closed, Zo gestured to the small table. "Can we have just one more minute of your time?"

"Sure." Cora scooted into the chair. "Is something wrong?"

"No," said Jules. "I didn't want to say anything in front of the Traceys, but I did find something in the house. Besides dust bunnies."

Cora's pale blue eyes widened. "What?"

Jules retrieved the nugget, wrapped in a silk cloth, from her purse. She gave Cora a peek at what was beneath.

"Is that what I think it is?" Cora asked.

Zo studied her reaction. "What do you think it is?"

Cora tilted her head to one side. "Gold?"

"Right," said Jules. "We found it in the office attic, behind a bookcase. You didn't know about it?"

"Of course not." Cora shook her head. "I mean, it doesn't surprise me, because of who Aunt Vera was, but I had no idea she was hiding gold." She reached out to touch it, and Jules yanked it back, folding it in the cloth.

"Let me get this straight. You find a piece of gold in my aunt's house, yet you're not here to give it back?"

"Right again," Jules said.

Zo gave Jules a look, mentally asking her not to add fuel to the fire. "We think it might be the reason my friend was killed."

"I get it now." Cora huffed. "This is about the hidden treasure, isn't it? The one you *didn't care* about." She made air quotes.

"Do you know anything about it?" asked Zo.

Cora stood and pushed back her chair. "Aunt Vera was right, about all of it. I thought you were different, but you've been seduced by greed, just like she said you would be. She said it was the root of all evil, and I guess she was right."

"Wait, Cora," Jules interrupted. "It's not like that."

Cora held up her hand. "Save it for my attorney. I'm done here." She stalked out of the lobby, looking older than her twentysomething years.

Jules tucked the gold into her purse and stood. "That went well."

"Actually, it did." Zo followed Jules outside.

"How can you say that?"

Zo waited to answer until they were in the parking lot. "She didn't mention the treasure map, which means she must not know about it."

Jules popped open the car doors. "Probably not."

Zo rolled down her window as they pulled away from the Waterfall Inn. "I have a good feeling about this."

"Not me."

Zo looked at her friend. Her face was tight with worry. "Why?"

Jules took off for Main Street. "Because I'm getting sued."

Chapter Twenty-Seven

Zo and Jules returned to Happy Camper just as spectators were beginning to line Main Street for the Fun Run, and Jules had to park several blocks from the store. The race would begin at high noon with the firing of a gun. The irony wasn't lost on Zo, who couldn't imagine a better amalgam of the past and future. Shoot-outs at high noon were part of history. Today, residents spent their lunch hours hiking, running, and biking. But the town would never entirely shed the yoke of the Wild West. It was part of its history, a history that was still alive and well if Mayor Murphy's dress was any indication. She'd traded in her Patagonia fleece and hiking boots for chaps and a ten-gallon hat. Though they weren't dressed in Western attire, the runners wore gold bib numbers that sparkled in the summer sunshine. En masse, at the starting line, they were every bit as shiny as the nugget in Jules's purse.

"Hold the door, will you?" Zo asked, as they hurried to join the spectators.

"No problem." Jules held open the front door of Happy Camper.

Zo and Harley scooted past her with the wheeled cooler they used for large events. Together, they pushed it two blocks to their designated station, where participants and onlookers would enjoy the drinks. Sponsored by businesses, the community center, and the historical society, locations were set up all along the route. Since the runners weren't professional athletes—mostly members of the community, sprinkled with a few tourists—they would be stopping frequently for ice-cold water or sports drinks. The event was the kind of fun activity that brought together everyone in the community, which was why Zo was surprised when Jules said she wasn't staying.

"I can't," Jules explained. "I have an appointment with a California wine vendor at one o'clock. He's very well-connected."

Harley frowned.

"Sorry," Jules apologized. "I've had it on the books for a month."

"It's not you," said Harley. "It's *him*."

Zo followed her gaze. Chance was coming toward them on roller skates and gaining speed. She was no expert, but she was pretty sure roller skates were meant for indoors, not the busy streets of Spirit Canyon. Groups of people were shifting to get out of his way, but he still clipped several elbows as he careened forward, stumbling on a crack in the sidewalk.

Harley held out her arms to stop him, her strong muscles flexing as she caught him, spinning to a stop. "What are you doing?"

Chance smiled at Jules and Zo in between breaths. "Hi." He swallowed hard.

"How about a water?" Zo opened the cooler.

"That would be great. Thanks, Zo." Chance gulped down half the water bottle in one swig.

Harley was waiting for his explanation. "Well?"

"Oh, the skates." Looking too tall for his skinny legs, he adjusted a knee pad. "I decided the best way to learn a sport is to do it. I thought we could skate together." He twisted his hips. "You could show me a few moves."

"I think it's a great idea," Zo interjected.

"Never do that in public again." Harley waggled a finger at him. "The thing with your hips."

"Fine, but you have to promise me we'll skate."

Harley's lips turned up slightly as she grasped his hand. "Okay."

"I'd love to stick around and watch the start of the race, but I have to go." Jules hiked her purse over her shoulder. "See you tonight?"

"I'll call you."

Mayor Murphy checked the microphone, and even more people crowded the street. Zo waved at Cunningham, who was manning the Black Mountain College table. Her smile disappeared when she spotted Justin from KRSO a few yards away. From the looks of it, he was giving his cameraman a hard time, probably about the lighting, as if the poor man could do something about the bright yellow sun in the sky. Justin was interviewing Sue Archer, who was under the dark-green historical society banner. In a matching green T-shirt, she was handing out pamphlets to visitors.

The crowd quieted as the mayor began to speak.

"Now, listen here, all you outlaws, you'd better listen up because I'm the one with the gun!" Mayor Murphy flashed the old-time pistol in the air, and the crowd cheered. "Over a hundred years ago, a road bandit held up this very street, filling his pockets with Black Hills gold. Today the fine folks of Spirit Canyon have taken up more cultured pursuits." *Well*, thought Zo, *some of them*. Maynard Cline's murderer still went the way of the Wild, Wild West.

"The race begins here and ends at Cascade Park, where I will officially open the carnival for business." More cheers assailed the mayor. She squinted one eye. "But you'd better leave the first funnel cake for me, or you'll be in trouble. Are you ready?" The runners got on their marks. "Let the thirty-fifth annual Gold Rush Days begin!" She fired the gun, and the runners took off, some running, some walking, and some waving for a picture.

After a few minutes, the crowd dispersed, chatting and enjoying free drinks. Zo would have enjoyed it, too, if Justin Castle wasn't headed in her direction. He had a pamphlet from the historical society sticking out of his fancy shirt pocket.

"Hi, Justin." She nodded toward the pamphlet. "Thinking about joining the historical society?"

"No." His answer was decisive. "Sue Archer was happy to report a huge donation came in a few days ago from the group Women for Historical Accuracy. She wants it on the five o'clock news. I couldn't get her to shut up."

Zo digested the information. The historical society's money troubles were solved, for now. She hadn't needed Vera's money—or book—after all. The Archer House would keep going despite the expensive upkeep.

Justin took a water from the cooler. "Sue said your upcoming column is about the founding fathers of Spirit Canyon."

"And mothers," Zo was quick to add.

"Right. Mothers." He bit his bottom lip, feigning puzzlement. "Will it have anything to do with *your* birth mother?"

A coldness sank into her chest. She couldn't breathe, let alone speak. It was a topic he could kindly take out of his stupid mouth.

"Because Sue said you inquired after a few books in her library." He twisted the cap off his water. "I'm wondering if they're for you or for the article. A family enigma can make people...desperate."

She wanted to react—how *badly* she wanted to react—but she couldn't. The cold had turned into anger, and she worried she would haul off and hit him across his smug chops.

"Cunningham said something really smart the other day." He leaned in. "Such a *nice* old man. He said we should collaborate." He took a long drink of his water. "I think it's a good idea. Maybe we could find the answers you're looking for."

She had to get out of there. She just had to. He didn't want to collaborate; he wanted her story. She racked her brain for a reason to get away. "I just remembered, I forgot to lock my store."

It was equivalent to the excuse of shampooing her hair, but it did the trick—and it was true. She told Harley and Chance to watch over the cooler, leaving Justin staring after her, as she rushed back to Happy Camper.

Walking helped the air reenter her lungs, and she felt better after a few steps. She remembered reading that walking reduced anxiety, and she believed it after her conversation with Justin. He didn't care about her or her birth parents. All he cared about was his next story and whether it would be better than her column. Not better—more popular. That was what he really desired. Popularity. It was silly that at her age, she was stuck in a popularity contest. It was better left behind with high school.

As she approached Happy Camper, she saw Jules's VW Bug high on the hill and frowned. She checked her watch. Jules should have been long gone by now. A visit with her coveted wine vendor was a meeting she wouldn't miss. Why was she still here?

Zo made a detour up the hill, her steps coming quickly as she neared the car. By the time she approached the driver's door, she was running. Her heart already knew what her eyes confirmed. Jules's head was bent over the wheel, as if her friend was asleep. But there was no way she was sleeping in a hot car with the windows rolled up in the midday sun.

Zo yanked open the door. "Jules! Jules, are you okay?"

Jules's hand twitched, and a moan escaped from her chest.

Thank God! Zo pulled out her phone and dialed 911. As she gave the operator her location, she checked Jules's face and body. "No, I don't see any injuries." Then she noted the dark-red spot in Jules's lovely blond hair. "Wait." Her fingers touched the bump, a large goose egg growing beneath the surface. "She's been hit in the head."

Jules winced. "*Ouch.*"

"It's okay, Jules. I'm here." Zo clicked off the phone. "The ambulance is on the way."

Jules leaned back in her seat, her eyes fluttering open. "What happened?"

"That's what I was hoping you could tell me." From the appearance of her eyes, Jules was having a hard time focusing. Her pupils were bigger than normal.

Jules blinked slowly. "I heard a gunshot."

"That was the mayor," Zo explained. "The Fun Run?"

"That's when something hit me." Jules squeezed her eyes shut. The pain in her head was obviously causing her trouble. "Or someone. They must have been in the car, waiting for me."

Zo checked the tiny back seat. She didn't see anything out of place. "Did you see whom?"

By reflex, Jules shook her head and cried out.

"That's okay," Zo quickly said. "Don't worry about that right now. Your health is the most important thing."

"My...p-p-purse."

Zo noted Jules's handbag on the passenger's seat. "It's right here, beside you."

Jules fumbled for the strap, pulling the purse onto her lap. Opening her eyes, squinting to focus, she unfastened the large gold buckle. She pushed aside papers and a wallet, her movements weak and clumsy. Her hands fell to her sides, leaving the bag gaping open. But Zo didn't need to see inside to know that what she was looking for was gone.

The gold nugget had been stolen.

Chapter Twenty-Eight

Jules was in the ambulance on her way to the hospital before Zo took her first real breath. The paramedic had said she would be fine, but they would keep her several hours for observation. She had a concussion, which could turn serious quickly. The possibility struck Zo deep at her core. Jules was her closest friend. They'd weathered bad boyfriends, bad business decisions, and bad haircuts together. She couldn't lose her.

Zo should have left well enough alone. But always on the hunt for the truth, she had wanted to see Cora's reaction for herself. She wanted to *know* if Cora knew about the gold. Now her friend was hurt. "This is all my fault."

Max, who'd heard the call over the radio and raced to the scene, put his hands on her shoulders. "Don't say that. You know it's not true."

"The gold has disappeared, and Jules is on the way to the hospital." She searched his eyes. "How have I helped anyone?"

"Your tenacious spirit is a help to everyone." Looking over her shoulder, Max blinked. "Well, maybe not everyone. Here comes Merrigan."

Zo followed his gaze down the hill, where Brady Merrigan was talking to the first officer who'd arrived on the scene. The young officer was probably relaying the details Zo had already given her while two other officers searched Jules's car. Zo's eyes met Brady's, and he frowned and marched up the hill. Max dropped his hands.

To her surprise, Brady's first question was about her health. "Are you okay?" He gave her a once-over. "I heard your friend Jules took a pretty good knock to the head."

"She did," answered Zo. "The paramedic said he thinks she has a concussion."

"It's not good, but she'll be all right." Brady stood with his arms crossed, legs shoulder-width apart. "You told me about the treasure map. Why didn't you tell me about the gold? After all this time, don't you trust me?"

It was a hard question to answer. Their relationship had changed. It was more...amicable. They'd shared resources. But trust? She skipped over the subject. "It wasn't my secret to tell. It's Jules's gold, and you know how weird she is about money." It probably came from not having a lot of it growing up. Neither one of them had a dime to their names when they were younger.

His eyes moved to Max. "And you're here in the boyfriend capacity. Is that right?"

"I heard the call over the radio," said Max. "Of course I came."

The friction between them was palpable, and Zo worried her relationship with Max was putting a strain on his place in the police force. Brady preferred Max to stay in the forest. Spirit Canyon was his domain. "The important thing is that the gold is gone," she interjected. "Who stole it?"

"Before we can ascertain that, I need to understand who knew about it." Brady wagged a finger between them. "Obviously you two. Who else?"

Zo shrugged. "Not many people. Duncan Hall, Harley, she's my employee—" She smacked her forehead. "Oh my gosh. Cora Kingsley. We were at the Waterfall Inn just this morning. We showed her the gold. She had to have followed us. That must be it!"

Brady wasn't as enthusiastic. "Let me guess. You decided to question her about the break-in, even after I promised you I would."

"Yes, no. I questioned her about the gold." Seeing Brady's blank expression, she filled in the missing detail. "We found the gold with the treasure map. But Cora didn't know anything about either one. I don't think she was the one who broke into Jules's house."

"But you *do* think she conked Jules over the head and snatched the gold," said Brady.

She nodded. It sounded less convincing when he said it.

"I'm happy to ask Cora a few questions," Max offered. "I can see you'll be here for a while."

"Zo will need a ride to the hospital to visit her friend." He squinted down the hill at the Happy Camper parking lot. "I don't think she should be alone right now, and she definitely shouldn't drive."

"I'm fine," she argued. "Let him go."

"He's right," said Max. "Let me take you to the hospital. I want to see how Jules is doing anyway."

Brady made a brushing motion with his hands. "Get going."

Max gave her a little push before she had a chance to respond, which was probably a good thing. She didn't like Merrigan deciding what was best for her—or Max. She could have had Harley, Chance, Cunningham, or anyone drive her to the hospital. For that matter, she could have driven herself. She felt fine.

Except she was still shaking. Max must have noticed, because he put an arm around her as they walked down the steep incline of the hill. His warm hand steadied her as she watched the rest of the town, all along Main Street, enjoying the Fun Run. It was the middle of a sunny day in a small western town. How could someone have gotten away with stealing a small fortune in gold? The idea was baffling, but perhaps it shouldn't have been, seeing as most of the police force was at the Fun Run. If Zo didn't know better, she would have thought it was planned.

When they returned to Happy Camper, Zo called Harley and explained the situation. Harley said she would leave Chance in charge of the cooler and come back immediately.

Five minutes later, Harley arrived, her pixie cut flying in different directions. She gave Zo a hug.

Zo was surprised. Harley was not a huggy person.

"I'm here, so go." Harley caught her breath. "Tell me right away how Jules is doing."

"I will," Zo promised. She and Max hopped into his beat-up pickup truck and started toward the hospital. Because of the event, they had to zigzag down side streets, avoiding the main routes. By the time they arrived at the hospital, Zo was on edge. The drive had taken what seemed like forever, and she was desperate to see Jules. She needed to know she was okay.

Max pulled up to the entrance. "I'll park. Should I call Duncan?"

"You'd better." She opened the car door. "Jules will want him at the meeting with the wine vendor, if it's not too late. He'll need to meet the man at the store or close it. Tell him we can help if we need to." She shut the car door, and he sped off toward the parking lot.

Thankfully, a volunteer was staffed at the information desk. Zo asked her about Jules.

"She's in ER room eleven." The efficient volunteer gave her a visitor sticker, and Zo pressed it on her shirt. "Right through those double doors." She buzzed Zo in, and the doors clicked open.

Zo was happy to see Jules awake and sitting up. A thick bandage was secured by a gauze wrap that covered a third of her head. She rushed to her side. "How are you doing?"

"Better," said Jules. "I was out of it for a few minutes. It was weird."

Zo noticed her eyes were clearer and her pupils less dilated. Jules really did look better. "How's the bump?"

"It hurts." Jules touched the bandage at the back of her head. "I wonder what they hit me with?"

"Do you remember anything?"

Jules rearranged her pillow. "The doctor told me not to try, but I've been racking my brain since I got here." Her eyes searched the room as if the thief might be lurking somewhere. "I remember the hotel, Happy Camper, the Fun Run... After that, it's a big blank. Nothing." She clenched her hands into fists. "So frustrating."

Zo decided it was time to change subjects before Jules did her recovery any harm. She put a hand over hers. "The important thing is that you're safe. Do you know when they'll let you out?"

"I need to have a CT scan. If that checks out, I'll be home before dark." Jules lowered her voice. "At least, I'd better be. They move as slow as my imported wine around here."

"Hey, Jules." Max popped his head in the door. "Mind if I come in?"

"Not at all." Jules waved him in. "Did you find the missing gold nugget?"

"I'm a forest ranger, not a miracle worker." He tossed up his hands. "It's been like, an hour. How are you feeling?"

"Fine," said Jules. "How about Duncan? Did you tell him what happened?"

Max looked to Zo. "Why do I feel as if I'm getting the third degree? Shouldn't it be the other way around?"

Zo gave him a little friendly advice. "You'd better just answer her question."

"Yes, I talked to Duncan, and he's at the store right now." Max bit the corner of his lip. "He says he's going to try to get you a discount with the wine vendor."

Jules closed her eyes. "Heaven help us."

"What happened at Happy Camper?" asked Max.

A short nurse walked in carrying a black binder. She had ruddy round cheeks, a button nose, and a bright smile. "Hello!"

They returned her smile.

"Do you remember?" Max continued.

"No, no, no." The nurse wagged a thick finger at them. "Ms. Parker needs to rest."

"Did you hear that?" Jules said to Zo. "*Ms. Parker.* When this ordeal is over, I'm going to buy new wrinkle cream. The expensive one, on the end-cap."

Zo chuckled. "I think they're all pretty much the same."

"I'm going to have to ask you to leave for a little while." The cheerful nurse opened the binder to a plastic-covered page of letters, numbers, and animals. "We have an evaluation to complete, don't we?"

"How is that rest?" asked Jules.

Max and Zo inched toward the door. Zo could see Jules was doing just fine. "No problem. We'll check back later."

"And give me a ride!" Jules added before they could shut the door.

"Thank goodness she's okay," Zo said when they got to the lobby. "Do you think she'll be able to go home?"

Max lowered his lashes. "Go home? I wouldn't be surprised if she isn't selling Spirits & Spirits' wine in the gift shop before she leaves."

"True." She smiled.

Max held open the front door for her. "Did she say anything before I got there, about who hit her?"

"No, she said the whole thing was a blank. She doesn't even remember going to her car."

"It'll come back to her," he said. "Don't worry. I've seen this before, with concussions."

"In the meantime, we could ask Cora."

Max paused next to his truck. "You heard Merrigan. He told me to take you to the hospital."

"And do you always do what you're told?" She waited patiently for his response.

"You're a bad influence on me, Zo Jones." He pointed to the door. "Get in."

Chapter Twenty-Nine

Zo and Max drove to the Waterfall Inn, where they found Cora getting into a car. Zo was sort of disappointed in Officer Merrigan. She really thought he'd have Cora in handcuffs by now—or at least in his police cruiser, talking, like he promised. He was letting her get away. Jules was in the hospital with a bandaged head and a blurry memory. Zo was determined not to let Cora off so easily.

"Cora, hold up," Zo called out. "I need to talk to you."

"I have nothing to say to you," Cora shot back. Her hair was aflame in the sunlight, flickering orange and red. "You lied to me."

Max hustled to catch up. "We need to discuss your whereabouts this afternoon."

Cora ignored him. "You pretended to care about my aunt. All you really cared about was the gold. You've got it now, so stay away from me."

"That's just it," breathed Zo. "We don't have it."

Cora turned from the door. "What do you mean?"

"It was stolen. Jules is in the hospital."

"When?" Cora asked.

"A few hours ago," stated Max. "She was hit over the head, and the gold was taken from her purse."

Cora covered her mouth. "That's awful. I didn't mean what I said. I'm sorry."

She sounded sincere, but maybe it was her youth. She had a fresh young face that made trusting her easy. Still, Zo believed her.

Max didn't take her apology at face value, however. He continued with a question. "Where were you between twelve and one o'clock today?"

"That's funny." Cora sputtered a laugh. "You think I stole my own gold?"

He waited for an answer.

"I was right here, packing to leave." Cora put her hands on her hips. "I had to meet with the Tracey brothers this morning, as Zo knows. She can vouch for me. I was supposed to check out at noon and needed a time extension." She pointed to the hotel. "Ask the hostess."

"I'll do that," said Max.

Zo hung on Cora's words, replaying the morning's events. The Tracey brothers were at the hotel. What if *they* saw Jules show Cora the gold? What if they were the ones who had hurt her?

"Wait here," Max instructed. "I don't want you leaving until I talk to someone."

"Fine, but make it quick," Cora said. "I have a plane to catch, and I have to drive all the way to Rapid City."

After Max left, Zo asked Cora about Cedric and Sean Tracey. "Do you think it's possible they saw Jules showing you the gold?"

She considered the question a moment before answering. "That didn't happen until after they left."

True. Jules didn't get to the gold until after the papers were signed.

Cora raised a finger. "But if they were outside, they might have seen it from the street. We were in the lobby."

The lobby had floor-to-ceiling windows, and the gold nugget was large enough to see from a distance. If Cora didn't take the gold, it had to be them. Unless Duncan had told someone… She didn't even want to go down that road, which, if true, might lead to Duncan's immediate eviction.

"But why would they steal the gold?" Cora shifted her carrying case to her other hand. "They came highly recommended from my aunt's estate attorney. He said they were very knowledgeable when it came to antiques, and by the looks of their business, they are very successful."

"I don't know," Zo admitted. "Gold makes people a little crazy. You've heard of gold fever? It might have been the case here."

"That was a thousand years ago," said Cora. "People aren't like that now."

Not a thousand, Zo thought but remained silent. Maybe Jules was right. Maybe they were older than they felt. "You'd be surprised what people are capable of."

The back door opened, and Max returned, speaking to Zo. "She's telling the truth. The hostess said she's been here all morning."

"So, am I free to go?" Cora asked.

Max nodded.

"I'm sorry about the questions, and I'm sorry about your aunt." Zo tried to strike a conciliatory tone. She knew the girl wanted to get away from here and be done with this town. "She was an incredible woman, and she'll be missed."

"Thank you for that." Cora opened her car door. "And if you find the gold, tell your friend to keep it. Aunt Vera was right. It only brings heartbreak and trouble."

Zo watched her speed away, perhaps for the last time, putting a good distance between herself, the parking lot, and her past. She turned to Max. "I have another idea."

"Let me guess: the Tracey brothers."

She slipped on her Ray-Bans. "Are you taking lessons from Jules? Are you reading my mind now?"

"I wish it were that easy." He pulled out his keys.

They hopped in Max's truck and headed toward the Tracey brothers' brokerage house, which, according to Max's phone, was located on Twin Rivers Road. It was a beautiful area of town, tucked away at the edge of the forest at the fork of two fine rivers. Eclectic but pricey. Though Zo didn't frequent the area often, she did buy her favorite body care nearby at the Dope Soap. Their products were locally made and suited her sensitive skin.

"What have you heard about the Tracey brothers?" Max asked. "I know you go to a lot of estate sales."

"That's a good point. Why isn't their name familiar?" Zo shook her head, not coming up with a reason. "They must be new to the area. Either that, or they only offer their services to private estate sales."

"How do those work?"

"Don't ask me," she answered. "I've never been invited to one." She watched Main Street disappear in the rearview mirror. It was replaced by a curvy road that skirted the tiny town, one that was perfect for motorcycles, not so much old trucks. Max's green-and-white classic truck sputtered around the uphill bend.

"Regardless, they must be pretty good at their jobs for Vera's attorney to recommend them." He shifted to a lower gear. "How did they seem at the sale?"

She thought back to the auction. "Adequate. Stuffy..."

Max nodded.

She landed on a word. "Pretentious. But they knew their collectables, I'll say that. They had to be the ones who appraised *My Journey West*. Cora wouldn't have known its value on her own."

Descending the hill they'd just climbed, Max slowed the truck as he approached the address. Tucked near a smattering of small businesses was a custom cottage that looked more like a home than an office. Zo squinted at the ornate hanging sign. Was that really it? It must be. But where did customers park?

"Drive around back." She pointed to a side street. "There must be an alley." He turned the corner, and when he did, her jaw dropped. Standing tall, like an oak tree, Officer Merrigan was interviewing Cedric Tracey. At least that's what it looked like. He had out his battered notebook, the one that was too big for his shirt pocket that he stuffed in there anyway. "Oh no. It's Merrigan. Turn around."

Max threw her a look. "Yeah, I would if I could, but where exactly would I do that?"

They were on a single-lane road that led to the parking lot of the posh establishments. They only way around was a U-turn. "Just try."

Merrigan shaded his eyes with his notebook, his hat not completely protecting his face from the brilliant sun.

Zo scooted down in her seat. No way was she going to let him see her here. He would know what they were up to.

"What are you doing?" Max asked.

"Hiding."

"You realize I'm the one who works with him, right?" He spoke out of the side of his mouth. "It's no use. He's walking this way."

Zo froze. If she sat very still, maybe he wouldn't see her. She'd heard that worked, but where? She remembered just as Officer Merrigan was approaching the door. *Jurassic Park*. Hardly a credible source...though Brady *did* look a little like a T. rex.

"I thought that was you, Max," said Brady.

Max tried a chuckle. "You were right."

"And hey, there's Zo."

At her name, she had no other choice but to acknowledge him. She turned her head. "Hi."

Brady dipped his chin. "Why are you sitting like that?"

"Just tired," she lied.

"Really?" Brady put a hairy arm on the window. "It looks like you're hiding."

"Why would I be hiding?"

"Oh, I don't know." Brady looked over his shoulder at Cedric Tracey, who was waiting in the parking lot, staring at his phone. He returned his attention to her. "Maybe because I told you specifically to stay out of this. To leave it to the professionals."

Zo nodded toward Max. "He's a professional."

"A professional who's not acting very professionally," countered Brady.

"That's not true," Max defended.

She sat up. "Look, it was my idea. He had nothing to do with it. After we talked to Cora, I knew—"

"Excuse me?" Brady blinked. "You talked to Cora, too?"

"My friend's in the hospital," Zo said. "What am I supposed to do? Sit on my hands and wait for the truth to come out?"

"You're a business owner," said Brady. "Go run your gift shop. I've got this under control. I made it here all by myself, didn't I?"

Zo considered his words. "You must have come to the same conclusion: the Tracey brothers stole the gold."

He looked at a spot somewhere over her head. "They're new to the area. Of course I'm going to check them out."

Ah, yes. He'd done the same thing to her friend Beth when she first arrived at Spirit Canyon. Newcomers were suspect until proven otherwise.

He pulled his gaze out of the sky. It landed on her. "Why is this so important to you? And don't say Maynard Cline."

Zo opened her mouth and then shut it. She knew the answer. She'd told him part of it already: her friend had been hurt, and she wanted to know why. The other part she'd kept largely to herself. The idea that her birth mother's surname, Hart, was mentioned in the book wouldn't leave her mind. The gold, the map, and the book were tied together. If she could find one, she just might find them all.

"If I find the book, you're the first person I'm coming to," promised Brady. "I told you that. You have my word."

She smiled. "Nobody says that anymore."

"Well maybe they should."

She couldn't argue with that cowboy logic.

Chapter Thirty

Zo could hardly wait for dark. Jules was at home resting, with the handsome Duncan doing double duty as employee and nurse. The thought gave her pause. Picturing Duncan in scrubs came a little too easily. She shook off the image. It was time to close Happy Camper and get ready for the carnival. Max was picking her up, and she couldn't wait to stuff herself with hot dogs, nachos, and slushies—not to mention dessert. Besides funnel cakes, the carnival had the best deep-fried banana split in the world. Tomorrow would definitely require exercise. But tonight, she was going to indulge. After the week she'd had, she deserved it.

She flipped the OPEN sign to CLOSED and took George off the counter, tucking her fat orange cat under her arm. "Sorry, big guy. You're staying in tonight." With the streets full of people, she didn't want him outdoors, despite the beautiful evening. In the west, the sun was just beginning to dip below the hills, creating a soft glow that fell over the town in shades of pink and purple. With no cloud cover, the evening would turn cool, and she looked forward to a break from the heat.

Upstairs, she traded shorts for jeans, tucking a sweatshirt into her backpack just in case. She picked out a shirt she'd been saving to wear. George watched from the bed, judging her attire.

"What do you think?" She pointed at her new green boatneck T-shirt. "Do you like the color?" She batted her eyelashes. "I think it brings out my eyes."

George stood, turned in a circle, and faced the wall.

"Fine. Be that way. I think it's nice." Giving her blond do a tussle, she sprayed some dry shampoo at her roots. It was as close as she was getting to a shower. Then she added big gold hoops, because she was feeling fancy, and a dab of lip gloss.

The ping of her phone announced Max's arrival, and she hurried to feed George before she left. He was already mad at being left inside. Hungry, too? Not a chance.

Outside, Max was talking to Cunningham, who was schooling him on garden pests.

"They eat certain vegetables, see. Like my cucumbers." Cunningham walked over to a bendy tangle of oversized leaves.

Zo skipped down the steps. "Those don't look like cucumbers to me. They look like the wallpaper from that creepy story you made me read. The one that strangles all those women." She made a choking gesture.

Cunningham took his hands out of his Bermuda shorts pockets, making a serious attempt to explain. "It was a metaphor, Zo. 'The Yellow Wallpaper' is a rebuttal of society's treatment of women."

"I know. I liked it."

"And these are green," added Cunningham.

"Well…" Zo walked over to the vines. "There are quite a few yellow leaves."

Cunningham blinked at Max. "Just take her away, will you?"

"I'm teasing you, Professor."

Max linked her arm through his, and they started for his truck.

"Have a good time, kids," Cunningham called after them.

As Zo suspected, the carnival was packed. The first night was always the busiest. Max had to park a block away, and the entrance had a long line of people waiting to buy passes.

"So," Max said as they were waiting. "Which one do you want to ride first, Ferris wheel or carousel?"

"Neither," she answered. "I want a hot dog and nachos."

Max's face broke into a smile. "I like the way you think."

When the line shifted, she noticed Olivia and Landon were a couple of spots in front of them, but she didn't call out because they were arguing. It sounded as if the dispute was about money. They were at the ticket counter, and the clerk was ringing them up. Nudging Max, Zo nodded toward them. He listened in, too.

"Like I can't afford a couple of carnival tickets?" Landon took out his wallet. "Give me some credit."

"I just meant I have cash." Olivia shoved a wad of money into her back pocket. "You're so touchy."

"When it comes to money, yeah, I am, because you're always throwing yours in my face," Landon said.

"That's not true." Wearing a trendy fleece, leggings, and a high ponytail, Olivia gave his arm a squeeze. "Come on. Let's have fun."

"Fine, just stop thinking you need to help me, okay?" He let out a breath, but by the sound of his voice, his teeth were still clenched.

Olivia reached up to kiss his cheek. "Deal."

Max and Zo watched the couple walk away as the next person paid. He slipped a hand in his jeans pocket and leaned closer. "If you want to pay, I'm totally cool with it."

Zo smirked. "Same. Neither of us makes enough money to throw it around."

He chuckled and took out his wallet. "I'll get the tickets; you get the nachos."

"Perfect."

The carnival didn't disappoint. Not only were there rides, but food and games with prizes that fit the Gold Rush theme. Zo won a very nice piece of fool's gold at the ring toss game. It was so big and shiny, she had to stick it in the largest zip pocket of her backpack to keep it safe.

Then it was off to the nachos, where she bought herself and Max their own baskets so they didn't have to share. After topping it off with a fried banana split, she didn't know if she should attempt the Ferris wheel, but the night was calm and the stars bright, so they went for it.

Hand in hand, they climbed higher and higher in the sky until she felt as if she could reach out and touch Jupiter, located to the right of the moon. When they stopped at the top, Max kissed her, ending the ride and melting her heart, which had started softening a long time ago.

As they descended, she touched her sun and moon necklaces. They were opposites, one shining during the day, the other at night. The same could be said about her and Max. Murder had brought them together, but justice made them stay. Even with Maynard's killer and Jules's thief at large, she knew they would find the answers, as long as they were together.

"What are you smiling about?" Max asked her as the left the ride.

"Nothing," she said. "I was just thinking about how so many things come in twos, as pairs." She stopped. Pairs. Two. *They.* She felt the smile drain from her face. Of course. Why hadn't she realized it before?

"What? What is it?"

She grabbed his arm. "In the hospital. Jules said she wondered what *they* hit her over the head with."

His brow wrinkled.

"Don't you see? Even though Jules can't remember yet, she remembers there being two thieves."

"The Tracey brothers."

Zo nodded. "The Tracey brothers. Our visit was cut short last time by Officer Merrigan. Let's go out there now, while it's dark. They won't see us."

"What are we going to do, peek in the windows?" he asked.

She shrugged. "Maybe. Their apartment is above the business. Maybe we'll see something." She could see he'd need a little convincing. "I'll let you drive my motorcycle…"

"Deal."

Fifteen minutes later, they had dropped off his truck, picked up her motorcycle, and were cruising toward Twin Rivers Road. Max was speeding around the twisty curves now, and Zo was holding on for dear life. "Slow down! You're going to kill us."

"Said the speed demon to the man without a single ticket," Max hollered over the wind. "I've got this. Trust me."

Normally, that was an easy thing to do, but he was feeling a little too confident for her taste. His squeaky-clean record might be smudged if he didn't lay off the throttle. Luckily, they were returning to the outlier of shops, and the Tracey brothers' business came into view. Mostly dark, it had a single light on. By the looks of it, Cedric and Sean were out for the evening.

"Drive by slowly," Zo instructed.

"It doesn't look like anyone is home."

"You never know." She studied the well-spaced buildings as they passed. They looked like tiny cottages, nestled into the hillside so as not to distract from the scenery. She noted the lawyer's name that Cora had mentioned above a brick abode. His office was a stone's throw away from the brokerage house. No wonder he was giving them business. It was probably a reciprocal relationship.

All of the businesses were well-equipped with security cameras. She spotted them from the street. Owners wanted to protect their posh investments. If the Tracey brothers had brought the gold back to their house, it might be on camera. As they stopped at a light, the thought brought her little recompense. She knew they stole it. Brady had to know, too. That's why he was here this afternoon. So why hadn't he arrested them or obtained a search warrant? She asked Max.

He spoke over the hum of the motorcycle. "Search warrants take time. It's not like the cop shows you see on TV."

Time for the crooks to get away, she was thinking when she saw something move out of the corner of her eye. Beyond the road was a bridge that spanned the two rivers the street was named for. The movement was on the bridge. A flicker of light.

She squeezed his sides. "Pull off here, near the bridge. I think I see something."

"Probably an animal," he grumbled but did as she asked and parked near the trees. "A wild animal with sharp teeth and claws." Obviously he didn't want to stop.

She took off her helmet, and he did the same. "I'm okay with that."

He leveled a look at her.

"What good is it dating a forest ranger if you can't have him stave off a wild animal now and then?"

Chapter Thirty-One

Wild animals were one thing. Mosquitos were another. Zo was starting to question their detour when the second one bit her arm. Stopping on the path, she took her sweatshirt out of her backpack and pulled it on. When they got to the bridge, the trees would clear, and the mosquitos might, too. She could hear the ripple of the rivers already. Then she heard an aerosol sound.

"What good is dating a forest ranger who doesn't carry bug repellent?" In his hand, he held a miniature can of spray. He gave her several shots.

She smiled as she continued toward a beautiful nature area that surrounding businesses capitalized on for events. The city put on a brown-bag lunch once a month here that was always well-attended.

The flicker appeared again. She stopped and ducked behind a bush. Her heart began to thump loudly. It wasn't her imagination. Someone was out there. "Do you see it?" she whispered.

"I see *something*," Max confirmed. "I don't know if it's a person."

"There are voices." It was hard to tell between the wind and the voice. After a few minutes, she decided the voices were male. For sure they were people. But why meet here so late? She could think of only one reason. "It's them. I'm going to get a closer look."

He put a hand on her shoulder. "Wait here. Let me go." Seeing her resistance, he added, "Please? It might be dangerous, and I can't let any harm come to you."

When you put it that way... She nodded. It was getting harder and harder to fight with him. It used to be so easy. But she wasn't a fool. She knew he was better equipped than she was to deal with criminals.

Max disappeared into the trees, and she could see nothing. Not even the outline of him. A massive cloud covered the earlier moonlight, and she cursed the state's unpredictable weather. It could go from clear to cloudy in a matter of minutes. She inched forward, but the dense brush was blocking her way. The only way to see anything was from above.

She sized up the tree near the clearing. From the time she could walk, she'd been climbing trees. As a young girl, nature was her refuge. It still was. Though it'd been a while since she'd climbed a tree (okay, twenty years), she had no doubt that she still had the skill.

That was until she got halfway up the tree, where she felt a bit unsteady. Her hands did not have the grip they used to. Or maybe it was her legs. Whatever it was—the nachos?—she was sure age had nothing to do with it. Thirty-four was not old. Then again, Jules was switching to that expensive wrinkle cream...

Locking onto a limb, she couldn't see Max, but she could see where the voices came from. One belonged to Cedric Tracey; she recognized his wingtip shoes. But the other person had his back turned to her. His build seemed familiar. Who did she know who would be out here in the middle of the night? *Turn around, turn around*, she willed him. They were talking about antiques. The man sounded like a collector. He wore an expensive black suit jacket, beret, and nice boots. If she could just see his face...

Her hand slipped, and a piece of bark fell to the ground. Cedric stopped talking. Had they heard her? She tried to stop breathing, which only made the sound of her breath louder in her ears. If they spotted her, what would she say? How would she explain her position in the tree?

The man picked up the conversation, and the noise was forgotten. His voice was clear and certain. Her breathing calmed again, until he pulled a stack of bills from his jacket pocket. When Cedric turned to the light to count the cash, Zo could see the arm of the other man. It was Peter Merrigan! The glint she'd seen from afar was the sparkle of his gold watch. She'd recognize the timepiece anywhere. She pulled her eyes upward. Sure enough, it was him.

It was just as she thought. The Merrigans were involved. From the day she'd read their name on the piece of notepaper, she knew something was amiss. Now Peter was paying Cedric for the book. That had to be it. Unless he was buying Jules's gold nugget. That was also possible. Though... Peter didn't seem like a thief, or any kind of criminal for that matter. She shook off the thought. It was the old Merrigan charm. It'd put a spell on her before. She wouldn't be fooled by it again.

Where was Max? She looked left and right. Peter Merrigan was going to get away with the goods, and Max was nowhere to be found. Was he behind her? Had she somehow gotten ahead of him? Carefully, she twisted her body, but not carefully enough. A leg unhooked from the branch, then another, and her legs swung down, dangling back and forth as she scrambled for a better grip.

It was no use. Her hand ripped away from the dry bark, and she was tumbling down, down, until she hit the dirt below. Someone hollered, and she looked up to see Cedric coming toward her, cash in hand. There was no doubt in her mind that he and his brother had stolen the gold. Well, she had her own golden nugget, and it was valuable in other ways. She opened her backpack and chucked the fool's gold from the carnival at his back. It hit him squarely between the shoulders, and he tripped on a tree root and fell.

"Nice shot! Are you okay?"

Zo blinked. It was Peter Merrigan. He was kneeling beside her. Then it was Brady Merrigan, running past her. What was this? A family reunion? Were they all in on it together? Wait. Brady was putting handcuffs on Cedric. Max was close behind him. *What in the world?*

Answering her unasked question, Peter replied, "It's a sting. I'm part of the operation. Don't you recognize me?" He nodded toward Cedric. "He certainly didn't, but he hasn't been in town very long."

Peter was wearing a beret. That's what threw her off. And the scarf, knotted closely at his neck. He looked like an art collector, not a cowboy. Except for the boots.

He helped her sit up. "Believe it or not, I used to be the chief of police. Way before you were born, about a thousand years ago." His eyes twinkled. "Those were the days."

But Zo didn't have time to go down memory lane. Brady was marching toward her with the oddest look on his face. She glanced at the bridge. Maybe she could jump off it and swim to safety.

"Nowhere to run, dear. You're going to have to face the music." Peter patted her shoulder. "But I'll stay here. I won't let him be too hard on you."

A few more steps, and Brady loomed above her, arms crossed. "Twice in one day? Really, Zo?"

She smiled sheepishly. "It must be your lucky day. Maybe you should buy a lottery ticket."

"You interrupted important police work," he said through gritted teeth. "That criminal could've gotten away."

"But he didn't." Peter gave Zo a hand up. "Thanks to her, and her good aim, he's going to jail, where he belongs."

"He would've gone to jail anyway, Pop." Brady crossed his arms.

Peter waved away the comment. "But it wouldn't have been as exciting."

"But definitely less harmful." Zo dusted off her rear. "I guess I'm not as young as I used to be."

"Who are you kidding?" Peter said. "You're just a whippersnapper. Climbing trees, knocking off criminals." He made a throwing motion with his arm. "What a night."

"Don't encourage her," Brady said.

"Phooey. We need to encourage people like her, with passion and bravery." Peter gave her a wink. "That's a winning combination in my book."

"Thank you," said Zo.

Red-cheeked, Max returned to the scene. It told a story without him saying a word. It relayed his concern for her, and she assured him she was fine. "The only thing hurt is my pride."

Max gave her a quick hug. "I thought you were going to wait for me."

"I was waiting for you," said Zo. "I was waiting up in that tree. It had a much better view, until I fell." She turned to Brady. "How did you know Cedric stole the gold anyway?"

"My earlier interview spooked him," Brady explained. "I could tell by the way he kept fidgeting. But I couldn't get a search order on a hunch, so I asked Pop here to pretend to be an antiquities dealer."

Peter tugged his suit jacket. "I clean up pretty good, don't I?"

"Very convincing." Brady smiled. "It was easy since the Tracey Brothers are a brokerage and deal with antiques all the time. There was nothing suspicious about Pop calling him. When he said he was in the market for gold, Cedric was in a rush to meet him tonight. He wanted to dispose of the stolen goods."

"I get that, but why?" Max shook his head. "They seem to be doing so well."

"Not everything is as it seems." Brady inclined his head. "Actually, it was Zo's comment about Cora's lawyer that tipped me off. Why was he referring people to a new auction house that hadn't been in town even a year?"

The group was silent, waiting for his answer.

"I decided to ask him, and his answer was surprising," continued Brady. "He said they owed him back rent on their place—six months' worth. He thought if he gave them the Dalrymple estate, they'd finally be able to pay their rent."

"But they didn't," Peter cut in. "So I did a little checking, and they left a trail of unpaid debts behind them in Colorado. I wouldn't be surprised if we didn't find other stolen antiques inside."

"Not *we*, Pop. Me," Brady corrected.

Zo remembered the missing jewelry. "Like Vera's cameo necklace. Cora couldn't find it and assumed Vera had misplaced it or given it away. But the cameo was special. When Cora was young, Vera told her it belonged to the Princess of Wales."

"And it probably did," said Peter. "But to the layperson, like Cora, its value wouldn't be known. It's the perfect theft—and probably inside their flat right now."

A flicker of hope alighted within her as she turned to Brady. "Could *My Journey West* be inside, too?"

Chapter Thirty-Two

With all eyes on him, Brady stiffened. He was not the type to take leads from inexperienced shopkeepers. Especially shopkeepers like Zo, who had skin in the game. But a flicker of acknowledgment flashed on his face. He, too, wondered if the book they'd been searching for was inside the Tracey brothers' apartment. She knew he did.

Brady's voice was cautious. "That's for the police to determine, through a legal search."

"Exigent circumstances apply here," Max argued. "If given a chance, Sean Tracey will sell or destroy the evidence. Either way, it gets lost before now and his brother's trial."

Peter nodded. "I agree."

Zo could see Brady weighing their opinions. He might not completely trust Max, but he trusted his father. Peter had been the police chief years ago. He knew the law better than any of them. Sure, he was excited to be chasing criminals again, but he wouldn't let that excitement cloud his judgment.

Brady made up his mind. "All right, let's go." He pointed to Peter and Zo. "You two wait here. An ambulance is on the way to check you out."

"I don't need a paramedic," Zo insisted. "I'm fine."

Brady adjusted his hat and started toward the brokerage. "I wish I could say the same for Cedric Tracey. He claims the rock you threw broke a bone."

"*Right*." Zo held Max's arm as they crossed over the gnarly tree root. "He's stalling for time. He doesn't want you to search the apartment."

"Either way, let them check you out," Brady called over his shoulder. "Pop can stay with you."

"I've been demoted to babysitter now?" Peter grumbled as they approached the pavement. "Thanks."

The parking lot gave them a better view of the upscale digs with a stunning deck that faced the forest. It was highlighted by flashing ambulance lights, which told her something about Cedric's condition. If he was seriously injured, they'd be on the way to the hospital already. As it was, two medics were examining him in the back of the van. He looked fine to her.

Peter touched her arm. "There's no way around it. You'll need to let them give you a look. Once my son gets an idea in his head, there's no going back. He can be pretty stubborn."

That's an understatement. But she knew he was right. It was best to get checked out so that she could be on her way to better things, like finding the book. The idea that it could be steps away set her heart aflame. The secret of her story could be revealed within its pages. She clung to the possibility as she approached the medics. "Officer Merrigan wants you guys to make sure I'm okay. I'm fine, but I fell from a tree." She showed them the palms of her hands. "A few scrapes, that's about it."

Cedric glowered at her. "*You,*" he hissed. "You could've killed me. If that rock had been thrown any higher, it would have hit my head. What was that thing?"

The medic pushed on his shoulder blade, and he yelped.

"Fool's gold," she answered. "And you got what was coming to you. You hurt my friend Jules. She has a concussion." Another medic stuck a thermometer in her mouth, forcing her to quit talking.

Cedric's lips turned into a thin line. "You can't prove anything."

Peter hopped into the conversation, pulling the gold from his pocket. "Oh, really? What about this? It proves you're a scoundrel and a thief."

The thermometer gone, Zo shot him a smile. She liked Peter. Dressed in a scarf and driving cap, with his white whiskers and mischievous eyes, he reminded her of an artist. And maybe he was, of sorts. He'd been a lawman and a legend in town, but he wasn't above taking risks if it meant getting the job done. Or talking smack to criminals.

"*My back...*" Cedric moaned, closing his eyes. "Take me to the hospital."

The medic slid the blood pressure cuff off Zo's arm, and Zo jumped forward. "Wait. I want to know about a book. It's important."

Cedric's eyes flipped open. "I don't have it."

Zo shook her head. "How do you know what book I'm talking about, then?"

"Because I've been asked about it a gazillion times," Cedric mumbled. "I wish I had it. Quite a few people in town want it. If only I would've known how much it was worth to them *before* the auction."

"Who?" Peter asked.

"Sue Archer, Jeffrey Davis, some angry college kid." Cedric sighed. "I really wish I could have sold it to the college kid. He would have bought it in a heartbeat."

Zo racked her brain. *Angry college kid...* A light went off. Thomas Lancaster. Did Cedric mean him? She asked. "Do you mean Tom Lancaster? He's a graduate student at Black Mountain College. His family owns a casino in Deadwood."

"Right," confirmed Cedric. "That's what he said."

Zo knew Jeffrey and Sue wanted the book for historical reasons. And Tom wanted to expose the cowboys as thieves and liars. "Did he say why he thought the book was so important?"

Cedric sat up. "What will you give me if I tell you?"

"How about my good graces?" Peter crossed his arms, looking more like a police officer than an artist now. Although he was older, he was in no way diminished. "How about that?"

Cedric leaned back. "For dirt on his father. He doesn't like the guy."

Or he doesn't like his business. Why did he hate gambling so vehemently, anyway? A personal reason had to exist. She reminded herself to find it. "So, you really don't have the book."

"No," answered Cedric. "Now, can I please go to the hospital?" The medic pushed the stretcher into the van and closed the door.

Zo and Peter were left staring after him.

"Criminals lie. All. The. Time." Peter set his chin. "Don't give up."

She glanced up at the apartment, where the glow was no longer from the ambulance but the indoor lights. Brady and Max were inside right now. Maybe they'd find it after all. "I won't."

"Can I ask you something?"

"Sure," she said, still scanning the apartment windows from afar.

"Why is the book so important to you? Is there something besides your friend's murder?"

She lowered her gaze to Peter. She knew *of* him, but she didn't know him that well. Something in his eyes told her she could trust him. He cared about the reason, and it didn't have anything to do with police work. It had to do with her. "I was orphaned. It's a slim chance, but my birth mother might be mentioned in the book."

Peter rubbed the whiskers on his chin. "You're the girl Brady found at the police station."

"That'd be the one." A smile spread across her face. "I've been a menace to him ever since."

Peter shook his head. "Not true. That day affected him more than he lets on. He admires your grit."

"My grit?"

"Your perseverance," he explained. "I admire it, too."

Zo was not the blushing type, but his words humbled her, and she felt a warmth rise to her cheeks. They touched her somewhere deep inside. "Thank you."

He dipped his chin.

A holler came from the balcony, and they both looked up. For a second, Zo thought her wish had been granted and the book had been found. Then she saw Max's face, and she knew Cedric had been telling the truth.

"No book," he said. "But we did find this." He held up a string of gold. It was Cora's cameo necklace.

Chapter Thirty-Three

Cedric and his brothers were thieves, not murderers. Another door closed, and Zo wondered how many more doors she could open—and how much time she had left to open them. Today was Gold Rush Days' Arts and Crafts Festival, and the store would be hopping. Businesses welcomed shoppers who were browsing nearby tents and tables set up by local artisans. Although it was only ten o'clock in the morning, the streets were packed.

Zo propped her door open and hauled her sidewalk tent outside. Harley had scrawled, "COME IN. GET YOUR HAPPY ON!" in colorful bubble letters. Before Zo could scoot back inside, three customers wandered in, and she handed them shopping baskets. Harley was busy opening the till and preparing to ring up their first sale of the day. Meanwhile, George had crawled to the top of the tallest bookshelf, his two front paws tucked safely beneath him. The busyness was getting on his nerves. His tail switched back and forth between Architecture and Astrology. The impudence of shoppers! To talk and browse while he was trying to digest his breakfast.

"Is that your cat?" a woman asked.

"Yes." Zo smiled.

"He's beautiful." The woman reached up to touch his tail, but he curled it around his body before she had the chance. "What's his name?"

"George," Zo answered.

The woman frowned. "Oh."

"It's a good solid name," said a male voice behind her. "A name fit for a king."

George squinted in approval.

"Cunningham," Zo greeted. "Good morning."

"Good morning." Cunningham was dressed in his summer attire: khakis, a Hawaiian shirt, and slip-ons. He gestured to the store. "A pretty good crowd in here already."

"I know."

"I got your message about that student." Cunningham raised a bushy eyebrow.

She knew he meant Tom Lancaster. Before work, she'd texted him, asking if he knew anything about him. Leave it up to Cunningham to come right over. He wasn't very good with technology, especially technology that cut his verbosity in half. "Let's go to the back room."

She smiled at a few familiar shoppers as she zigzagged to her small storage area. "Cedric Tracey mentioned him name last night. Tom asked after *My Journey West*."

Cunningham glanced at her shelves, perhaps thinking up a new organizational system while he considered his response. "That doesn't surprise me. The Lancasters are a well-known name in town, as I'm sure you are aware."

"Right." She'd lived here her entire life. Obviously, she'd heard the name. What she wanted from him was particulars.

"I first heard the name when I did a presentation on notable writers of the West. The conversation veered to gambling and money's impact on the noble art." He straightened a roll of wrapping paper. "The problem with art is the same as with crime: It doesn't pay. Many a desperate artist has turned to a different master to earn his keep."

A burst of chatter announced another group of shoppers, and she was stuck in the back with a garrulous professor. She tapped her foot. "*And?* What happened then?"

"A young man raised his hand—this was three years ago, when students used to raise their hands and ask questions politely—and said that gambling not only ruined artists, it also ruined lives. I asked him how he knew, and he announced his father was Lawrence Lancaster, the casino mogul in Deadwood."

Zo could hear the press of the buttons at the cash register. She hoped Harley was doing okay. The store was a flurry of activity, and she was getting a lesson on academic chatter. "I knew Lawrence Lancaster was his father."

He held up a stubby finger. "Ah, but what you don't know is that the ruined life was someone very near and dear to Tom."

"Who?" she asked.

Cunningham waved away the question. "Well, I don't know *who*, but it was someone close to him. I could tell by the emotion in his voice."

Zo let out a breath. "I see. Okay. Good to know." She motioned toward the door, and they started for the store. "I'd better get back at it. I'm hoping for a break so that I can ask Tom why he asked after the book." She glanced at the crowded room. "Who knows when that will be?"

He paused near the register. "Why not let me help? I've been here lots of times. I know Harley. I work well with young people." He gave Harley a salute. "She and I will be compadres in our labor."

Harley pointed a thumb in his direction. "Is there a reason he's speaking Spanish?"

"Not that I'm aware of," Zo answered. "Maybe he ran out of words in English."

"I beseech you, Zoelle," Cunningham said. "Put this old man to good use. Let me show you what an old-timer can do." He picked up the gift-wrapping scissors and spun it around his pinkie. It fell to the floor with a clunk. He retrieved it sheepishly.

Harley looked at her like *Don't you dare*. But Zo was desperate. She needed to know if Tom had killed Maynard and stolen the book. It could be in his hands right now, and the mystery of her birth and the murder of Maynard might be solved by lunchtime.

"Okay," Zo agreed. "But you need to wear a name tag." She took out the stick-on tags she used at events and handed him a Sharpie. Giving Harley a sympathetic smile, she reached for her backpack beneath the counter. "I won't be gone long, I swear."

As she walked away, she heard Cunningham say, "Do you know the name Russell means *red*? Not unlike our word *russet*…" Oh boy. She would need to bring back lunch from the Chipped Cup, their favorite sandwich and tea shop, if Harley was ever to forgive her.

Zo stood in the crowded street. It was summer, so school schedules were flexible, but Tom and Professor Davis were working on his thesis at the library last time she'd checked. It was possible he was there right now. She dialed the library.

Agnes answered. "Spirit Canyon Public Library."

Zo recognized the nasal voice. "Hey, Agnes, this is Zo. Is Hattie there?"

"She's here, but the phone is not to be used for personal business—"

A scuffle, then Hattie's voice came on the line. "Hello?"

"Sorry, I should've called your cell," Zo apologized. "By chance is Tom Lancaster there?"

"He's in the Special Collections room. Why?"

"Good." Zo hopped on her motorcycle. "Keep him there. I'm on my way."

"What's this about?" asked Hattie.

"Cedric Tracey said Tom asked after the memoir." She took out her spare key.

Hattie lowered her voice. "You think he killed Maynard?" A muffle came over the mouthpiece. "I said I prefer mustard! Quit listening to my conversations."

"It's a possibility," said Zo, swallowing a laugh. "I'll see you soon."

She shoved her phone in her pocket, slipped on her Ray-Bans, and pulled onto Main Street. Thankfully it was a short drive. Retrieving her helmet was not an option. She didn't want to get between Cunningham and Harley and the meaning of *Russell*.

A loud bark announced she'd been caught without her safety equipment. She looked to her left to see Max next to her.

"What do you think you're doing?" hollered Max over Scout's barking.

"I'm headed to the library. I'll call you when I get back."

"I'm going to tell Brady about this," he warned, pointing to her head.

She flashed him a thumbs-up and took off. Remarkably, helmets weren't required in South Dakota. With lack of restrictions on, well, just about everything, it really did feel as if she was living in the Wild West some days.

With the arts and crafts festival happening, Hattie's Gold Rush book display wasn't as busy as it had been, and the library was quiet and calm. It was a nice break from the noisy streets outside. The only sound was the clap her flip-flops made against her feet. It echoed through the building, and Agnes glared at her as she walked up to reference desk.

"Shh!" Agnes put her finger to her lips.

Zo blinked. "I haven't said anything."

"Zo," Hattie called. "Back here."

Zo met Hattie at Periodicals. "I can't even walk by that woman correctly."

"She's a pest, but she's not a killer." Hattie was wearing a gray I READ PAST MY BEDTIME T-shirt that matched her spiky, silver hair. "She was telling the truth about the damaged book."

"How do you know?"

Hattie shelved a copy of *Good Housekeeping* on the metal rack. "You'd be proud of me. I did a little investigative work of my own. The last book Maynard checked out was a hardcover about Frank Lloyd Wright, a beauty that cost me one hundred and twenty-five dollars. Agnes wasn't lying. Red wine was spilled on a page, and several others stuck to it. It's completely unusable."

"Wow. Good work." No wonder Agnes had revoked his library card. Zo just wished they'd investigated it sooner. In a tiny corner of her mind, she'd wondered if Agnes was capable of the dastardly deed. "What about Tom? He's still here, right?"

"I brought him a new book about online gambling just to make sure." Hattie leaned closer. "He was very interested in the new text. I imagine he won't be leaving for a while."

Zo gave her shoulder a squeeze. "Thanks, Hattie. I don't know what I'd do without you."

"You wouldn't read as many books, I know that." Hattie winked.

In the Special Collections room, Tom was hunched over a brown leather book that spanned half of the table. It appeared to be a collection of maps. Could he be looking for Ezra Kind's gold right now? She tried to silence her flip-flops as she crossed the room, gliding across the low-profile carpet.

He heard her and looked up. Shadows hovered below his eyes. It looked as if he'd been reading a lot. His face, too, was unshaven, and thick stubble accompanied his goatee. "Hi."

Zo tucked her fingertips in her jeans, trying to appear casual. "Hey, Tom. What are you looking at?"

He pressed his palms into the pages. He wore a large silver ring engraved with a peace symbol. "Land grants. Professor Davis is going to be very interested in what I found."

"Why?"

"The survey shows his family was one of the first families to lay a claim in the area." Tom traced the outline with his pointer finger. "This is from 1877." He said the words with awe.

Zo looked over his shoulder, recognizing a lot of the names in town, including the Merrigans, which took up a large portion of the map. "Cool." Her eyes wandered over the page. "I see your family is mentioned, too."

"Right," he said. "But they didn't strike gold in Lawrence County—not until they built the casino, over a hundred years later. Ironic, isn't it?"

"I guess." Zo didn't know what else to say. It was obvious he had a vendetta against his family. She needed to know why, and whether or not it had anything to do with the book. "Can I ask you a question?"

He looked up from the map. "Sure."

"Last night, Cedric Tracey was arrested for selling a piece of stolen gold—which happened to belong to my friend," she quickly added. "Before he was arrested, he told me you asked after Charlie Clay's memoir." She studied his hazel eyes. "Is that true?"

He didn't flinch. "Yes. *My Journey West* is one of the first histories of Spirit Canyon. Of course I wanted it for my research, and Professor Davis didn't have the money."

"So you offered to pay for it?"

"Why not?" His pointy shoulders moved up and down under his shirt. "I might as well put my dad's money to good use, and I know if I asked, he would lend it to me. I would have donated the book to the college—where it belongs—when I was finished. It was promised to Professor Davis. Ask any of the history professors."

"So, what happened?" Zo pressed.

"The Traceys had already sold it to the highest bidder," he said. "And couldn't get it back. If only I'd been at the auction... But Professor Davis didn't have any reason to believe Professor Dalrymple would sell it."

Zo knew he was telling the truth. The day of the auction, Jeffrey Davis was shocked that the book was for sale.

Tom pursed his lips. "The Traceys did have some necklace they tried to pawn off on me. But it was so ugly. I don't know of any girl who would wear it." He paused and a smile crept on his face. "Leslie would have hated it."

Zo wondered if he was talking about the cameo necklace. Cedric would want to get rid of it as fast as he could. "Who's Leslie, may I ask?"

He pulled at his goatee. "Leslie was my best friend. Smart, passionate. Much smarter than I am." His eyes glistened. "She was really special."

Zo could see she meant a lot to him. Though she'd asked Tom a lot of questions, she couldn't ask the one on her mind now. It would be too painful for him to respond.

Surprisingly, he continued on his own. "She took her own life after losing her savings in the slot machines. It'd been happening all semester, but she hid it from me." He shook his head. "I didn't know. I should have seen the signs."

"You can't blame yourself." Zo repeated the words she'd heard many times but knew they must sound hollow to a best friend. If it were Jules, she'd be wrecked.

He pointed to the book on gambling Hattie had given him. "A lot of young people gamble online. When it's in the next town, though, it makes it really convenient."

She nodded. *This* was why he was so adamantly opposed to gambling. Everything clicked into place. His friend had taken her own life, possibly after spending her money at his own dad's casino. No wonder he wanted to stop students from gambling.

It was clear to her then. He didn't steal the book, and he didn't kill Maynard. He was a passionate student who would probably turn into a hip professor someday. In the meantime, she was stuck with a question: If he didn't kill Maynard, who did?

The question plagued her all the way to the library parking lot, where she turned the key of her motorcycle but didn't move. There was no one left. She'd come to the end of her ideas.

Unless—one tiny clue remained. Olivia's barrette. It proved she'd been in Jules's house, and she hadn't attended the auction. She'd been at the astronomy fund-raiser. So, when had she dropped it, and why had she lied?

The *whoop, whoop* of a siren went off behind her. Startled, she looked over her shoulder.

"I thought that'd get your attention." Brady's head was hanging out the window of his police cruiser. "Where's your helmet, young lady?"

Zo looked around for Max. He was probably hiding somewhere close by, laughing at her. She'd get him back for this. "It's at Happy Camper. I was in a hurry."

"All it takes is one accident."

"Aww," Zo said. "I didn't know you cared."

"Of course I care. What's your hurry?"

She turned off the bike, threw up the kickstand, and walked over to the patrol car. "Actually, I'm glad you're here. I wanted to talk to you about Olivia Nesbitt. Remember how I told you we found her barrette at Jules's house?"

"Yes, and remember how I told you to let me do my job?"

She ignored his comeback. "I know, but just hear me out. Olivia was with Landon—that's her boyfriend—at Black Mountain College the day of the auction. She couldn't have lost it then, like she said she did. I saw a picture of her eating a cookie at the college fund-raiser."

He looked skeptical.

"It was in the shape of Saturn," she added. "I have a picture if you want to see it."

"Oh, well, if it was shaped like Saturn," Brady teased.

"I'm just saying, what do you have to lose?" Zo pressed.

"Just a long-term friendship. The Nesbitts have been our neighbors since I can remember."

Zo crossed her arms. "Breaking and entering is against the law."

"I'm well aware of that." Brady tipped his black hat, smoothing the black hair beneath it. "I'll go check it out. Maybe I can bring out a pan of Mom's apple cake. Butter him up before accusing his daughter of a crime."

"Sweets always work for me." Zo smiled.

He didn't smile back. He buckled his seat belt and said, "Next time, wear your helmet." Then he was gone.

Chapter Thirty-Four

Zo returned to a busy Happy Camper with a to-go bag from the Chipped Cup. Inside were sandwiches, chips, and the store's famous chocolate-chip cookies. She insisted Harley and Cunningham eat first while she staffed the register. Although Harley was grateful for the break, Zo knew she was growing weary of Cunningham's verbosity. The man didn't stop talking! But Zo thought most everything he said was interesting, so his garrulity didn't bother her. Yet for Harley, who listened to lectures all year long from her professors, another half hour with Cunningham might be too much.

Busy ringing up purchases, Zo soon forgot about the problem and immersed herself in conversation with her customers. Mrs. Bixby, who was one of her frequent shoppers, was asking her when holiday décor would be in. "I understand your excitement, but it's only July!" Zo laughed.

"The roads ice up early in the canyon. Don't forget." Mrs. Bixby snapped her tiny wallet shut. It carried a one-hundred-dollar bill at all times. She'd told Zo once she didn't believe in credit cards. A woman of seventy-five with strong opinions about everything, she could believe whatever she wanted. Zo was just happy to see her in the store.

"I won't forget." Zo placed Mrs. Bixby's candle in a brown paper sack. "I'll call you when it comes in."

Mrs. Bixby took the bag. "Just put it on Facebook. I follow your page."

"Okay," said Zo, a smile still on her face as she watched her turn down the street. A sparkle caught her eye, and she left the counter for a closer look. Gold was on her mind all the time these days. But this jewel was familiar. It was the barrette they'd found in Jules's house, and it was on the head of its owner: Olivia Nesbitt.

Olivia wouldn't miss an opportunity to shop. By the look of her designer clothes and handbag, it was her favorite pastime. Wearing a yellow polo shirt and plaid skirt, she was with Landon, skimming the used book cart Zo had displayed outside under the window. *Shoot.* Brady wouldn't be able to question her after all. *Oh well. I'll just have to do it myself.*

She pushed open the door. "Hey, Landon. Hi, Olivia. Thanks for dropping by."

"We couldn't go to an arts and crafts fair without stopping at one of the Zodiac Club's stores." Landon grinned, looking young, happy, and carefree in his rugged jeans and faded T-shirt. He picked up a used book. "What gives? No books on astrology?"

"I do. They're new, so they're inside." Zo pointed toward the indoor bookshelf.

"Ah," said Landon, and put back the book.

Olivia lifted her face. "Go ahead. I'll wait here."

Landon shrugged. "Okay, I'll be right back."

After he left, Olivia said in a low voice, "If he finds one he likes, will you give him a discount? I can pay you back."

Landon was short on funds, but if he'd heard what Oliva had asked, he'd be offended. If she thought throwing money around would solve all his problems, she was wrong. Although poor, he was proud and hardworking. "Sure, but you don't need to pay me back."

"Thanks."

Zo glanced at the counter. Harley was finished with lunch and stationed at the register, and Cunningham was returning from the back room. He could help customers if needed. Zo took the opportunity to ask Olivia about the barrette. "I see your dad returned your jewelry."

Olivia gave her a sheepish smile. "He might talk a big talk, but he's a softie. He wouldn't really take it away."

Zo had a feeling he would do anything to make his daughter happy. After all, she was all he had left. That and his ancestral home. Which was probably why he clung to both so desperately. "You said you lost it at Jules's auction."

"That's right." She blinked. "Thanks again for returning it. It means a lot to me."

"I'm not in the habit of keeping things that aren't mine," said Zo.

She shifted her feet. "What does that mean? Have I done something wrong?"

Zo lowered her voice. "I know you weren't at the estate sale. Landon showed me a picture of you at the college fund-raiser, with him."

Her pink lips trembled. "Does Landon know?"

"Not yet."

"Don't tell him—please," she whispered. "I'm begging you." Her blue eyes were wide and desperate.

"Then tell me how it got there. The truth this time, or I'll tell Landon everything."

"It's stupid, really." She shook her head. "It was a dumb idea. That book you mentioned, at the library, *My Journey West*? I found it at our community guesthouse. Landon and I were swimming one afternoon, and I stumbled on it when I stopped to use the shower."

Zo's heart thumped in her chest. "Where?"

"On the bookshelf in the living room. Anyone would have seen it if they knew what they were looking for. Then again," she added, "no one was supposed to be there." She shrugged. "Landon and I use the house sometimes since my dad doesn't want him in our house."

No better hiding place existed than one in plain sight. Whoever had put the book there—and Zo had a good idea who did—knew exactly what he was doing. If the police did find it, the thief and murderer wouldn't be incriminated. The property belonged to the community, not an individual. It would be hard to prove a certain person had taken it.

"Anyway," Olivia continued, "the map Professor Scott mentioned is missing, torn out of the book. I saw where it should have been. I thought if I could find the map at Vera Dalrymple's house, I could give it Landon. He won't take money from me, but if he found it on his own…who knows?"

She took a shaky breath and swallowed. "I know you think I'm terrible person."

"I don't," Zo said. "I think you're a very brave person who cares about Landon a great deal."

"I love him." Her blue eyes turned gray with tears. "I don't want him to go, and Black Mountain is expensive. If he doesn't get that graduate stipend, he'll have to leave. I can't lose him. He's changed everything for me. I feel alive again."

"Is that why you stole your dad's cuff links? To sell them?"

Olivia nodded at the ground. "I didn't go through with it, though. I realized Landon wouldn't take the money, so I put them back. My dad just hasn't found them yet."

"I understand," said Zo, and she did. Olivia had taken great risks to keep Landon in her life. That counted for a lot in her book. "Do you still have a key to the guesthouse? I'd like to take a look at the book myself."

She dug through her expensive bag and handed Zo a key. "You won't tell him?"

Zo shook her head. Telling Landon about Olivia's break-in was the least of her worries right now. She had more pressing concerns, like Brady Merrigan and his trip to the Nesbitt house. She needed to get ahold of Max and quick.

"Everything okay out here?" Landon was back.

"Better than okay. Olivia's great." Zo smiled with more enthusiasm than she felt. Her mind was on her next move. "Did you find anything you liked, on astrology?"

He clasped his hand in Olivia's. "Oh, I found lots of good stuff, but nothing I need today."

Olivia opened her mouth, looked at Zo, then closed it. "Anything good is worth waiting for."

Landon beamed at her, and they turned toward the street.

The second they were gone, Zo grabbed her phone out of her pocket and dialed Max. "We have a problem."

"Okay, okay, I'm sorry," Max apologized. "I meant it as a joke."

Zo frowned. "What are you talking about?"

"Merrigan? The helmet?"

"Never mind that," she said. "I think he may be in trouble."

"Why?" Max asked.

"Pick me up. I'll tell you on the way." She ducked inside the store to tell Harley and Cunningham she had to leave again.

"If you're late, feel free to pick up dinner, too." Cunningham, who was organizing the bookshelves, was excited to be playing shopkeeper.

Harley not so much. "Please don't be late."

"That new pizza place my students are always raving about," Cunningham hollered as Zo spotted Max's truck. "Mile High Pie!"

She gave him a thumbs-up and walked out the door.

"Hey," she greeted as she climbed into Max's truck. She patted Scout's head before giving her a gentle push to the middle seat.

"Where am I going?" asked Max, wondering which way to turn out of the parking lot.

"Carl Nesbitt's house."

Max flipped on his blinker. "Carl? Why was Merrigan going out there?"

Zo put her hands over her face. "Because I told him to. I wanted him to question Olivia, about the barrette. In the meantime, she and Landon stopped in my store. She admitted to being in Jules's house, looking for the map, but she didn't kill Maynard."

He gave her a curious glance. "How do you know?"

"Olivia knew about the missing map because she's seen the book. It's at their community guesthouse, and I think her dad hid it there."

Max tapped the steering wheel with his dirt-caked fingertips. She must've interrupted his work outdoors. "So, Carl Nesbitt has the book?"

"Right," she answered.

"Find the book, find the murderer." Max said this more to himself than to Zo. He turned toward the forest. "But why? What did Carl have against Maynard?"

I've been asking myself the same thing.

For the next several minutes, she considered the question while ponderosa pines whirred by in a streak of hunter green. It reminded her of an old-fashioned movie reel, rewinding the last few days, which had been a blur. She kept coming back to a map—but not the treasure map. The map Tom Lancaster had shown her in the library. "It wasn't what Carl had against Maynard. It was what Maynard had against Carl."

"I'm not sure I'm following." His old pickup chugged up the hill.

Even from a distance, she could see Brady's police cruiser parked in the Nesbitts' long driveway, the gates hanging open. The pang in her heart reached deeper. He was a trained police officer. She told herself he knew how to take care of himself, but it didn't ease the feeling. If she had put him in harm's way, she'd never forgive herself.

"Zo?" Max pulled to the side of the road, several feet from the house.

She faced him. "This isn't the Nesbitts' land."

He furrowed his brow, not following.

"It's the Merrigans'."

Chapter Thirty-Five

She didn't have time to explain. Brady needed to know what he was getting into. She briefly told Max about the land grant map in the library and how the Nesbitts' name wasn't on it. The Merrigans' name, however, covered the entire area. It didn't prove the land was theirs, but the missing book probably did. At least, that was her best guess. They wouldn't know for sure until they read the pages, but why else had Maynard written Merrigan's name on a notecard? Maynard worked for the government as a land surveyor. He would have come to the conclusion right away.

Max agreed it was a solid possibility. "Carl won't try anything funny with a second officer there. But just in case, I'm calling it in."

Zo waited while he phoned the police, the seconds creeping by like hours while he relayed the details. Then he reached for the door handle, and she did the same. "I'm coming with. This affects me, and I'm not staying behind."

"You'll get the book," Max promised. "You know that."

"It's not just the book. It's Brady. I've gotten him into this mess. I need to be there when you get him out of it." She climbed out of the truck, and Scout scooted over to her seat.

"Thanks, loyal friend," Max grumbled, shutting his door. "Fine. But keep Scout with you, and don't get in the way. There's a chance this could get dangerous."

"I will. You won't even know I'm there."

"I doubt that." He marched toward the front gate, looking very much like a solider going into battle.

Zo and Scout ducked into the forest. She knew the Nesbitts had a security system that would announce Max's arrival. If it caught her approaching from the rear, Carl would be too busy with Max to notice. At least that was her hope.

Scout was one step in front of her, as if she was testing the uneven ground. Her demeanor had changed, and she looked physically larger. Her tall ears stood at attention. As they approached the brush that signaled the clearing, Scout looked back at her. Her deep brown eyes seemed to ask if Zo was ready.

"As ready as I'll ever be," she answered out loud. "Let's go."

As they closed in on the mansion, Zo assuaged herself with the knowledge that the Nesbitts and Merrigans had been neighbors for years. They knew each other as well as any neighbors could. Brady had called him a friend. But Zo knew even friends could turn on each other when something they loved was at stake, and it was obvious Carl Nesbitt loved his land very much. It was perhaps the only thing, besides his daughter, he felt connected to.

Her muscles tightened as they climbed the hill on which the house rested. She didn't need to worry about fences. There were none. The wild grass gave way to a rustic yard, more rock than turf. Like most houses in the area, the Nesbitts' place had a large deck and walkout basement, capitalizing on the beautiful views of the forest.

Seeing no one through the sliding glass basement door, she inched her way up the hill, sticking close to the stone façade. As she neared the front, she heard voices. She flattened herself by the window, which was open. Her chest heaved up and down, and she waited for it to quit rising and falling so quickly. She swallowed, wishing she had something to drink. If Scout's hanging tongue was any indication, she could use a drink, too.

"I know we can talk about this like gentlemen, Carl." It was Brady's voice. "There's no need for that."

No need for what? Oh no. What if he had a gun?

"Absolutely," agreed Max. "No one's accusing you of anything."

Whew. At least Max was there. He wouldn't let anything happen.

Scout made a tiny whine.

"It's okay." Zo patted her head. "He's going to be okay."

Carl chuckled. It wasn't a happy sound. "You know, Merrigan, I've watched your family for years on this hill. The parties. The dinners. The birthdays. Do you know what I would give to have one more birthday with Mandy?"

"I'm sorry for your loss," said Brady. "You know that. Mandy was a dear friend of ours, too."

"But do you know what it's like to go through that kind of pain?" Carl demanded.

"Not exactly, but I know loss." Brady's voice caught in his throat.

"You know nothing!" Carl shouted. "You have everything. You're not getting this land, too. It's all I have left of her."

"I don't want it," Brady was quick to answer. "It doesn't matter what the book says."

"You lie!" spat Carl.

"Brady doesn't lie," said Max. "You can trust him."

"Ah yes, the Merrigans and their Irish honor." Another chuckle stuck in Carl's throat. "It makes me so sick I could puke."

"Careful with that…" said Max.

Zo sneaked a glance. It was just as she thought. Carl had a gun and was waving it toward Brady, who was near a bookshelf. Max, however, was in the doorway. Carl couldn't keep the gun pointed at both of them at the same time, so he took turns pointing it at each of them.

She racked her brain for a way to help them. One wrong move and Carl could end up pulling the trigger. If only she practiced karate instead of yoga.

"You mind your own business, Ranger," Carl warned.

She peeked another look and sucked in a breath. Now he had the gun on Max.

That's when Scout jumped into action.

Literally.

Knowing Max was in trouble, she busted through the window screen with her massive body, the mesh twisting around her body. Like a slow-motion video, Zo watched as Scout took Carl to the floor with her two front legs. Max scrambled for the gun, which lay on the floor, and Brady followed with handcuffs.

Brady pulled Carl's hands behind his back and fastened the locks. He patted Scout's head. "You are a good boy, you know that?"

"Girl." Zo threw her leg over the windowsill, joining them in the library.

"Excuse me." Brady smiled at Zo. "Girl. Where's this dog's police vest, Max?"

"She's not officially a police dog," Max answered.

"Well, she is now." Brady tugged Carl to his feet. "As for you, all you had to do was come to my family. Did you ever think about that?"

"I'd rather hang." The bitterness in Carl's voice was palpable, his large black glasses magnifying the slits of his eyes.

Zo remembered Maynard's shoe, sitting on the edge of the cliff. With Carl's bad eyesight, he hadn't seen it in the dark mountain night. She should have thought of that sooner.

A siren sounded outside. It was the backup Max had called in. He grabbed the cuff of Carl's arm. "And hang you might. Come on."

Chapter Thirty-Six

Zo watched as Scout followed Max and Carl outside. Then she and Brady followed, too. It had been a heck of a couple weeks, and she'd learned so much. Carl had killed Maynard to protect a family's secret: his land wasn't actually his land. It was the Merrigans.' But it was all he had left of his wife, and that was worth committing murder. His daughter had moved on, creating a new life with Landon, which made him cling to the past even harder, determined not to let go of the last memories of them in their home. It reminded Zo how important family was and just what lengths people would go to protect it. In a way, she was almost jealous. She'd never had that in her life.

Walking to the community guesthouse with Brady, which wasn't far from Carl's place, she took the opportunity to apologize for putting him in harm's way. "I'm sorry for sending you here. You might have been killed. I never dreamed Carl was the murderer, until Olivia stopped by my store. Then I called Max, and well, you know the rest."

"Don't worry about it. It's my job to investigate bad guys."

"Still, I feel responsible." The crunch of her shoes on the dry path was the only response.

After a moment, Brady answered, "You sort of are."

She stopped short of the guesthouse door.

Seeing her pained face, he added, "Responsible for solving Maynard's murder, that is. I'm sure I would have found out eventually, but it might have been later, rather than sooner. Who knows what Carl might have done with the book by then?"

"Thank you, Brady. That means a lot." She turned the key in the door, noting the slight scent of disuse as she entered. The house was magnificent, with a floor-to-ceiling fireplace and crown molding, but it must not have been occupied often. Residents in this area probably had guestrooms galore for their visitors.

She turned toward the fireplace in the great room, which was home to three bookshelves. She scanned each one carefully. Brady did the same. The collection was an assortment of old and new books, probably castoffs from the residents' own collections. It was the reason the book was so well disguised. But Olivia was right. Zo found it on the last shelf after scanning it twice. *My Journey West* was in plain view.

She reached for it.

"So, that's the little book causing all the big problems," Brady mumbled, reading over her shoulder. "Carl told me what's in it. He thought I'd found it, which, of course, I let him keep on thinking."

She thumbed through the pages. "What did he say?"

He paraphrased the account. "The Nesbitts were hung up near Murdo, South Dakota, where Carl's kin did some jail time for stealing a horse. He didn't come with my great-grandfather, like they'd originally planned, or stake a claim together. They were friends, and my great-granddad leased him the land. The Nesbitts never owned it at all."

"And that was worth murdering Maynard over?"

Brady nodded. "You'd be surprised at what people will do when it comes to protecting their land or their heritage."

She probably would be.

"Maynard's not completely blameless, though," explained Brady. "He blackmailed Carl with the information. He wanted a cool one hundred thousand dollars to keep his family's secret. He knew Carl had the funds and would pay. Carl decided to put an end to the extortion before it began by killing Maynard and burying the evidence." Brady shook his head. "Greed is a dangerous vice. It grows like a wildfire."

"Consuming everything in its path," she added.

"It's a story that's well known in these parts." Brady paused. "But I know another story you're probably more interested in." He took a step back. "Have at it, kid. Don't let me keep you."

Zo's pulse raced, and she couldn't hold back. Smiling, she flipped to the index to see if "Hart" was mentioned in the index. *Dang.* There wasn't an index. She flipped through the chapter headings. Nothing stood out. She zeroed in on businesses and the opera house. Her mom acting in the theater was all she had to go on. Her finger traced paragraph after paragraph, finding nothing relevant. She released a breath, losing hope.

"What name are you looking for?" Brady asked. "Maybe I can help."

"Maybe…" Her eyes didn't leave the pages. "Hart is the name." She flipped a few more pages, quickly scanning for clues. "Ever heard of it?"

"What name did you say?"

"Hart." She flipped to the missing pages, marked by the torn paper. This must have been where the map was. Although its promise, like the cave, had turned up empty. Maybe she shouldn't put too much faith in the book. It hadn't been wrong about the Merrigans, however. Which reminded her, Brady hadn't answered. She met his eyes, and something in them frightened her. "What?"

"I knew a Hart," he said.

"Great, was he a loser or something?" That'd be just her luck. Their feud probably went back centuries, and the gulf, which they'd recently bridged, would widen again.

"It wasn't a he." Brady suddenly looked very young. His eyes lightened, like a lamp had been turned on. "It was a she."

Oh no, oh no, oh no. Zo kept repeating the words in her head. But why? What did it matter if he knew her? Any information was welcome, wasn't it? "What was her name?"

"Elle." Brady smiled when he said it.

At that moment, she realized she'd never really seen him smile, not like this, with his teeth showing and even a little dimple near his eye. He was lost now, in another time. It was as if he'd forgotten she was there.

"Years ago, when I was a young man, Elle Hart was my girl," he said to no one in particular. "She performed every weekend at the opera house, and suddenly I liked theater very much." He sighed. "A beautiful woman and an incredible voice. Like an angel sent from heaven to grace our tiny town."

"You dated?" Her voice was incredulous.

He nodded, looking like a sheepish schoolboy. "For a season. It was quite serious. I thought…" He pushed the thought aside. "Well, it doesn't matter what I thought. She obviously thought differently. We didn't see each other after that."

"Elle was my mother," Zo revealed.

He pulled his mind from his memory, focusing on her now.

Zo held up her sun and moon necklaces, trying to connect to something tangible. If she could hold on to something real, it might help. "Zo and Elle. That's me."

"She didn't have a daughter." His dark brow furrowed with confusion. "Elle was an actress," he repeated.

"I know." She decided *they* were like actors, stumbling through a play they'd never heard of, the lines fumbling on their tongues. "I found the Elle half in the theater last fall, when the opera house did the renovation."

"She came for a spring and left." He blinked. "I couldn't follow her. I wanted to. But I'd just started with the police force, and she wasn't the type to settle down. She was a free spirit, like you."

She couldn't believe he was telling her this. *Why* was he telling her this?

"How old are you?"

She didn't want to tell him. The words came out anyway. "Thirty-four. I don't see why that matters. None of this matters."

"But it does." He closed his eyes. He opened them again, and the truth reflected like mirrors. They were the same emerald-green eyes. "She left you at the police station because she wanted *me* to find you."

Zo shook her head. Why would Elle want Brady to find her? Unless... It couldn't be. Brady Merrigan was her father? Even inside her head, the words sounded wrong.

Yet something also felt right.

He'd been there since the beginning. When she was abandoned at the police station, he'd found her. When she was a teenager in trouble, he'd corrected her. When she was attacked by a mountain lion, he'd helped her—he'd saved her. Maybe her mom knew he'd be there for her all along. Of course she did. Deep down, Zo did, too.

"Think about it," he suggested. "It makes sense."

Despite her understanding, the physical urge to flee took over. She glanced around the empty house. "I need to go. Max must be looking for me."

"Zo, wait." Brady reached for her hand.

She paused.

Now was not the time to flee. Now was the time to stay. She stood still, allowing the realization to sink in. She could do this. She *would* do this. She had found the truth for others. She needed to discover it for herself.

For as long as she could remember, she'd been looking for her mother, a woman she could connect with. Someone who knew her. Someone who was like her. Now she was standing in a front of a man who was different.

She wore flip-flops; he wore cowboy boots. She drank tea; he drank beer. She bent the rules; he followed them to the letter of the law.

She was okay with different. Her life had been different, and that difference was good. Was he?

She met his gaze.

To her surprise, he smiled.

She allowed him to take her hand, then, closing the chapter in one book and opening another. Who knew where the pages would lead? No one, least of all her. But like most readers, she welcomed the new journey.

A Note to Readers

I love history, so when I came across the legend of the Thoen Stone, I knew I wanted to include it in *Mining for Murder*. I also love mixing fact and fiction, however, so some clarification might be needed. The Thoen Stone I include in this book is real, and interested parties can see the actual stone at the Adams Museum in Deadwood, South Dakota. The only book-length work I've found on the stone is *The Thoen Stone: A Saga of the Black Hills* by Frank Thomson, which is not widely available, and I count myself lucky to have secured a copy. Ezra Kind, the person who purportedly struck gold with his friends and carved the stone, is also real, according to accounts from his descendants. The story of Charlie Clay, however, is just that: a story. He is a figment of my imagination and my idea of what might have happened had Ezra Kind written home to friends and family about his newly found riches. To the best of anyone's knowledge, Ezra Kind's gold is still hidden deep in the Hills.

Katie Merrigan's Irish Apple Cake

Cake:
½ c. butter, softened
½ c. sugar
2 tsp. vanilla extract
2 eggs
1¼ c. flour
1 tsp. baking powder
1 tsp. cinnamon
1/8 tsp. salt
4 tbsp. milk
2–3 Granny Smith apples, peeled and sliced thin

Streusel topping:
6 tbsp. butter, softened
½ c. sugar
1 tsp. cinnamon
¾ c. flour
¼ c. rolled oats

1. Preheat oven to 350 degrees.

2. Spray a 9-inch cake pan with Pam Baking Spray (or prepare pan with butter and flour).

3. To make the streusel topping, combine the flour, oats, sugar, and cinnamon. Cut in the butter until the topping resembles bread crumbs. (I use a pastry blender.) Set aside.

4. To make the cake, cream together butter and sugar. Add eggs one at a time. Add vanilla.

5. In a separate bowl, combine flour, cinnamon, baking powder, and salt. Fold into the wet ingredients, alternating with milk.

6. Pour into prepared pan.

7. Peel and core apples. Slice thinly and add to cake in an even layer.

8. Top with streusel.

9. Bake for about 70 minutes, or until a toothpick comes out clean.

Acknowledgments

So many people make the dream of writing books possible, but space allows me to include only a few here. My parents were my first writing cheerleaders, and I am eternally grateful to both of them for encouraging me to follow my heart. My husband, Quintin, continues to champion my work, especially on the days when I need it most, and that means everything. My friend Amy Cecil Holm reads whatever I ask her to, which included the first draft of this book, and I am forever indebted to her reading and writing expertise. My agent, Amanda Jain, has been a confidant in my publishing journey, and I love having her in my corner. Norma Perez-Hernandez has been one of the most supportive editors I've had the pleasure to work with, and for her and all the wonderful people at Kensington, including Rebecca Cremonese, my production editor, and copy editor Christy Phillippe, I'm incredibly thankful. And to readers who have followed this series, thank you. You've made me a very happy camper.

Printed in the United States
by Baker & Taylor Publisher Services